THE
NEW
HOME

BOOKS BY CHRIS MERRITT

THE
NEW
HOME

CHRIS MERRITT

bookouture

Published by Bookouture in 2021

An imprint of Storyfire Ltd.
Carmelite House
50 Victoria Embankment
London EC4Y 0DZ

www.bookouture.com

ISBN: 978-1-80019-334-5
eBook ISBN: 978-1-80019-333-8

To Fiona, and domestic bliss.

In memory of Bill Moodie.

CHAPTER ONE

Saturday, 13 March

I'm good at imagining things. Psychologists call it visual thinking. To me, it's like a movie screen's been set up in my head, but the projectionist has long since left and nobody else knows how to turn it off; certainly not me, the sole audience member, sat there with my box of popcorn. I've been like that since I was a little kid and, thirty-something years later, nothing has changed. A vivid imagination can be scary at times, but I wouldn't want to live without it. Everything would just be so much less interesting.

My fiancé, Jack, says it's my imagination that has brought us here, to Sunningdale Road in the London suburb of Weybridge. To the small, dilapidated middle-terrace house that is number twelve, with its peeling paint, warped window frames and loose, creaky floorboards. It'd been on the market for over a year, and the owner had already dropped the price three times. Jack said they must be desperate to sell; I suggested that the place was overvalued at the beginning, that they were probably given bad advice by an aggressive estate agent. That it gave us the chance for a bargain.

As soon as we viewed it, we could see why no one had even made an offer. Cracks ran over the walls and ceilings like lightning strikes captured in photographs. Blooms of black mould gathered in the corners like a thousand tiny Rorschach inkblots. Every room was old-fashioned, not in a boho-chic way, just in a hadn't-been-upgraded-since-the-seventies way. We couldn't see the end of the garden through the tangle of head-high weeds, so thick you'd need a machete to get through them. The trap door to the loft didn't even open, despite the estate agent's best efforts (he assured us there was enough space up there for an extra bedroom, though, maybe with an en-suite bathroom). In short, the place was a complete shithole. And I loved it. Because I could picture its potential.

On those property TV programmes, they'd call it a doer-upper. Most people wouldn't look past its photos on the website. But I could fast forward in my mind through months or perhaps years of hard work, after which we'd have a beautiful house we'd created ourselves. And – even though the phrase makes me cringe a little – what I saw on that first visit was our forever home. A place into which Jack and I would pour our love and energy as our family grows to fill it. A puppy, then a child, maybe two… all of us playing together in the garden on long, warm summer evenings. I let myself get carried away, as usual. We put in an offer the next day and it was accepted immediately.

Last week, we exchanged and completed, and Jack went to pick up the keys. Today, we're moving in. I'm so excited about the start of this journey that I can feel butterflies in my stomach right now, more even than the moment I realised Jack was going to propose to me, though I wouldn't tell him that. I'll keep it to myself, same as the clichéd thought that keeps popping into my head: this is the first day of the rest of our lives together.

I have a vision of the two of us, happily grown old, taking a break from tending our garden to drink tea and eat home-made cake. I see our evenings spent snuggled up by a wood-burning stove, reading and talking and watching films. I picture us still having a dance to our favourite songs while we cook dinner, just like we do now. And all this between lots of visits from our family; grandchildren tumbling through the door and racing into our arms…

'Freya,' says Jack beside me. I realise that he's stopped the car, and we've arrived. I turn to him, and he gives me a lopsided grin. They say we're meant to find symmetry attractive, but his off-kilter smiles were one of the first things I remember fancying about him. 'You were away in a little dream, weren't you?'

'Yeah, I was.' My gaze drifts to our new home. When I look back at him, I catch an expression in his features that might be apprehension. But it's gone so fast that I can't be certain.

He switches the engine off. 'Right, then.'

I inhale deeply. 'So, here we are.'

I secretly hope Jack will say something profound about the occasion that we'll remember for years to come. Something about love and hope and family and the future. Instead, pragmatic as ever, he nods to the van that's parked in front of us. 'Removal guys are already here,' he says. 'We'd better get inside and tell them where to put everything.'

An hour later, our house is full of cardboard boxes, Jack is sorting out the kitchen appliances, and I pop back outside to make sure we haven't forgotten anything. Satisfied that the truck is empty, I hand Pavel and Ondrej two hundred pounds in cash and a six-pack of Czech lager, and I thank them for their help. They insist on me taking one of the beers and, before I know it, we're clinking cans and drinking together. The slight awkwardness of this lasts for a minute before they tell me they have another job and they should leave. They jump back into the cab of their van, and I watch as they disappear around the corner, part of me wishing the pair of them could stay and help us unpack. Maybe even start renovating. But no, I remind myself, this is *our* project. I take a swig of the beer I didn't want, and it fizzes unpleasantly in my mouth. Then a voice calls out behind me.

'Hello!'

I turn to see a woman striding towards me, her shoes crunching on the gravel path of her own, neatly landscaped, front garden. She's beautiful, in a kind of effortless, natural way that's all bone structure and good genes. She's dressed casually, but I can tell it's nice stuff. Tresses of thick golden hair tumble around her shoulders as she moves. She's about my age, maybe a bit older; it's hard to tell. She's as radiant as a Hollywood star, and I'm suddenly ashamed of the shabby old clothes I chose for moving, embarrassed by the half-drunk beer can dangling at my side, and aware of the miniature jungle of a lawn between us, which is now my responsibility. But she doesn't seem to care about any of that; she's looking right at me and beaming, clutching an elegant green bottle topped with gold foil.

'Hi,' I reply.

Her eyes flick up to the 'SOLD' sign that's been tied to the rotting remains of what I guess was once a picket fence. 'You're moving in?' she asks.

'Yup. Literally just arrived.'

'Congratulations!' she exclaims, approaching and handing me the bottle as if I've won a prize. 'I'm Emily.' She nods towards the immaculate house from which she's emerged. 'We're the neighbours.'

'Freya.' I take the bottle from her outstretched hand and glance at the label. Pol Roger. It's champagne, not cava or prosecco. 'Oh, wow. That's very kind, are you sure?'

'Course.' Emily shrugs, as if she gives it out all the time.

'You really didn't have to…'

She flaps a hand. 'It's a pleasure. Welcome.'

'I don't know what to say.' I can feel myself blushing. 'Thank you.'

Emily gestures to our run-down house and starts asking what we're planning to do with it, when a child's voice calls from her open front door.

'Mummy! I can't find my swimming goggles.'

Emily looks at me, rolls her eyes and smiles indulgently. 'Have you tried your schoolbag, darling?' she calls back, then lowers her voice to me. 'This happens every Saturday.'

I laugh.

'But I don't know where my bag is,' comes the plaintive response.

'Okay, we'll find it in a minute,' says Emily. 'Sorry,' she adds for my benefit.

A little girl in a blue-and-white striped dress bursts out of the door and runs towards us. She's ridiculously cute, a miniature version of Emily. I'm already picturing them on a sun-drenched beach somewhere during a summer holiday, splashing in the waves and building perfect sandcastles. When the girl sees me, though, she freezes before taking cover behind her mum, clinging to her legs and peeking out at me.

'Don't be shy, Thea!' Emily ruffles her hair. 'Would you like to meet our new neighbour?'

Thea shakes her head slowly.

'This is Freya.'

'Hello, Thea,' I say, trying to be friendly but conscious that I have alcohol in both hands, and it's not even midday yet. 'Nice to meet you.'

Thea doesn't reply.

'How old are you?' I ask.

After a silence, Emily says, 'She's five, aren't you, sweetie?'

'Five and a half,' Thea corrects her.

'I like your dress,' I say.

Thea ignores this and stares at the can in my hand. 'She's drinking the same drink as Daddy.'

I'm saved from responding to this by Jack, who appears in our doorway and raises a palm in greeting. I do the introductions, pass him the bottle. But when I glance up, he's not looking at it. He's looking at Emily. There's something in his eyes, in the slight parting of his lips and the tiny hesitation before he says, 'Lovely to meet you.'

'You too.'

The brief silence that follows is broken by a deep male voice inside their house.

'Come on, we've got to go.'

'But I haven't got my goggles,' Thea reminds her mum. She sounds worried, now.

Before Emily can respond to her daughter, a tall man emerges from their front door. He's good-looking, in a kind of austere way, with a full head of dark hair that's grey at the temples. He wears a thin sweater over a collared shirt and chinos, and his brown deck shoes are buffed to a shine. He's carrying a small red rucksack that's designed to look like a giant ladybird. He stops and regards me and Jack as if we're a couple of trespassers. This time it's Emily who introduces us to her husband. His name's Michael. But that's all we get before his attention is elsewhere.

'You're going to be late,' he tells Thea.

'She can't find her goggles,' Emily says, hand on her daughter's shoulder.

Michael huffs his irritation and points a key fob at a Range Rover parked in the street. Its lights flash as the locks make a smooth clunk sound. 'Never mind. We'll get you some new ones at the pool. Let's go.'

As he bundles Thea into the vehicle and we watch them pull away, Emily chuckles and waves goodbye. I turn to Jack, wondering whether this might be us in a few years' time. But I can't catch his eye because he's staring at Emily.

He's got that strange look of apprehension once more; the same one I glimpsed in the car. And this time, I know I'm not imagining it.

CHAPTER TWO

Saturday, 13 March

By late afternoon, Jack and I are both knackered. We've lugged boxes, unwrapped crockery, hung clothes and stacked books for five hours straight, barely pausing to inhale the sandwiches we picked up at a petrol station this morning. But the place still feels half-empty. The few items of furniture we've brought from our one-bed flat in Hackney hardly seem to register their presence here, as if they've been plucked from a doll's house and dropped into a real home, their inadequacy exposed. The enormity of the task we've taken on begins to dawn on me, and the euphoria I felt this morning is starting to ebb away. I decide it's time for a break. I find Jack in the bathroom, eyes narrowed in concentration as he threads the rings on a shower curtain.

'Hello handsome handyman,' I say. 'Fancy a walk?'

'Sure.' He immediately drops the curtain into the old bathtub, metal rings clattering on enamel. 'Where do you wanna go?'

'I was thinking next door.'

He blinks. 'Again? I mean, already?'

'No, other side. We can introduce ourselves.'

'Oh, yeah. Course.' He looks relieved.

We make our way outside and towards the neighbouring property, number eleven. It has a large bay window at the front, but the curtains are closed. We exchange a glance as we move down the side of the house in search of an entrance, half-wondering if we're already intruding. It's not as run-down as our place, but nowhere near as nice as Emily and Michael's, either. Along a path of concrete slabs, weeds sprouting from the cracks between them, we find the front door. It's open.

'Hello?' I call out. There's no reply.

'Anyone home?' says Jack loudly.

Without stepping over the threshold, I crane my neck to look inside. I can see worn carpet, faded wallpaper and a couple of old framed photos of people whose faces I can't make out in the gloom. For some reason, I'm picturing an older woman who lives alone.

I point to the interior. 'Should we?…'

'No.' Jack takes a step back. 'If there's no one here, we should try again later.'

'But the door's open.' Suddenly, my curiosity gets the better of me and I step inside.

'Freya!' Jack hisses behind me. 'You can't just—' But it's too late.

As I walk through a narrow hallway, inspecting the photographs, I hear Jack follow me in. The lighting's low, but I notice that the people in the images on the wall are dressed as if from a bygone era. I move slowly towards a room at the back where there's a little more light, unsure whether I should call out in the silence. But something keeps me quiet, and even my footsteps become softer. I can feel Jack creeping behind me, matching my movement. We probably shouldn't be here, but now I have to know who lives in this house and why they've left their front door open.

Tentatively, we go into a kitchen, and I see the first sign of life since entering: a kettle on a lit gas hob. Is someone here? I'm trying to take in the other features of the room when something flashes at the corner of my vision. There's a scraping sound and I don't even have time to turn my head before a dark shape rushes at me from above. Instinctively I scream and shut my eyes and raise my hands to shield my face.

But the attack never comes. Breathing heavily, I lower my hands and open my eyes again. A large black cat has landed on the linoleum floor, and it's staring up at us with undisguised hostility. It snarls briefly before nonchalantly slinking away.

'Jesus,' says Jack. 'Bloody thing scared the living shit out of me.'

'I reckon we probably frightened it too.' I could almost laugh, but my heart is hammering in my chest. 'We're the ones who turned up unannounced.'

'Must've been up on those cupboard units,' he observes. 'You okay?'

'Yeah, fine. Nearly had a heart attack though.'

'Don't do that, it's my day off.'

I turn and he's giving me that lopsided smile. I've just started to relax slightly when a piercing shriek cuts through the air, and my heart leaps into my throat once more. It's the kettle, steam billowing from its spout. Decisively, Jack moves past me and switches off the hob. The screeching dies down, and the low rumble of boiled water is the only noise until the words cut through the air like a scalpel.

'Who are you?'

I whip round to the doorway where a tall old woman is standing with hands on hips. Her jaw is set firm, her back is straight, and she seems completely undaunted by the presence of two strangers in her house. She has a mane of long white hair, and her eyes are a cold, pale blue. She's enveloped in a thick grey cardigan that extends almost to her bare feet.

'What are you doing here?' she demands.

'Sorry,' I blurt. 'We're, um, the new neighbours. We just came to say hello and the door was open and…' I falter and try a smile. I want to show her we mean no harm. But she isn't paying attention to me any more. She's staring at Jack, wide-eyed and fearful, as though she's seen a ghost.

'Henry?' she says.

His features crease in confusion for a moment. 'No,' he replies. 'I'm not Henry.'

'This is Jack, my fiancé,' I explain.

The woman shakes her head, pinches the brow of her nose and shuts her eyes. 'Of course,' she says when she opens them again. 'How silly of me.' Then she moves briskly towards the kettle. 'Right, then. Would you both like some tea?'

Cathy, as we've learned our new neighbour is called, pours the tea. It's old-fashioned, made in a pot with loose leaves, the proper way. As she places the little strainer over each of our cups in turn, I study her, trying to guess her age. Sixty-five? Seventy-five? Older? I can't tell. Her face is lined and weather-beaten, the skin dotted with liver spots. But her hands are strong, her grip on the full teapot steady, her movements assured.

'Sorry again,' I say, 'about coming in, uninvited.'

'I thought I'd closed the door,' she says, giving a tiny shake of her head, 'but it must've blown open.'

'How long have you lived here?' I ask.

'Henry and I bought this place in 1978,' she replies instantly.

Henry. I've been wondering who he is since she mistook Jack for him. 'Who's Henry?'

'My husband.'

'Oh, is he?—'

'He's not here now.'

I'm not sure what she means. Is Henry dead? Are they separated? Or has he just popped to the shops? I look at Jack, and I can tell he's trying to work it out, too.

'Seventeen thousand pounds, it cost then.' She finishes pouring and pushes the cups towards us. 'And we thought that was a fortune! But we fell in love with it, so we put on our smartest clothes and made an appointment to see the bank manager. He took some convincing, but we persuaded him to give us the mortgage, and that was that.'

Jack says something about house prices and times changing. I'm picturing this meeting, though, the formality of it, the lost age when people had a personal relationship with their local bank branch and mortgages weren't simply decided by an algorithm processing reams of online data about credit cards. I see Henry, tall and broad, dressed in his best suit, Cathy straightening his regimental tie before they go in. She's feeling that same sense of anticipation as I felt today, moving house with Jack: the start of a future together.

'Why did you come here?' she says suddenly.

'We wanted more space.' I squeeze Jack's hand under the table. 'You know, for the future…'

'Yes, of course. Same as Henry and I did.' She pauses. 'I mean, why Weybridge?'

'I've got a job,' says Jack. 'Up the road, at St Peter's hospital. Starting tomorrow.'

'You're a doctor?'

'Cardiologist.'

I think back to the day Jack was offered the position as a consultant, five months ago. He punched the air with both fists and threw his arms around me. I knew how hard he'd worked to get the opportunity, how many years of specialist training he'd slogged through. I was so happy for him. The only problem was that St Peter's was in Surrey, thirty miles away, on the other side of London – a four-hour round trip – and he'd be on call-out. With my work being freelance and mostly remote, the sensible decision was to move so he could be near the hospital. It was a no-brainer, but in this moment I feel a pang of loss for my friends in Hackney. For the canal, for Broadway Market and the marshes.

It's replaced quickly, though, by the thought of hanging out with Emily. I'm already imagining us chatting easily over coffee, as if we've known each other for years.

'Neighbours seem lovely,' I say when there's a lull in the conversation a bit later.

'Neighbours?' Cathy frowns.

'On the other side.' I point in what I think is the right direction. 'Emily and Michael.'

'Who?'

'You know, er, at number thirteen. They have a daughter, Thea.'

Cathy purses her lips, narrows her eyes and holds my gaze. 'Just be careful,' she whispers. 'They're not...' but I don't catch the end of her sentence.

'Not what?' I ask, suddenly anxious.

Cathy doesn't reply. Instead, she stands and carries her cup over to the sink. 'I should be getting on,' she says.

Jack and I have a lazy, decadent dinner of takeaway pizza and champagne. I wonder if we should invite Michael and Emily over to share the bottle, but Jack says that we deserve to celebrate together, just the two of us, and I don't take much persuasion. We're both exhausted from the move, and we eat the pizza straight from the box without plates or cutlery. Midway through my second glass of champagne, I ask him the question that's been niggling at me since this morning.

'This is going to sound strange,' I say, 'but you haven't met our neighbours before, have you?'

Jack barks a laugh. 'What? No, course not. How would I have done that?'

'I don't know.' I'm less sure of myself, now. 'Maybe you treated them at hospital once...'

'In Homerton? Why would they be up there?' He reaches for another slice of pizza. He's right. It's miles away.

'Could've been somewhere else,' I add hastily. 'You do locum shifts, and you've worked all over London at some point in the last fifteen years.'

He crams in half of the slice and shakes his head.

'Friends of friends?' I suggest. 'Uni, maybe?'

'Nope.' Jack arches his eyebrows. He thinks I'm being weird. 'What makes you say that?'

I take a swig from my glass. 'For some reason I just got the impression that you recognised them.' Recognised *Emily*, I want to say.

'I've never seen them before,' he says firmly, staring at the remainder of his slice. But I know what I saw. At least, I think I do. I wait, but he doesn't elaborate.

'What about Cathy?' I ask.

'Crazy old cat lady?' Jack snorts. 'Do you reckon I've met her before, too?'

'No, I mean, what do you think she meant when she told us to be careful?'

He stops chewing. Looks at me sceptically. 'Come on, Freya.'

'What?'

'She's not all there.'

'What do you mean?'

'She leaves a gas flame unattended, claims her door blew open on a day with no wind and doesn't remember the names of the couple who've lived two down from her for the last however-many years?'

'Maybe she got distracted by something, lost concentration. Happens to all of us.'

He ignores my suggestion. 'And it's obvious there's no one else in that house, even though she talked about her husband like he was still around. She thought I was him, for God's sake!'

'You think Henry's dead?'

'I don't know about *dead*, but he's not there.' He sighs. 'I'm not an old-age psychiatrist, but I've seen the onset of dementia enough times. Early MCI, it's called. That's how it started for my dad. Small lapses that got bigger and more frequent until they were the norm.' There's pain on his face.

I nod. I never knew Jack's father; he died before we met.

'I'm worried about her, if anything,' he continues. 'I mean, are we gonna find her wandering around in the street at night, disorientated, or wake up to our house burning down?'

'She seems pretty capable of taking care of herself,' I counter.

'Don't be too sure. When someone's mind goes…'

Maybe Jack's right. Perhaps I was too busy imagining Cathy and Henry at our age, dreaming while Jack was analysing. It wouldn't be the first time. But, despite his logic, I can't shake her words of warning.

Just be careful.

CHAPTER THREE

Saturday, 20 March

It's a week since we moved in. We've been invited to Michael and Emily's house for dinner, and it sounds silly but I'm almost as excited as the day we arrived. I'm anticipating a fun night that's not only the start of a close friendship, but also a step towards being accepted in our new community. Jack, on the other hand, was a bit funny about it at first, saying he might need to work or be on-call, claiming he'd be tired from a busy first week at the hospital. But I'd already accepted for both of us, so I batted back his excuses one by one until, eventually, he gave in and agreed. Would it have killed him to be a bit more enthusiastic, though?

Now, as we stand on the doorstep and tap the knocker, brandishing a bottle of wine that's twice as expensive as one we'd have taken to our friends in Hackney, I recall his expression as he looked at Emily that first day. I wonder if it has anything to do with his apparent reluctance to be here now. But the thought goes out of my head as the door opens and Emily is there, beaming at me and pulling me into a hug. Her perfume is gorgeous.

She looks stunning in a full-length emerald-green dress that makes her hair seem a deeper shade of gold and even more lustrous. She ushers us into a warm, well-lit entrance hall and pauses to give Jack a quick hug and double air-kiss. He seems to go slightly rigid, mumbling a hello, and when she waltzes off, telling us to come through, I shoot him a glare: an unspoken reminder to make an effort because this is important. He frowns, as if he hasn't understood me.

The interior of the house is as pristine as its outside, the décor and furnishings as beautiful as the occupants. At the back of the ground floor is a large extension I've glimpsed through the overgrown vegetation of our garden. It contains a kitchen-diner, with full-length glass doors onto a patio, and an island on which a pair of Le Creuset cast-iron casseroles are steaming and bubbling gently. The smell is incredible. It's as if I've been transported to a fantasy world of how our home might look one day, but my heart sinks slightly when I realise how much we've got to do before we have a space like this to entertain guests.

I hand the wine to Emily, and she thanks me, studying the label with wide-eyed appreciation. She pours us both deep glasses from a bottle of red she's already opened, and I feel the first smooth mouthful of it flow down and into my tummy, warming and delicious. I can hear small, quick footsteps upstairs that must be Thea's, but Michael is nowhere to be seen.

'Michael's just finishing off some work,' explains Emily, as if she's read my mind. 'He's got a pretty massive deadline coming up.'

'What for?' I ask, noticing Jack wandering off into the open-plan living area that stretches all the way back to the front of the house.

'He's a computer programmer,' she says, 'and they're delivering version one of a new app, some time next week, I think.'

'Amazing! I'd love to hear about it.'

Emily laughs. 'Don't get him started on coding. Not if you want to talk about anything else tonight, anyway.'

'Thanks for the tip. Jack can be the same with his medical stuff.' I look over, expecting him to protest or tease me back, but he's oblivious, silently examining a set of framed family photos on the mantelpiece. He's staring at a large one that shows Michael,

Emily and Thea with a dog that's so big and hairy it's more like a bear. The perfect family.

I ask Emily what she's cooking, and she tells me it's paella, made to a special recipe they brought home from a trip to Valencia, where the dish originated. I'm picturing her and Michael there, cooling off in the shade of an airy waterfront restaurant, all blue and white tiles and ceiling fans, the smell of sun cream and the sound of waves washing on the shore beside them. But my dream is interrupted by the patter of feet on stairs, and Thea runs in, wearing her pyjamas.

'Er, excuse me, young lady,' says Emily with mock outrage. 'You're supposed to be in bed.'

'Can you read me a story?' Thea's holding tightly to a doll of a baby.

'You've already had a story,' Emily replies.

'I want another one.' The girl twists left and right, grinning, knowing she's pushing her luck. 'Please.'

'I can't now, darling. We've got guests. You remember Freya?'

Thea nods. This time, though, instead of hiding, she comes over to me and hands me the doll. It's naked, except for a nappy.

'Thank you!' I exclaim. 'Is this for me?'

She nods again. 'It's your baby.'

Emily shakes her head and smiles. Then Thea wraps her arms around my leg and, all of a sudden, I'm standing in my ideal home with a small child hugging me and a baby in my arms, albeit a plastic one. I blink at this vision of the future, and check to see if Jack's watching, but he's just browsing the bookshelves. He's nearly finished his glass of wine already.

Twenty minutes later, Thea has been packed off to bed again and Emily serves the food as we take our seats. I hear a door open and close and, right on cue, Michael enters the kitchen, as if he knew the exact time the plates would be put on the table. He grunts some sort of greeting but doesn't shake hands.

'Emily said you were working on an app,' I try. 'How's it going?'

'We're behind schedule,' he says irritably. 'One of the dev guys has fucked something up and it's going to take me hours to fix it. I would actually kill him if we shared an office, but he's all the way over in bloody India. Useless bastard.' He sighs and wipes a hand over his face, taking the plate of paella from Emily without a word of thanks and immediately digging in with his fork.

'Sounds really tricky,' I offer. When he doesn't respond, I tell him that I sympathise with hard deadlines, having had quite a few myself. Emily asks what I do.

'I make documentaries.'

'Oh my god!' she says. 'Seriously? What, anything I would've seen?'

'Maybe.'

'She had something on BBC Two last year,' says Jack. 'It was nominated for an award.' I feel a little glow of pride, and my cheeks getting hotter.

Emily looks astonished. 'What was it about?'

'Gender-based violence,' I reply.

'Such an important topic.' Emily takes a sip of wine. 'So, what else have you done?'

'Mostly other crime and social justice issues affecting women. Trafficking, sex work, forced marriage, that kind of thing.'

'Incredible!' Her face lights up with interest.

Emily asks me more about it, and I describe a few projects I've worked on. She seems fascinated and hungry for details, but after a while I realise we've been mostly talking about me and start to feel a bit uncomfortable.

'How about you?' I ask her. 'What do you do?'

'I used to work at the British Museum,' she says.

'Cool.'

'Voluntarily,' says Michael, his mouth half-full. It's the first word he's said since he started eating.

'Er, well, towards the end it was, yes.' Emily sounds slightly defensive. 'But only because our funding got cut when we were midway through curating an exhibition, and I wanted to stay on, see it through till it was open to the public. Aztecs,' she adds, for me and Jack.

'Super-interesting,' I say, although I don't want to admit that I've never actually visited the museum, and I don't really know anything about the Aztecs, either. 'So, what happened? You left?'

'Thea came along, and we decided that I should quit to be a full-time mum.' She smiles, but it doesn't quite reach her eyes. 'I can always go back there later if I want.'

'I'm sure you could.'

There's a brief silence, then Emily nods at Michael. 'It's how we met.'

'Really?' I'm struggling to imagine him doing anything in a museum other than IT maintenance.

'Didn't we, darling?' Emily prompts him.

'My firm was sponsoring an exhibition there,' Michael eventually replies, his mouth full of food, 'and I went along to the opening night drinks reception. We got chatting.'

'Swept me off my feet,' says Emily, though I find that hard to believe.

'We didn't get together right away,' Michael adds flatly.

'But, once we did, we had Thea not long after.' She smiles, lifts her wine glass. 'What about you two?'

I glance at Jack. 'Oh, we just met online,' I say, still slightly embarrassed about the fact, even though something like a third of all romantic relationships start with internet dating, now.

'I've never dated online.' Emily sounds intrigued. 'Did he live up to his profile?' She winks at me.

'Just about.' I laugh and reach for Jack's hand.

'It's mad, really,' says Jack. 'To think we'd never have met without that app.'

'I know.'

I do remember being a bit surprised that Jack and I didn't have a single mutual friend. He's only three years older than me, and the way people are randomly connected in London, I'd have expected us to know at least one person in common. Even a distant acquaintance on social media. Someone I met at a party who goes to the gym with someone he used to work with… but there was nothing. I don't mention that right now, though.

The conversation meanders on through renovations, extensions and knock-throughs. Michael advises us not to bother with a loft conversion (the ceiling's not high enough, apparently), although he does tell us he's turned the cellar into an office. He can recommend a damp-proofing firm if we want to do the same.

'Did you know we had a cellar?' I ask Jack.

'Yeah.' His eyes dart around like it's a trick question.

'I must've missed that in the floor plans.'

'It was in the survey, too,' Jack says, as if I'm being particularly dappy. I want to move on from my oversight, so I ask if they know the woman at number eleven.

'Oh, Cathy.' Emily makes a sad, empathic face. 'She's sweet.'

'How old is she?' I ask.

'No idea,' Emily replies. 'Seventies, maybe? She's pretty sprightly.'

'Is her husband still around?'

'Don't think so…' Emily turns to Michael. 'I've never seen anyone else there. Have you, darling?'

Michael looks as though he's smelled something bad. Shakes his head. 'He obviously croaked years ago.'

'That's what I thought,' offers Jack.

'Older people have always got good stories,' I say cheerily. 'I bet she has some.'

'She has.' Emily lifts her wine glass, leans in. 'She's lived through a lot, like—'

'She's losing her marbles,' says Michael, interrupting his wife. 'Plain and simple. Being on your own will do that to someone, especially a woman. Which reminds me' – he clicks his fingers – 'we should get our spare keys back off her. She can't be trusted to look after them.'

I bite my tongue. He's starting to piss me off. I want to call out his casual sexism and lack of humanity. But I'm also aware that we don't know this couple, and we're guests in their house. Even if I never speak to Michael again, I still want to be friends with Emily. What I can't really understand is why they're together, but I guess I'll find that out soon enough.

Two hours later, Jack and I are back home. We've barely shut the door when Jack speaks.

'Well, he's utterly charmless.' He sniggers, and I can tell he's drunk too much.

'Michael's not the only one who could've done with a bit more charm tonight,' I say quietly.

'What? Are you seriously comparing me to that fucking robot?'

'Keep your voice down.' I hook a thumb at the wall to remind him they're just on the other side of it.

'He's not going to hear me.' Jack waves a dismissive hand. 'He'll be back down in the cellar, doing his coding or whatever.' He mimes an exaggerated typing action.

'I don't care.' I slip off my heels, relieved to take the pressure off my toes. 'Anyway, you hardly said a word tonight.'

He shrugs. 'I was knackered.'

'It was almost like you didn't want to be there.'

'That's not true. I was listening.'

'Hm.'

'I was! You're always telling me I should do that more, so there you go.'

I'm not in the mood to argue; apart from the men being a bit odd, the evening went well, and I feel as though Emily and I are becoming friends. I drop my voice to a whisper. 'Okay, I admit it: he's a bit of an arsehole. But Emily's lovely.'

'Yeah. I just don't know what she sees in him.'

That makes two of us, I think. I have the slightest sense that something's not right, and I'd love to know what it is. Same as I want to know what Jack saw in Emily that first day.

CHAPTER FOUR

I'll never forget the first time I saw you. You were just standing there, casually holding your drink, looking a little nervous, and the second I clapped eyes on you, something happened to me. It's hard to put into words, to describe exactly what took place. A poet would no doubt be able to craft some beautiful lines to capture that moment with an appropriate level of romance, but that's not me. I prefer a more scientific account. I think it probably comes down to basic biology: a chemical reaction that was encoded into my genes long before I knew you even existed. Information stored in the nuclei of my cells, waiting for you to come along so they could communicate an urgent, powerful message to me that we should be together. That you were an ideal mate for me. For me, that's a more convincing explanation than stars aligning or love at first sight or any of that crap.

I'm theorising after the fact, though. In that moment, it was just a feeling, a lurching and shifting inside me that grew until it seemed to take over my whole body. The only thing I've experienced like it was the time on holiday, years ago, when I was standing in the sea but facing towards the beach. I didn't see the huge wave until it was almost on top of me, signalled seconds in advance by the rapid pull of water away from around my waist. Next I knew, it had completely covered me, lifted me off my feet, swallowed me up and swept me along with it, helpless. By the time I was spat out and dumped on the sand, coughing up water and gasping for breath, I felt as though that wave had nearly killed me. I hope you coming into my life doesn't kill me either; although, if it did, at least I could say I died happy. Well, happier, at least.

Once the overwhelming physical shock of that first encounter had passed, I knew that I had to find out more about you. I had to get to know you. The real you, not just the one that everybody else sees. I wanted to gather every single detail, each little piece of the jigsaw that makes up you. I didn't care how long it took. It became a project, as all-consuming as that feeling of seeing you for the first time. I began dedicating spare time to it, carving out space here and there in the day, when I could, alongside longer sessions at night when I could get more privacy. The more I looked, the more I discovered. And the more I discovered, the more my desires crystallised. I had to be with you. But I knew even that wouldn't be enough.

I couldn't let anyone else have you, either. I had to have you all to myself, exclusively and permanently. I had to possess you.

And I knew I wouldn't stop until I did.

CHAPTER FIVE

Wednesday, 14 July

It's a warm, summer's day and I'm working from home, engrossed in some research on my laptop, when I hear the knock at the door. Three sharp taps – *rat-a-tat* – and I think it's probably Emily because that's normally how she knocks when she drops round. I quickly check my phone, wondering if I've missed a text from her, but there's nothing.

I call out: 'Hey, just coming!' as I push my chair back and pad into the entrance hall. On the way, a crack in the wall catches my eye and I wonder if it's new or just one I've seen so many times that I've forgotten I knew it existed. Whichever it is, it's a reminder that Jack and I have so much work to do. We've been here four months now and it feels as though we've barely scratched the surface of our renovation plans. Loft conversions and cellar repurposing flit through my mind, projects-within-a-project that we haven't yet started, but the images are gone in a second as I open the door and it's not Emily.

It's a middle-aged man and a smartly dressed woman who looks improbably young. He's standing slightly in front of her. And they're both holding up little wallets with the card-and-badge combo I've seen a hundred times in crime dramas, but never once in real life. My eyes zero in on the words *SURREY POLICE*.

My first thought is that it must be Jack. Maybe he's had a car accident. My throat instantly constricts as I picture firefighters cutting him out of the twisted metal wreckage of our Volvo. Or something at the hospital, perhaps; a drug-abusing, wild-eyed patient lunging at him with a stolen surgical scalpel. I swallow and blink a few times. The man opens his mouth to speak, but before he can say anything I blurt out: 'Is it Jack? What's happened to him?'

His eyebrows draw together and his head tilts slightly. He looks tired, like he hasn't slept properly in years, and his tie knot is already loose, even though it's only ten a.m.

'No, madam,' he replies, 'it's not about, er, Jack. I'm acting Detective Inspector Henderson. This is Detective Constable Willis. We're from Surrey CID. We're investigating the disappearance of Emily Crawford and her daughter Thea.'

'Oh my god,' I exclaim, and now new images are forming quickly in my mind, unbidden, each more unpleasant than the last. A twisted body lying in undergrowth, torn clothing revealing pale, lacerated skin. I can taste a bit of bile at the back of my mouth. 'Disappearance?'

'Yes. We're just going house to house on the road and speaking to residents. Would you mind if we ask you a few questions, Ms—?'

'I… of course,' I stammer, trying to push away that scene. 'Freya Northcott.'

Henderson lowers his ID. 'It'd be easier if we could speak inside, if that's all right with you, Miss Northcott.'

I usher them in and, absurdly, I feel embarrassed about the fact we still haven't yet sorted out our living room. There's a two-seater sofa opposite the TV that I offer to Henderson and Willis. They perch on it while I drag over a dining table chair and sit down. Willis has her notebook and pen out already and looks bright and keen, full of vigour. I'm only thirty-five, but she's making me feel old. And that's two ridiculous thoughts in the space of a few seconds, when the real issue here is that my neighbour and her little girl are missing.

'Did you know Mrs Crawford – Emily – and Thea?' asks Henderson.

'Yes, Emily and I were friends.' I catch myself. 'We *are* friends.'

'How long have you known her?'

'About four months, since we moved in.'

'And how often do you see her?'

'To talk to, do you mean?'

The detective clasps his hands, nods.

'Oh.' I blow out my cheeks. 'Once a week for a chat or a drink, you know?'

Willis is furiously scribbling notes, as if she wants to record every word.

'How would you describe your friendship?' he asks.

'Good,' I reply. Is that accurate? We hang out, we speak – usually about our houses or local shops or something Thea is doing – and we have a bond, for sure. But I always get the impression that Emily keeps a part of herself at arm's length. I'm sure she has secrets, same as all of us, but maybe she needs a bit more time before she can tell me about them. There are hints of something deeper – something not right behind the perfect exterior – but she never fully gives voice to that, whatever it is.

'Just... good?'

'Yeah.' I shrug. 'I mean, we only met four months ago, but we get on really well. We're in and out of each other's houses, for coffee or a glass of wine. I like her.' I'm not sure why I say that, as if I need to prove something. 'What happened?'

Henderson leans forward. 'Okay. Well, what we know so far is that Emily and Thea left home on Monday afternoon to walk to a kids' summer holiday activity club. That was the last anyone saw of them, far as we can tell. They never turned up at the club.'

'So, who—?'

'Mr Crawford – Michael – reported them missing the next day. Yesterday.'

The next day? I hope that when Jack and I have children, if we didn't come back, Jack would do something about it there and then. Not go to sleep in an empty house without us and then perhaps get round to calling someone about it a day later.

Then I remember what Michael's like. The aloof, irascible man who I've spoken to a handful of times in as many months. My cheerful offerings to him met by grunts and mumbling and excuses about needing to do something else. The harsh, unfriendly way he seems to treat Emily and Thea. Maybe it took him a day to realise they weren't actually there, I think, uncharitably.

Then a darker thought occurs to me: does he know something about it? Is he responsible? Oh God, has he?...

'Are you all right, Miss Northcott?'

I blink a few times, but the grizzly scene is still there in my mind. 'Yes, fine. Thanks.'

'What's your impression of Mr and Mrs Crawford's relationship?'

'It's okay, I guess. Hard to know, isn't it? I mean, Michael tends to keep to himself. But they seem fine, more or less.'

I don't want to point the finger directly at Michael. Not yet, at least. I expect they'll be looking closely at him anyway. They always look at the husband. The stats about that kind of thing don't lie. Memories of conversations with Emily are flooding back to me; I'm desperately trying to remember if she said anything that indicated problems with Michael, or the threat of violence. I'm sure there was something...

'Did you see or hear anything unusual on Monday afternoon, Miss Northcott?'

I try to recall where I was, what I was doing, but my mind is racing. I was at home, obviously, as I have been most of the days since we moved in. Trying to do some stuff on the house and working on new pitches for documentaries and not really succeeding at either.

'No, not that I know of,' I say. 'I was here, but I didn't see them leave.'

'And any suspicious activity in the street or around the Crawfords' house in the preceding days or weeks that you're aware of?'

I shake my head. 'Nothing. Suspicious? What, do you think something's happened to them?' I can hear the shock in my own voice.

'We have to look at every possibility.' Henderson takes out a card. 'Well, if anything else comes to mind...'

I take it from him, turn it over. There's a mobile number written by hand on the back.

'I'll let you know,' I say. I assume he isn't talking about the gruesome thoughts I've been having pretty much since I opened the door to them.

His gaze roams around the house, and I see him take in a photograph of me and Jack, as well as a large pair of work boots in one corner, clearly too big to be mine. 'Who else lives here?'

'My fiancé, Jack. He's at work at the moment.'

'Right. We'll need to speak to him later on.' Henderson's tone is casual, but it still makes my heart thump.

'Why?' I demand.

He gives me a weary smile. 'It's completely routine, Miss Northcott. Like I said, we're just speaking to everyone in the area. Anyone who might have relevant information.'

'But Jack won't have anything useful to tell you,' I insist. 'I mean, he'd have been out at work at the time they went missing, anyway.'

Henderson sighs. 'We'd still like to make contact with him. Would you mind giving us his number, please? DC Willis will follow up with him at a more convenient time.'

'Um... okay.' I grab my phone and find Jack's details.

They get up and we exchange a flurry of pleasantries about me getting back to work and them continuing their inquiries and all of us having nice days and so on. Then the door shuts and their footsteps fade and I'm alone in the hallway, wondering how the seemingly happy woman and girl next door could just vanish without trace. Imagining how easily Michael could become intimidating, violent, even. And asking myself why the police think Jack would be able to help with the investigation into Emily and Thea's disappearance.

Instinctively, I grab my mobile and call Emily, but it goes straight to voicemail.

CHAPTER SIX

Wednesday, 14 July

In the afternoon, I make the short walk over our scrubby front garden and across the neatly raked gravel next door to see Michael. It's an unscheduled trip, since I don't even have his number to text ahead, but I think he's in because his Range Rover is parked outside. Jack is still on shift at the hospital, as usual, so I'm on my own.

I've debated whether Michael will appreciate me calling round and concluded: probably not. But, since the police visited this morning, I've not been able to think of much else besides Emily and Thea. I've tried a dozen more calls to Emily, with the same result each time: instant voicemail, as if the phone's switched off.

I can no longer resist the tug of curiosity which has already turned into suspicion. I want – *need* – to know what's happened to them. Whether there's anything I can do to help, whatever form that might take. And whether Michael might be hiding something about them.

I knock on the door but there's no response. I wait, then try again, with the same result. I take a few steps to my right, to the side of the house where there's a path that I know runs to their garden. But the gate is shut. I try to peek over the top of it on tiptoes, but it's just too high for me to see anything. I reach out to try the latch when I hear a lock snap and the front door is snatched open beside me. Michael's long, lean face shoots out and stares at me with obvious disdain.

'What the hell do you think you're doing?'

My hand drops to my side, like a guilty child trying to pretend they haven't just been caught stealing. 'Hi, Michael, sorry to bother you. I just… the police were here earlier, and—'

'I know.'

'Of course. So, um, they told me about Emily and Thea, and I just wanted to say how sad I was to hear what happened. I hope we find them really soon.'

He doesn't reply, just follows me with watchful eyes as I step across to stand in front of him. With the extra height of the doorstep, he towers over me by more than a foot.

'I can't imagine what you're going through,' I add. 'It must be so difficult.'

He makes a noise that's somewhere between a snort and a grunt.

'Okay, well, if I can help in any way then, you know, just ask.'

'Right.'

'And the same goes for Jack,' I add. I'm not sure why I've brought him into this; maybe I'm subconsciously trying to tap into some kind of male bond, since I seem to be failing to make any connection with Michael myself. But that's clearly a bad idea, since Jack and Michael don't particularly like each other. 'We're here for you.'

Silence.

'Is there anything you need?' I ask.

'I'm fine,' he replies, looking through me rather than at me. The strange thing is that, other than dark smudges of tiredness under his eyes, that sounds about right. In fact, Michael barely seems to be experiencing any emotion at all. I imagine the range of shock, anxiety, panic and grief I'd be going through if Jack went missing. But Michael appears to be his usual taciturn self; it wouldn't surprise me if he was just working from home today, like any other day, doing emails and coding while the police search for his missing family. Is that because he knows?…

I'm trying to work out what else to say when his head jerks up and he looks over my shoulder. I see his eyes narrow, and I turn, following his gaze to the front window of one of the terraced houses opposite, whose drapes are closed but still rippling, as if they've hastily been pulled shut while we were talking. I feel a tiny burst of irritation at the curtain-twitchers before I wonder whether I'm any better. Then I remind myself I'm here for Emily, for Thea, and not out of some morbid curiosity, but out of a desire to help my friend and her daughter.

I gesture inside. 'If you'd prefer to talk in private, we could—'

He thrusts out a hand and grips the lintel, his arm barring the doorway. 'No,' he says simply.

Instantly, I imagine he's concealing something, and another of those horrible images pops into my head. It's Emily, her hands bound, a gag in her mouth, writhing on a dirty floor... Just the thought of it gives me a stab of adrenalin and I have to pull myself back into the moment.

'Sure, sorry.' I hold up my palms to show him I'm not a threat. 'I don't mean to intrude.'

I try to peer past him into the hallway, as if that's going to hold the key to their disappearance, but I can't see anything that's different to usual. I glimpse a pair of Thea's little shoes. 'Well, you know where we are if there's any—'

But Michael closes the door in my face before I can finish repeating the offer of help. I hear the key turn in the lock, and a bolt slide across.

It's late by the time Jack gets home. I've made dinner for us – which is gradually becoming the norm, since we moved here – and already eaten mine. I've been feeling a bit more hungry than usual lately. I'm not going to apologise for cracking and dining alone; he's the one who's late. I know he's helping people, and his shifts can be unpredictable, but he could've at least texted to let me know he was on his way back.

'Hey,' I call out.

I look up from my laptop as he comes through and chucks his keys and bag down on the dining table. 'All right?' he says. I wait for him to come over and kiss me, but he doesn't.

'Have you heard?' I ask.

He frowns. 'Heard what?'

'Emily and Thea.'

'No. What about them?'

'Seriously? The police didn't call you?'

Jack shakes his head, half-smiling as if he thinks I'm winding him up. 'What're you on about?'

'They've gone missing.'

His initial reaction is to give a short, breathy laugh, which seems inappropriate. 'Really?'

'Two detectives came round this morning to talk to me.'

'Why you?'

'They're asking everyone. They want to talk to you, too.'

'Me?'

'Yes, *you*.'

'What do they think I'm gonna be able to tell them?'

I throw up my hands in exasperation. 'I don't know. Whether you saw anything or whatever.'

'I was at work,' he replies instantly.

'How do you even know what time they went missing?'

He opens his mouth but doesn't say anything for a second. Then he shrugs one shoulder. 'I just guessed... I mean, I'm at that bloody hospital most of the time, now.'

'Yeah, I know.' I don't mean for my reply to sound chippy, but it does. Jack and I stare at each other for a few seconds, then he pulls his phone out of his pocket and checks it.

'Oh, I had a missed call while I was in clinic,' he says. 'And I've got a voicemail.'

'That'll be them. You should ring back.'

'But I don't know anything,' he protests.

I point to the phone. 'Tell them that.'

'How'd they get my number?'

'I gave it to them.'

'What?' A look of annoyance flashes across his face but it disappears quickly. 'Sorry, I'm just stressed. Long day, again. I'm a bit hangry. Barely ate all shift.' He gives me that lopsided grin I can't resist.

I soften immediately. 'It's all right,' I sigh. 'There's a plate for you in the kitchen.'

'Legend.' Now, he leans over and kisses me.

I want to tell him, but I can't. Not yet.

While Jack shovels in the chicken stir-fry I made earlier, I talk him through my chat with the police, as well as what's appeared in the news (which he's been too busy to read), and my abortive attempt to offer sympathy and help to Michael.

'Christ,' he says when I've finished. 'Hope they're all okay.'

'Me too. Don't you think Michael's reaction was a bit strange, though? I mean, he literally shut the door in my face.'

'You've got to make allowances, Freya. He's probably in pieces.'

'Seemed like he didn't give a shit.'

'People express distress and grief in different ways. I see that all the time at work.'

'I still think he was behaving weirdly. Like he had something to hide.'

Jack lifts his fork. 'You don't know that.'

'Why are you defending him?' I ask. 'You don't even like him.'

'Neither do you. All I'm saying is, he might be an odd guy, but it doesn't mean he's done anything wrong, until the evidence proves otherwise.'

'What evidence?'

'I don't know. If they find that, you know…' He tails off, the unspoken implication clear.

'I just want to know what happened to them,' I say. 'Don't you?'

'Course I do.'

'A woman in her thirties – my friend – has gone missing from our road. I mean, what if it was me?'

'Come on, Freya.'

I can feel my face tightening, my eyes prickling. 'No, Jack. What if it was me and our child? What then?'

'We don't have a child.'

I don't reply right away. I'm close to tears as my hand goes to my belly. Jack looks at me for a long moment.

'Yes, we do,' I say, eventually. 'I'm pregnant.'

CHAPTER SEVEN

Tuesday, 10 August

It's almost a month since Emily and Thea disappeared. Four weeks of long days sitting at home on my laptop, with sore breasts and nausea, while Jack is at work. He's so busy in his new consultant role that he's barely had any time to spare for serious house renovations. I keep meaning to make a start on things, but I'm either too tired or too distracted, flitting between half-hearted research into possible documentary topics and news about Emily and Thea Crawford.

In the first week or two after they went missing, the media carried almost daily coverage of their case, posing questions about the reclusive husband and father, and offering theories that ranged from the conspiratorial (they're lying low abroad as part of a life insurance scam) to the absurd (alien abduction, according to one psychic). Even the serious news outlets couldn't resist running articles plastered with photos of mother and daughter looking gorgeous together: Thea a perfect mini-Emily. It sold copies and got attention, for a short time.

But, as July turned to August, and there were no new developments in the case, the story started to fade from the press, quickly replaced by newer and – as far as editors were concerned – more exciting things. It seemed as though people were forgetting about Emily and Thea, almost as if they'd never existed at all. That made me feel even sicker, scared for myself and my unborn child at the thought that, one day, you could just vanish and, a month later, the world has moved on without you. I'm determined not to let that happen.

Yesterday, I phoned that detective, Henderson, from Surrey CID. Twice. I didn't get through either time, but I left a message and this morning he called me back to repeat, like a weary parrot, the lines he'd given in the most recent press statement, last week: *We have no credible information as to their whereabouts, and we are not currently pursuing any active leads.* I tried to push him; what had the leads been? How thoroughly had they looked into Michael's background? But he just exhaled long and hard, and said he couldn't discuss details with me. If I had any new information, he added, then they'd take it into consideration. But I had nothing beyond my suspicion of Michael. And, as Jack pointed out to me, that's not based on anything more than the fact he's a bit grumpy and doesn't like small talk.

I decided it was time to speak to someone else who might be able to tell me about the Crawfords, because she's lived next door-but-one to them since they moved in six years ago. I can still recall her cryptic words of warning about them on that first day we arrived here: *Just be careful.*

Cathy's door is open again – as it has been on most of the half-dozen times I've called round in the past five months to say hello and see how she's doing – but I knock loudly and find her in the kitchen, washing up. She makes tea and we sit down together. It's turning into a hot day, but somehow her house is still chilly, and I'm glad of the warm drink. I ask if she's been following the news about Emily and Thea.

'Terrible business.' She shakes her head, gripping the cup firmly in one hand. 'Terrible.'

'What do you think happened?'

She lifts those ice-blue eyes to me. 'It's obvious, isn't it? It was him.'

'Who?' I know who she means, but I want to hear her say his name.

'The husband. Michael.'

'He forced them away?' I suggest, though I've read that, apparently, none of their personal items were taken beyond what they left with for the activity club.

'No, dear.'

'You think he's... *done* something to them?'

She gives a single, deep nod.

Part of me feels like a gossiping busybody, but I press on. 'What makes you say that?'

'He's not right.' She tilts her head. 'You must've seen it too.'

I have – at least, I think I have – but I can't put my finger on what it is. 'I've only met him a few times, and we've barely spoken. He's very reserved, maybe even rude, at times. When you say "not right", though?...'

'Well, he's tall and nice-looking, and he's got plenty of money, but he's got a temper, and he hated that little girl of his.'

'Really?'

'Oh, yes. I'd hear him shouting at her in the garden. "Holly! Get inside, now!"' she snarls, her craggy face twisting malevolently. '"No dinner again for you tonight, you stupid little bitch."'

'Holly?' I blink. 'Don't you mean Thea?'

'Who?'

'Thea, that's the name of the girl at number thirteen.'

'Is it?'

I pause, sip my tea and wonder how much I can trust what Cathy tells me. 'You heard Michael shouting at someone in the garden?'

'Not just out there.' She waves a hand vaguely towards her back window. 'Inside the house, too.'

'How did you hear that?'

'Do you think I'm lying?' Cathy gives me a rigid stare, her lips tight.

'No, God, no, Cathy. Of course not. Sorry.' My brain feels as though it's operating on half-speed, and I'm struggling to sort fact from fiction.

She wags a knowing finger at me. 'The police need to look at him. Good and close. That's what I told them.'

I calmly explain that it was reported that the police found no signs of violence in the house, and apparently Michael had a rock-solid alibi for the time of their disappearance, on a three-hour video call with some clients of his in the US.

She barks a laugh. 'You'd don't believe that, do you?'

'Is there something else?'

Cathy slowly raises the cup to her lips, drinks and replaces it in the saucer. 'That fancy man of hers.'

'Who, Emily?'

'Yes. Used to come and visit her when Michael was out.'

'A man?'

'Quite a handsome fellow, he was, too.'

I came here for information, but now I'm struggling to make sense of it all. Was there another girl called Holly, or is it Thea, and Cathy's mistaken? And who is the man who used to visit Emily? Was she having an affair?

'What do you remember about the man?' I ask.

She pushes her lower lip out. 'Not much. Always very well dressed, like my Henry is.'

I'm pretty sure Henry is dead, but I don't want to upset Cathy, so I leave it. 'Go on,' I urge.

'Usually came around the same time each week,' she continues. 'Her husband would go out somewhere, I don't know where, and the girl would be at nursery or school.'

'When was this?'

'Oh, years ago.'

'How many years ago?' I need to know if this is relevant or not.

'I can't remember.' She shakes her head, as if the memory has evaporated, like steam from a kettle. Then her gaze drifts away, out of the window, like I'm not there any more.

'Cathy?'

'Hm?' She turns back to me.

'When I was round here with Jack, months ago, the first day we moved here, you told me to be careful.'

'Did I?'

'Yes, you said I should be careful, and you were talking about the Crawfords. About Michael and Emily.'

'Was I?'

I nod encouragement. 'What did you mean by that?'

'Well, probably exactly what I said.'

I can feel my face getting hotter as my frustration grows. But I need to be patient. 'Why me, though, and why do I need to be careful?'

She sniffs, lifts her teacup again and looks at me over the brim. 'Well, it's probably because you're a lot like her. And you're pregnant, too, same as she was when they moved in.'

Jack is home at something approaching a normal time that evening, and I make us dinner; a feta and squash salad, perfect for a hot day. It'd be nice if we could eat in the garden – as I'd pictured us doing this summer – but it's still a tangled mess that we haven't sorted out yet. I put two plates down on the dining table, where Jack's already sitting in anticipation of being served food. I feel a surge of resentment at the realisation that I seem to have slid gradually and unconsciously into the role of housewife, dutifully cooking meals for my working man, tidying up and nursing an invisible bump.

Jack examines his salad and doesn't even try to hide his disappointment. 'Is that it?'

'It's good for you,' I reply. 'I've been trying to eat better, now that I'm doing it for two. 'Aren't you always telling your patients to eat healthily?'

'Yeah, but...' He prods the leaves and vegetables with his fork, as if he's hoping to find something hidden underneath, like a steak or a secret layer of mac 'n' cheese.

'What's wrong with it?' I demand.

'Oh, nothing. Just...'

Something inside me snaps at his lack of gratitude. 'If you don't like it, you can make your own bloody dinner.'

'Sorry.' He puts his fork down and reaches over, lays a hand on top of mine. 'I didn't mean to sound... Guess I'm still a bit in stressed-out work mode. It's lovely. Thank you.'

But the damage has been done. We eat in silence for a minute until I tell him that I went to see Cathy earlier, to chat about Emily and Thea.

'She thinks Michael might've been involved in it, too.'

'Based on what?'

'She said that Michael hated his daughter, and that Emily had a man who used to visit her.'

'Who was he?' Jack sounds intrigued.

'Cathy didn't know. If I'm honest, she wasn't completely making sense.'

'I'm not surprised,' he says, spearing some rocket leaves. 'I wouldn't rely on her as a source of information. Why are you so concerned about it, anyway?'

'Why am I concerned?' I can hear my own voice go up an octave. 'Why do you think, Jack? My friend and her child have gone missing and no one seems to care. No one's looking for her. For all we know, they've been murdered, and their bodies are lying somewhere undiscovered.'

'Don't be ridiculous, Freya. They haven't been murdered.'

'Haven't they?' I hold his gaze, challenging him. 'You're the one who always talks about evidence-based stuff. How do you *know* they're still alive? Where are they?'

'I haven't got a clue!'

'Well, then. At least admit it's a possibility.'

'Okay, fine.' He holds up his palms, a half-surrender. 'Maybe they have been. Or maybe they finally had enough of living with Michael and they buggered off somewhere!'

'I've researched this, Jack. I made a documentary about gender-based violence, for God's sake. It's nearly always the male partner who's responsible. But I've barely seen the police go into their house. I'd have expected them to be digging up the garden by now, sending those forensic people in white suits in to search the loft and the cellar.' I'm aware that my pulse is racing.

'Freya,' says Jack calmly. It's the tone I know he reserves for his cardiac patients, soothing and reassuring. 'I completely agree with you that it's shocking that two of our neighbours seem to have just vanished into thin air. But that doesn't mean they've been murdered or abducted, and it doesn't mean you're in danger.'

I take a deep breath. I want to believe him, but my instincts are telling me otherwise.

'We've both got a lot on right now,' he adds. 'There's the house, there's my work and there's…' He gestures to my stomach. He's still yet to show any real enthusiasm for our baby. We hadn't planned to have one yet, not until we'd fixed up the house. *A happy accident*, we call it, although that's not quite true. But it's the reference to *his* work that really grates on me, as if working is no longer something I do. It's not my fault the recession seems to have cut broadcasters' budgets for factual programmes.

'I'm just saying,' he concludes, 'that you – we – have got other things to worry about.'

I nod. He's right. But I already know that I can't let this go.

'I have to find out what happened to them,' I tell him.

He gives a quick, incredulous shake of the head. 'It's not up to you, Freya. Let the police do their jobs.'

'They're not doing anything! No active leads, that's what they said.'

'Well, if that's the case, then there's nothing to investigate.'

He's wrong. There's a story here, I know it. Something that's been covered up. Silent victims who need someone to fight for them. If Henderson and his mates in the police aren't going to do it, then I will. There's a woman and a girl who need me.

Emily once told me how alone she sometimes felt. We were walking in the park on a sunny day in April when she opened up about her background. She was an only child, and her parents had died together in a car accident while she was at university, leaving her well and truly on her own, not to mention inheriting their debts. I sympathised; I'm an only child, too, and after my parents separated my dad moved overseas and I lost touch with him. At least I still had my mum, though. Emily joked that the only person she had (apart from Michael, she added hastily, and somewhat unconvincingly) was her therapist, a lovely local guy. I said that, even though we'd only met recently, she had me, too. She thanked me but said that she didn't deserve that. I wasn't sure what she meant.

Emily's got other friends, of course, people who've known her for years, from university or work. But, perhaps, like me, she's drifted from them as they've moved and started their own families. She knows the other parents in Thea's class at school, but I don't think they're particularly close. That's why she needs me. Because, right here and right now, I'm the best friend she's got.

And I won't stop looking until I find the truth, wherever it takes me.

CHAPTER EIGHT

Those early months of getting to know you were one of the happiest times of my life. Each new day brought another discovery, and I took immense pleasure in even the smallest of these things as I gradually worked out what makes you tick. You like jogging? So do I! You take oat milk in your coffee? Me too! You prefer Instagram to Twitter? Same here! I couldn't believe how much we had in common, once I really started looking. You adore small children and animals, and they clearly love you, too; those were two very good signs for me. And there was so much more besides.

The more I found out about you, the closer I felt us becoming, and the stronger my desire for you grew. Quite simply, you were perfect. At that time, I couldn't find anything wrong with you at all. Everything confirmed what my subconscious had told me the very first moment I laid eyes on you: that we were made for each other. I was certain that nothing could get in the way of that outcome of our paths crossing. It was just a question of when, rather than if, we would be together. If I was religious, I'd say our union had been predestined by a higher power; that's how inevitable it felt.

I can only describe that feeling at the start as like taking cocaine while lying in a warm bath: at once intoxicatingly exciting and blissfully relaxing. The deepening realisation that I had found my perfect partner combined the thrill of what lay ahead for us with the knowledge that everything was going to be all right. Others must have noticed a change in me, too; a tendency to smile more often or a lightness in my step that signalled a drop in my usual stress levels.

Obviously, I couldn't tell anyone the reason for that happiness. I had to keep it under wraps, at least until I'd had a chance to set things up a little more, and to find out how you felt about me.

Of course, there was only ever going to be one right answer to that.

I couldn't accept anything else.

I wouldn't.

CHAPTER NINE

Monday, 23 August

It's mid-afternoon at the start of the week and I'm back working on my laptop after a weekend of actually doing something on the house (I know, it only took us five months to get going). Jack and I managed to paint one whole bedroom, including the ceiling: a gender-neutral green-grey colour in anticipation that it'll be our baby's room, once he or she is old enough not to sleep next to us. I felt great about it, and not only because we got it done.

Jack and I had been drifting a bit. That was partly the product of his new job, with its long, endlessly busy hours crammed with demanding, draining tasks that could mean the difference between life and death for his patients. I'd seen in Jack's previous positions how carrying all that on his shoulders takes its toll, and now he's a consultant, the burden's heavier than it's ever been. Meanwhile, my own professional situation is the exact opposite; pitch after pitch rejected by production companies who like my ideas but have no money to make them, or by broadcasters who have money but want to make something else. It hadn't just been work, though. It was also our baby.

I'd told Jack that I was on the pill. I'd been taking it since about a year into our relationship, and we'd talked about me coming off it when we both felt that the time was right for us to try for a baby. I thought arriving here was the best time to try. Jack disagreed. We debated it for a week or two. But then I decided to stop taking the pill without telling him. I said to Jack that it must have been an accident, that the pill doesn't offer total protection. As a doctor, he should know that. Does he suspect I stopped taking it? Maybe. Once I was pregnant, though, he seemed to accept it. But his response was to distance himself slightly from me, as if he was letting me know that *he* still didn't feel it was the right time. I called him out on that, but he denied it, of course, and blamed his behaviour on work. I knew the baby was a part of our problems, though.

However, as we painted the room last weekend, something seemed to shift, just a little. I started to feel closer to Jack, again, and he touched me more on those two days than he had in the whole of the previous month. We kissed, our faces splattered with tiny droplets of paint, as passionately as we had on some of our first dates. Whether it was the physical task, the ability to chat or be silent as we wished, or the chance to throw our favourite tunes on the Sonos and bop in time to the music as we painted that did it, I don't know. But, as the paint dried and we stood back to admire our handiwork, his arm around my shoulder and mine around his waist, I started to picture our future as a family once more. Our baby – a little girl, I reckon – standing up in her crib, gripping the sides of it with chubby fingers, slightly unsteady on bandy legs, gurgling at us and laughing.

I can't let my imagination run away with me, though. There's still a very long way to go. I'm only ten weeks, by my calculations, and our twelve-week scan is booked for a fortnight. I can already see the shape of our little girl moving on the ultrasound scanner. But I remind myself that, in the meantime, I need to come up with a documentary pitch that no one can turn down, and I've got to keep looking for leads on Emily and Thea. I can't just let them disappear.

To fuel these tasks, I've made myself a plate of boiled eggs with hot sauce and mayonnaise. I wasn't particularly into any of those things before I became pregnant, but I've read about some really mad cravings (chewing on cigarette butts, believe it or not) and aversions (*all* sweet things, which is unthinkable, even with my imagination) that other women have had during their terms, so I guess it's not that bad. Eggs are healthy, I suppose. The strange thing is that, having made the snack, I now don't really feel like eating it. I'm as tired as ever, but at least my breasts don't feel so swollen and tender as before.

I turn my attention back to the laptop screen. Unsurprisingly, there's been no real news over the weekend about Emily or Thea. A possible sighting in Cornwall last Monday turned out not to be them, just like the one in Oxford a week before that. I run a hand over my bump – which is starting to show, now, through anything but the baggiest tops – and wonder about poor little Thea. Had Emily needed to protect her, perhaps, from Michael? I can see myself defending my child's life with my own, if necessary, with an elemental ferocity that would be almost outside my control, when—

My muscles tense as a cramp seizes hold of my stomach. My lower back goes rigid and tight, and the stab of pain reaches my pelvis and vagina. I gasp aloud, gripping the edge of the table and bending forward, biting my tongue until, eventually, it passes.

It's not the first time that's happened and, same as the occasional spotting of blood I've noticed, apparently it's not uncommon in the early stages of pregnancy. I told Jack about it, and he said it was fine, that there was nothing to worry about. He's not an obstetrician, of course, but he's still a doctor, and he's my fiancé, so I trust him. I've had no other complications or issues so far. I try to get back to work.

Half an hour later there's another cramp. It's bigger and more painful than the last, and I feel as though I need to tense everything to fight it off, clenching my teeth and willing it to subside. As it fades, I feel an overwhelming urge to go to the toilet and relieve the pressure. When I do, I notice blood on the toilet paper, more than before, and it's a reddish-brown colour. I know something's not right.

I'm drained already, and now I'm starting to panic. I drag myself back into the living room and grab my phone, jabbing at the screen to call Jack. I hear my own heavy breaths over his ringtone as I wait for him to pick up. But he doesn't. It goes to voicemail. I hang up and try again. Same result. Shit. He could be in clinic, on a ward round, or telling a patient's loved ones that they didn't make it – who knows? – but I just really need him now. Right now.

'Answer the fucking phone, Jack!' I yell as I call him one more time.

I put my left hand inside my pants, and when I take them out again, my fingertips are red and slick with my own blood. This is not good. This is really not good.

Jack's voicemail kicks in again, and I hear myself saying: 'Call me back as soon as you can, Jack, I think I might be losing our baby.'

At those words, my throat begins to tighten, a lump seeming to form in it as my lips compress and twist and I try not to cry. I need to hold it together. I need help. I call my mum.

'Hello, darling,' she says, and immediately starts explaining how she needs to go into the other room to get the cordless phone because the reception is better on that in the kitchen, where she's in the middle of making scones, and—

I cut her off and tell her what's going on. Her reply is swift and clear.

'Call an ambulance, Freya. I'm going to hang up now while you do that, and I want you to ring me straight back as soon as you've done it.'

I mumble my agreement before she ends the call, and then I dial 999.

But part of me feels as though I'm already too late.

That my little girl is already gone.

CHAPTER TEN

Friday, 10 September

'So, just tell me in your own words, Freya, what happened after that. Take your time.'

Laurence, my new therapist, leans slightly back in his chair, notebook propped on crossed legs, pen poised above it, ready to write. He tilts his head forward and to one side, giving me his full attention. I know we've only got about half an hour left of our fifty-minute session, but it's like we have all the time in the world. More importantly, I feel as though someone is actually listening to me for the first time in almost three weeks. That I don't have to pretend I'm okay.

I begin describing the day I realised something was wrong, and Laurence listens carefully, nodding every so often, and making small 'mm' noises to show he's heard me. He jots a few notes, but not excessively. As painful as it is to go through this, I know that I need it, and now I'm here, I'm actually starting to relax. Laurence's presence, his smart-casual outfit, his neat-yet-cosy consulting room – all of it evokes a sense of calm for me.

On several occasions since I found Laurence (on one of those websites that lists therapists near you), I've felt a pang of guilt about the cost. His sessions aren't cheap – £130 an hour, in fact – but he has great online reviews, a ton of letters after his name, and I can walk to his office easily. More than that, he was able to start seeing me immediately, versus the one month wait just to get an assessment in the National Health Service. Even with the supposed priority they give to perinatal patients, I could still have finished a course of treatment with Laurence before I've even had my first proper NHS appointment. And I need his help right now. I've needed it since the day I lost my baby.

It's not that Jack isn't helping. He is – he's paying for this. In some ways, I'd rather have his time or empathy, even just a consoling touch. Perhaps if I'd had that three weeks ago, I wouldn't need Laurence. Instead, my fiancé's contribution to my recovery – money – becomes another reminder of the space between us, of the growing power imbalance as his income shoots up and mine dwindles to almost nothing. And I get to pour my heart out to a total stranger.

That said, there is something different about talking to Laurence. He's got a distance from my miscarriage that Jack will never have, because it was his baby, too. In some ways, it's easier to speak to my new therapist about it *because* he's a stranger. He has no preconceptions or biases or history; I feel that he just accepts who I am, here and now. It's only our first session, but we're already covering things that Jack and I haven't yet properly discussed.

With a few careful prompts from Laurence, I go on to describe the hospital visit the day that I started to get cramps and bleeding. The ultrasound scan where I knew it was the worst news because the sonographer said she needed to fetch a doctor. Being told gently but clearly that my baby had no heartbeat. The tablets to speed up the miscarriage, which happened at home about eight days later. Feeling like a failure because I was in so much pain that I couldn't catch what came out of me in a sieve to collect it for testing. That awful moment of wondering if I was just flushing my baby down the toilet.

Laurence asks if I had anyone with me at that time. I shake my head. Jack was at work, as usual, saving lives, while I was expelling one from my body that had ended before it even began. My mother offered to travel down from Cheshire to stay with me, but she's semi-housebound with her lung problems, and I didn't want to drag her away from home, where she's got everything she needs, and make her sleep on a sofa bed in an unfurnished spare room. And my friends in Hackney were too far away to make it across town in time. Besides, the only one I've told about it so far was Bea, and she's got her own baby, now, which is taking up a hundred per cent of her time and energy.

'That sounds as though it was incredibly difficult for you, Freya,' says Laurence with genuine warmth. 'And that you've had to be extremely resilient to cope with most of that alone. How do you feel, talking about it now?'

'I… well, part of me knows that miscarriages are more common than everyone thinks, because it's not talked about much. What is it, something like one in four pregnancies?'

'I think so.'

'But even knowing that figure, reading it, you don't think it'll be you.' I pause, feeling myself well up a bit. I don't want to break down crying in front of Laurence at our first session; I don't want him thinking I'm some mad woman who's emotionally all over the place. And, yet, I know that he won't judge me for it, that he'll say the right thing. I stop resisting and feel the muscles of my face squeeze tight as warm tears fill my eyes.

'Take all the time you need. This is very recent, Freya; it's completely normal for it to feel so raw.'

He's right, it is raw. Hearing him say that does something to me. Like I have permission to grieve, now. Jack is such a pragmatist that he was back at work the next day, dealing with it in that matter-of-fact way that medical professionals do so well, because they have to. But I can't do that. And I feel bad for not having dealt with it already, even though it hasn't yet been three weeks. I explain this to the therapist.

'Everyone needs to find their own way of processing an event like this,' he replies. 'And that's what I'll try to help you with.'

He asks what I'm doing with my time at the moment, how I'm spending my days.

'I don't really know,' I say. 'I get up at a different time every day, walk around the house a bit, eat, watch TV…'

He nods, scribbles a note or two.

'I just don't think I can work at the moment,' I add. 'I can't think clearly enough, you know?'

Laurence tells me about the psychological approach called 'behavioural activation', which suggests that doing things, even when you don't feel like it, improves your mood, which gives you more motivation to do other stuff you enjoy, and so on. There's good evidence behind it, apparently. He asks if I'd be willing to try something. I say yes, I just can't think of what to do. I can't do serious exercise, because my body's still recovering. I can't face house renovations; that's just too big a task. I ask if he's got any ideas.

'Actually, there is one thing I've been thinking about, as we've been talking,' Laurence says.

'What's that?'

'Well, you mentioned before that your garden is a bit over-grown.'

'Did I say that?'

'Mm. You were talking about things you had to do at home but hadn't been able to get around to. So, I'm just wondering whether there might be an opportunity to do one or two small tasks out there.'

He goes on to list the benefits: fresh air, sunlight and vitamin D, physical activity and sense of purpose and achievement if we set simple, measurable goals for it. Suddenly, I can picture myself out there, in nature, working, creating. Like the garden's a metaphor for nurturing my mind and body back to health. And I feel something I haven't felt for many days.

Hope.

CHAPTER ELEVEN

Friday, 17 September

It's a beautiful, sunny afternoon. I'm out in the garden, working away, and I feel good. Not yet completely back to normal (whatever that is), but certainly the best I've felt emotionally and physically since that weekend painting the bedroom with Jack almost four weeks ago. Laurence was right; this is the perfect activity to get me up, out and moving, giving me something to do that I can feel proud of when I've finished. I'd never have thought that, at age thirty-five, I'd be listing gardening among my favourite hobbies, but there you go.

My new pastime is going as well as our course of therapy; we've had three sessions together (Tuesdays and Fridays) and we're making great progress. Earlier today we were talking about traumatic triggers that remind me of the miscarriage, and how I can separate them in my mind into 'then' and 'now', so that they don't set off my fight-or-flight system. My therapist has a way of explaining things that makes them easy to understand, and never makes me feel as though there's something wrong with me. I wish I could say the same for my fiancé.

I know Jack loves me, but being a medical doctor, his mentality is about diagnosing problems and fixing them. You find out what's wrong, and you sort it out. There's no room for grey areas, for messy, complex feelings and tricky, irrational thoughts. He variously suggested that I try anti-anxiety medication or antidepressants, maybe even a mood stabiliser. I was really pissed off with him.

Deep down, I'm sure Jack did that out of a sense of care, of wanting to make sure I was all right. But in the process, he forgot that I'm his fiancée, not one of his patients, just another sick woman to be medicated. If the problem was inside my aorta, he'd be all over it. He'd know exactly what to do. When it comes to my mind, though, sometimes I think he doesn't have a clue. I accused him of wanting to drug me up; he protested, and we had a row.

His way of apologising, a day later, was to buy me a present. In fact, he went a bit overboard with it, supporting my new pastime by buying me a load of gardening equipment. Spade, fork, wheelbarrow, gloves, kneelers and – the main event, despite being the smallest item – a pair of secateurs. Jack was particularly pleased with the secateurs. They're Japanese steel, apparently: razor-sharp and super-expensive. I was grateful, of course, but when I queried the cost of it all, Jack's response was to joke that I was cheaper than paying a gardener.

I was furious with him, again. He'd managed to take something that was playing a major role in my recovery and turn it into another example of the difference in financial power between us.

'I didn't mean it,' he'd apologised, hastily. 'I was just trying to help you be more active, you know? Do something you wanted to do. That's all.'

But I already felt alienated and, as I tried to explain to him that the damage was done, I started crying. His predictably male response was simply to tell me: *don't cry*.

Today, I cried in the session with Laurence. His reaction was totally different. He didn't intervene, didn't even offer me a tissue. Later, he explained that it was because the act of offering a tissue might imply that I should do something about my tears, that I should cover them up. He had a box of tissues, right there on the table, but he said that I needed to be the one to reach for them, if I wanted one. That tears were completely normal and didn't need to be stopped. That I didn't need to feel ashamed of them, or as though they represented a weakness. I liked that.

Now, as I snip at some overgrown brambles, I find myself thinking about Laurence. Wondering if he has the same capacity for empathy and compassion with the people in his life outside of work. Imagining who they might be. A special woman, or man, perhaps... I can't tell. He's hard to read. He's older than Jack, with a bit of grey in his hair, but he clearly looks after himself physically. I can picture him casually doing a triathlon at the weekends. Or pulling off some ridiculously difficult yoga pose: scorpion or peacock, maybe. While simultaneously meditating. I laugh to myself at the image and then think that, whoever he spends his private time with, I hope they realise how lucky they are. If he and I were together, I'd appreciate him as much as I know he'd value me.

I've been going steadily at the untamed jungle for about three hours, and the warmth of the afternoon is fading as the sun starts to dip towards the horizon. I've begun clearing a space towards the rear for a bonfire from the vegetation I've cut away. As I lug the collection of brushwood and brambles back, I realise that I haven't yet been to the very bottom of our garden. I decide to take a look.

I fetch the secateurs and have to cut away some branches and push others aside to get through. I get whipped across the arms and legs, and even full in the face on one occasion. On the other side, though, about eighty feet or more from the house, I can see that the fences run out. Maybe whoever installed them, years ago, didn't bother to take them all the way back to the rear wall. Perhaps there was some agreement that the end would be a communal space; I can ask Cathy about it, if she remembers. What it means, though, is that I can go into her garden as easily as she could enter mine. And the same goes for the Crawfords' house on the other side.

I walk towards Michael and Emily's land, peering through the vegetation. I can make out the perfectly landscaped space at the back of their house, and it reminds me of the time Emily and I drank gin and tonics out there. I complimented her on the garden, and she laughed, saying that she'd never laid a finger on it, and couldn't take credit for anything more than finding some decent gardeners online. I remember her self-deprecating smile as she admitted outsourcing all the best stuff in their home, and I feel a little jolt of sadness.

The landscaping extends around sixty feet back from the house. Beyond that boundary, in the area I can see now, they seem to have let nature take control. There's an old wooden shed that looks like it belongs more in our run-down garden than theirs. I really want to look more closely, but I know I shouldn't.

My guilty conscience at the prospect of trespassing makes me glance up at the windows of number thirteen to see whether I'm being observed, but they're all dark and empty. Michael's in his man-cave, I expect, coding away. I'm curious as to how much thought he gives to his wife and daughter. Whether, like me, he spends half of every day wondering where they are, searching the news for daily updates and calling Emily's phone, just in case she picks up. Or whether he was involved in their disappearance.

I step as far as I dare, imagining a line on the ground that marks the boundary between our property and theirs. *You shall not pass.* But I can't resist. I take one step onto it, then another, and another and, before I know it, I'm in their back garden, exploring. I duck beneath long, low tree branches, reaching out like spindly arms, their fingers clawing at my shoulders as I move towards the shed.

It's neglected, almost decaying. Tentacles of ivy snake their way around its splintered wood, moss grows in thick tufts on the ripped, dirty felt roof and the only window I can make out is completely opaque. As I get closer, I can see that the small pane of glass is covered with cobwebs and mould on the inside. It's horror-film creepy, but something about it is drawing me to it.

I recall a news article I read once about a man in South Carolina who kept a woman in a container in his backyard for months. Suddenly the scene forms in my mind: Emily, chained up inside. I feel the panic start to rise up and before I know it, I'm calling out.

'Hello, can anyone hear me? Emily? Thea?'

But there's no response. Just silence, punctuated by some distant conversation from another garden several houses away. I get a little closer, hoping I might be able to see inside, just to check, to make sure. My eyes are on the shed when my foot connects with something. Instinctively, I know it's not a leaf or a branch or anything natural. I look down.

It's a shoe.

One, single, tiny red shoe. I bend to inspect it more closely. It has a buckle, and a flower-petal shape cut into the material above the toes. But it doesn't appear old and discarded. It's clean, new and seems like it must have belonged to Thea. Why is there only one, though? And why is it all the way back here? I glance at the shed again, my pulse pounding at my temple. I poke at the undergrowth around the shoe with my plimsoll. And that's when I see it.

A ring.

It's a simple gold band, like a wedding ring. Maybe it is a wedding ring. Maybe it's Emily's. In that moment, the thought of what might've happened to her is too much, and I can't control my reaction.

I scream.

Only for a second, perhaps not even that long, before my hand shoots up and clamps over my mouth. I shouldn't be here. I freeze, rooted to the spot. I don't know what to do.

Then a sound comes from the house, like a window opening. My head jerks up and I scan the windows at the back of the Crawfords' house. I think I see some movement, but I can't be certain. Did Michael hear me? Has he seen me? The hairs on the nape of my neck are tingling and I have the horrible sensation that I'm being watched. I turn and run, twigs snapping under my feet and branches raking my skin as I head for the safety of my own garden.

I don't look back.

CHAPTER TWELVE

Saturday, 18 September

Michael's Range Rover pulls away from the kerb. I watch from the living room window as it roars off down the road, around the corner and out of sight. I half-jog through to the kitchen where Jack is reading the news on his tablet and drinking coffee. He's made it in a fancy new machine he's bought for us, one of those bean-to-cup things that's the size of a photocopier and cost £500. I can't complain – it is good coffee – but it's as though our old £10 cafetière isn't good enough, any more. Like a symbol of our simpler, past life that's gradually being jettisoned, piece by piece. And I don't like it, as if those old things represent a kind of security, from a time when I had more certainty about what was important. But I can't dwell on that right now.

'He's gone out,' I say. 'Come on, let's go.'

Jack compresses his lips for a moment and looks up from the screen. 'I don't know…'

'Don't you want to see?'

'It's trespassing.'

I shrug. 'Only if we get caught.'

'Well, what if we *do* get caught? What if he comes back and we're just standing there in the middle of his garden?'

'He's at the supermarket,' I counter.

'How do you know that?'

'He always goes there on a Saturday morning, so—'

'Have you been spying on him?'

'No!' My response is quick, outraged. 'Okay, maybe a bit.' I squint and make a finger-and-thumb gesture to show how little *a bit* is. 'But if there's even the tiniest chance he's involved in their disappearance, which I think he could be, then we need to check it out, and you said—'

'Freya.' Jack lays the tablet on the table and turns his body to me. 'I know what I said, but…'

Last night, when I told Jack what I'd found in the Crawfords' garden, he agreed to come and take a look with me, to let me show him. That wasn't his initial reaction. The first thing he asked was, 'Are you sure?', as if I can't trust my own senses. I might have overreacted slightly to that. I said that my eyes worked perfectly well, thank you very much, and we needed to go and see what else was in the garden and whether it might be connected with Emily and Thea going missing. To photograph the shoe and the ring, at the very least, so we can show the police. And check out the shed, to see if we can work out what's inside. Eventually, Jack said that he'd come with me. But, having slept on it, he seems to have changed his tune.

'You agreed.' I point an accusing finger at him. 'When we discussed it yesterday, you agreed.'

'I know, but…' He tails off, reluctant to tell me the truth.

'But what? Go on.'

'Nothing.'

'No. You mean: *but…* you only said that to shut me up, right? You didn't really want to go over there.'

'It's not that.' His eyes widen. 'It's just, you were getting really worked up about it.'

I take a breath. I need *not* to appear agitated now, even though I am. 'If I'm worked up, Jack, it's because I care about my friend and her daughter. No one else seems to. I want to know what the bloody hell happened to them, and this might help me – help

us – find out. The police clearly didn't even go to that part of the
garden, if they searched for evidence out there at all; otherwise
they would've discovered the shoe. And probably the ring, too.'

'That's a fair point,' he concedes. 'But those things aren't
necessarily connected with them going missing.'

'Aren't they? Surely it's worth a look. We document it, we
pass it on.'

'Ah...'

'Okay. If you don't want to come, I'll go on my own and film
it so you can see. Since you don't seem to believe me.'

'I do believe you,' he insists.

'Well, come and see for yourself then.'

Jack sighs. 'How long till he gets back?'

'Half an hour.'

He pushes back his chair and stands. 'You sure?'

'Yup.' I hope I'm right.

Hands on hips, Jack gives a long, slow breath out. 'Let me
get my shoes.'

We walk in silence, picking and pushing our way through to the
end of our overgrown garden. The vegetation gets thicker and more
impenetrable the further back we go, although this time I notice
how little of it seems to be alive. Brushwood crackles with almost
every step we take, as if announcing our intrusion as we near the
Crawfords' side. Jack and I exchange a glance. He looks apprehen-
sive, paler than he was in the kitchen, but nods quickly as I gesture
towards the shed. I'm already scanning the leaf litter for Thea's shoe
when there's a wet crack behind me and I hear Jack's voice.

'Jesus, fucking...'

I whip round, my heart already beating hard. He's looking at
the ground. I follow his gaze. But it's a false alarm. He's put his
foot through a large piece of rotten wood, which has disintegrated

under his weight and released a colony of woodlice that are now going berserk, running over his shoe as they flee for cover.

'You okay?' I ask.

'Fine.' He kicks out, shakes off the last few bugs. 'So, it's over there?'

'Yeah. Come on.'

I lead Jack over the invisible line that separates our property from next door's, under the scratchy branches and across to the old wooden shed. If it hadn't been for the shoe and the ring, I'd have said no one has been down here for years. The soil is hard and dry and compacted and covered with a layer of dead twigs and leaves. Above us, the tree canopies are conspiring to keep out the daylight, and in the strange gloom the shed is as foreboding as the first time I saw it, yesterday evening.

Retracing my steps towards it, I feel a coldness in my belly. I try to stay calm and keep moving. I can't see the shoe yet. A few yards further on, I reach the point where I found it and the ring.

But I can't see them.

'So, where are they?' Jack demands, suddenly right behind me. I can feel his breath on the back of my neck.

'They were just here.' I scan the ground. 'There's no sign of them. 'They must be...'

'Is this a joke, because—'

'I swear, Jack. This is where I saw them. A single, red, girl's shoe and a gold ring.'

He makes a teeth-sucking sound of scepticism. 'What, here?'

'Yes. Fuck's sake,' I mutter, prodding the leaves and twigs with my shoe, clearing them aside. 'I'm not making this up.'

'Well. There's obviously nothing here,' announces Jack. 'So, we should probably get off Michael's land and back inside before he comes home. Freya, what are you?...'

I'm down on hands and knees, now, scrabbling at the earth, shifting every bit of debris I can get my hands on in search of the shoe, the ring, or anything else that might belong to Emily and Thea. That might give an indication of what happened to them.

'They've...' I check around me, get my bearings. This is definitely the right place. 'They've gone.'

Jack is silent. And I know exactly what he's thinking. That it was my imagination. All in my mind. I dare him to say it. But he doesn't. Instead, he simply announces he's going.

'Wait!' I get up, brush all the crap off my elbows and knees. 'Let's take a look at the shed.'

'I don't think that's a good idea.'

'We're here now.'

He reaches out, and I feel his fingers curl around my arm. 'Freya, no, let's head back.'

'Come on.' I pull away from his grip and walk over. Behind me, Jack stands still. I hear him curse under his breath.

I keep to the back of the shed for extra cover, even though I'm pretty sure Michael's still out. I round the little building, not really knowing what I'm searching for. I reach the other side of it. Then I freeze.

'Oh my god. Jack!'

'What?'

'You have to see this.'

'What is it?' He crashes and snaps his way through until he's next to me.

My breaths are shallow, and I feel sweat prickle under my eyes. 'Look.'

On the far side of the shed is a metal fire pit. It's a low, broad dish mounted on a stubby tripod. And inside it is a mass of charred... stuff. Whatever it is, it's been incinerated. But that isn't even the thing that has my attention, now. It's what's next to the fire pit.

A large rectangular plot of bare earth. It looks as though it's been freshly dug. And it's about the right size for a human body.

My brain goes into overdrive as I imagine what lies beneath that layer of soil.

Then we hear the car engine at the front.

CHAPTER THIRTEEN

Before long, you were like a drug to me. The more I got of you, the more I craved you. When I wasn't finding out about you, I felt the urge to stop whatever dull or mundane thing I was doing and get back to that more important activity: you. I'd want to feel that sweet dopamine hit again, the one that flooded my brain each time I stepped into your world.

Soon, I began to notice that I was experiencing withdrawal symptoms from that sensation, just like a drug. If I wasn't immersed in you, discovering what made you tick, who your friends were, what your favourite outfits were, where you'd been, and all those other little things that made up your life, I'd start to become edgy. Anxious, frustrated, even angry. And me being angry isn't good for anyone. When I get like that, things have a tendency to… break. I quickly realised what was happening. I was becoming addicted to you.

Experts tell us that there are three parts to addiction: craving, withdrawal and tolerance. Pretty soon, I had the full house. I diagnosed myself with an acute case of dependency on you. Craving and withdrawal I could deal with; they were about wanting you. Feeling good when I was focused on you, and bad when I wasn't. Simple, really. It was the third symptom, tolerance, that changed everything.

Soon, just reading about you on social media and elsewhere wasn't enough. It stopped producing the hit. From what I knew about addiction, I understood that I had two choices. One, I could give you up. Break away, go cold turkey, put myself into a kind of monastic isolation as a form of rehab. Or, two, I could find a way to get a bigger hit. I thought about this for all of five seconds before choosing option two.

So, the question became: how to get a bigger hit of you? Well, there was one obvious answer to that.

Since our first encounter, I'd been keeping my distance. Staying in the shadows, mostly, until I knew more about you. Keeping my true intentions to myself. Now, it was time to get closer to you. To really get to know you, IRL – In Real Life. It was the obvious next step in our lives together.

But I wasn't prepared for what my new proximity to you would reveal, or the events it would set in train. If I'd known then what I know now, would I have stopped? Gone back and selected option one instead?

Not a chance.

We were meant to be, and no way was I giving you up.

Not for anything or anyone.

I'd accept the consequences of my addiction.

Whatever they were.

CHAPTER FOURTEEN

Monday, 20 September

I'm lying on my back, completely still. It's dark, and I can feel the ground beneath me, cold and hard. I know something's wrong because I can't move. My legs and arms are completely rigid, and all I can do is look up, past deep, dark walls and into the oblong of night beyond. A ragged cloud drifts across the blue-black sky and I focus on it for a moment, until I hear the snick of spade cutting soil. Seconds later, the first shovelful of earth tumbles over the sides and onto me. Then another, and another. I try to scream, but when I open my mouth, there's no sound. I try harder, but all I get are lumps of dirt and little stones in my mouth. No sooner have I spat them out than more cascade in. Soon, my mouth is full and I feel as though I can't even breathe. Then it stops. A figure looms over the side of my grave. I can't make out his face, but I know it's a man. He looks at me, pauses. Then he disappears from view and the digging starts again, faster this time, more urgent, the earth piling up on me until—

My eyes open and I'm in bed. My breathing is super-fast, and it takes a second to realise it wasn't real. That I'm safe. I wipe my hands over my face. I was so shit scared that I could almost laugh now, if my heart wasn't beating so quickly.

'Oh my god,' I whisper to myself, rocking over and getting up. I check the clock on my phone: 8.03 a.m. Jack's nowhere to be seen, but then I catch the sound of his coffee machine rumbling, whirring and hissing in the kitchen. I throw on my dressing gown and pad downstairs.

'Morning,' I say.

'Sleep okay?' he asks, barely glancing up from his phone. I can see he's on WhatsApp. He's fully dressed in a pale blue shirt and navy chinos.

'Er, no, actually.' I grab a bowl from the cupboard. 'Just had a horrible dream.'

Jack sips his coffee. 'Was it about, you know?…'

'My miscarriage?' I call it what it was; I don't want to refer to it as an *accident* or an *incident* or anything else that somehow plays it down or stops it being talked about properly. My therapist encouraged me not to be afraid to do that.

'Yeah.' He casts a quick glance at the phone screen.

'When we lost our unborn child,' I add.

'Freya.'

'Our little girl.'

'We don't know it was—' Jack stops himself, goes quiet.

It's strange how, since the miscarriage, it's my pragmatic, medic fiancé who's the one that tiptoes around it. The man who routinely tells people that their hearts don't work, or that their loved ones have died, doesn't want to discuss the death of our ten-week-old baby.

'No, in fact it wasn't about that. I had a nightmare that I was being buried alive.'

'Christ.'

'I know. So…' I start spooning granola from the big tub on the side into my bowl. 'Not sure which of those is less awful. Guess it shows what's on my mind, though.'

Jack takes a big gulp of coffee. 'We talked about this yesterday,' he says warily.

'Probably why I was dreaming about it. That, and the fact that I reckon my friend could be buried in the garden next door. Maybe with her child.' I don't mean to sound flippant. It's just that Jack doesn't seem to be taking this anywhere near as seriously as I am.

'There was a patch of ground that might've been dug. We have no clue what's in it, if anything.' He finishes his drink and slaps the cup down on the side with unnecessary force.

'Do you know what percentage of female murder victims in this country were killed by their partner or ex over the past decade?'

'Okay, but—'

'Sixty-two per cent.' I stare at him. 'Sixty-two.'

'Freya...'

'Why aren't the police doing anything about it? All you have to do is google this stuff and there are examples from all over the world of men murdering their female partners and burying them in the garden. Australia, Israel, France, the US. Police fail to spot it all the time.'

'You might be exaggerating a bit, there.'

'I don't think so.'

He huffs a breath of frustration. 'Well, obviously the police have had a look at Michael, and they don't think there's anything else to investigate.'

'That's because we haven't told them about the stuff we found.'

'What, the ring and the shoe that aren't there?'

I fold my arms. 'You still don't believe I saw them, do you?'

'I'm not saying that.' He shoves his phone into his pocket, then he comes over and clamps his hands on my shoulders. 'I just think, you know, spending so much time worrying about Emily is stressing you out. Now it's affecting your sleep. You need to look after yourself. Stop thinking about them and focus on your recovery,' he adds, gently, touching his fingertips to my collarbones.

He might be right. But he's missing the point. For me, finding the truth about Emily and Thea isn't an obstacle to my recovery. It's part of it.

*

It's the middle of the day and the house is quiet. I'm upstairs in the room that we call the 'spare' bedroom – a title given because it's empty, rather than because you could sleep in it – dutifully doing the laundry. I've taken the dry clothes off the rack and am hanging up a new load that's just come out of the washing machine. I'm feeling bored. And a tiny bit resentful.

I know laundry is part of the chores of running a household, a job that has to be done, but it seems to be me who does most of it these days, same as the food shopping, cooking and cleaning, while Jack is working at the hospital. As if there was something in the small print about staying at home after a miscarriage which says that I also have to act as a domestic servant while I recuperate.

Part of me longs to rewind a year, to the days when I made documentaries, having a big, meaningful project to get stuck into, research and interviews. But I know that's not realistic right now. I need more time, and besides, no one seems to want to make documentaries at the moment. Not mine, at least. The thought gets me down a bit, and next thing I'm remembering the baby I lost, the role I could've had as a mother. The sadness of that threatens to envelop me.

I try to distract myself by looking out of the window and down into the garden, to choose which part of it I'm going to tackle this afternoon. But my mind immediately goes to the rectangle of earth on the other side of the shed. I can't even see the shed from here; it's masked by thick bushes and trees at the back of Michael and Emily's garden. I can picture it so clearly, though, and the dark remnants of a fire beside it. Then a memory of my nightmare comes to me, and I stop what I'm doing, a ripple of fear slithering through my stomach until a deep, disembodied voice pulls me out of it.

It's Michael. He's on the other side of the wall.

'…the signal's better up here,' he says loudly. There's a silence before he speaks again; he must be on a mobile phone. He says something I can't quite catch, so I get closer to the wall.

'Yeah, well, you know what she was like.' His tone is calm, matter-of-fact. He agrees with something a few times in quick succession, in that way that people (usually men) do when they don't really want to listen to what the other person is saying. When they think they already know the answer. I realise how Jack has been doing that more, recently, when I hear the next thing Michael says: 'It had to be dealt with.'

You know what she was like.

I can't help thinking that he's talking about Emily, and perhaps Thea. That it was his wife and daughter who *had to be dealt with*. It gives me a chill that Michael might be no more than a few feet away from me. I can picture his smug face as he brags to someone about what he's done.

I've abandoned the laundry completely, now, and I'm pressed to the wall, my ear against the old wallpaper we haven't stripped yet, holding my breath so that I don't miss anything. But there's just some mumbling and a sniff, followed by a sigh, and I can't work out what he said.

Then he's clear again: 'There was no love. None at all.'

Is he still talking about his family? He must be; it makes sense if, as Cathy and I both think, he had something to do with their disappearance. I recall a conversation I had with Emily, one afternoon in late spring. I'd run into her on my way back from the post office, and she'd invited me in for a cup of tea. We'd talked about children, and I asked if she and Michael planned to have any more. She didn't answer directly; instead, she said: 'It's a wonderful thing to have a child with the man you love.' Now I'm wondering what she meant by that. Is it possible that she loved Michael and he didn't love her back? That seems the wrong way round. She was the catch; he was the one lucky to be with her. I'm still trying to work it out when I hear Michael again, from beyond the bedroom wall.

'He was just there, you know? He was in the way.'

I blink. He definitely said *he*. Who's he talking about? But there's no more detail. Michael makes a few affirmative noises and then signs off. I catch what sounds like some muttered profanity: short, harsh sounds. Then I hear his footsteps leaving the room and fading away. I can't make sense of the snippets. But overhearing Michael has done nothing to ease my suspicions of him. I know enough, at least, for one thing to be clear now. I need to take what I've got on the Crawfords to the police.

I jog downstairs to fetch my phone. Detective Henderson's number is already stored in my contacts list.

CHAPTER FIFTEEN

Wednesday, 22 September

I'm sitting on a metal chair that's bolted to the floor in the waiting area of Staines Police Station. I've made the half-hour train journey here, to the building that houses North Surrey CID, to see (acting) Detective Inspector Paul Henderson. It's taken me two days' worth of calls to his mobile before he eventually rang me back and bluntly asked me to give him the new information I *claimed* to have. But I insisted on meeting face to face, because I didn't want him to fob me off like he did the last time I called him. When you've got someone there, in person, you can pin them down, make sure they're recording it, that it's all official.

I check the time on my phone. He said to come at 11.30, which I did. It's 11.47, now, and there's still no sign of him. He knows I'm here because I texted him, as well as letting the person on the desk know I'd arrived. I'm about to get up and ask them what's happening, to tell them how important this is, when a door opens and Henderson appears. He sees me and lumbers over.

He looks dishevelled, like one of those overworked cops in a movie who's entirely neglecting his private life to pursue a case that his uptight boss is threatening to take him off. I wonder if that's true; if it is, it's certainly not the case of Emily and Thea's disappearance. He's dressed identically to when he came to our house, down to the loose tie knot, and I imagine him having a wardrobe full of the same outfit. Apparently, Obama did that when he was in the White House. I realise that, in Henderson's case, it's far more likely he's just wearing exactly the same clothes. That this *is* his entire wardrobe.

'Miss Northcott,' he says. 'You said you've got something for us.'

'*Ms* Northcott.' I stand. 'Yes, I have.'

'Okay.' He nods once. 'So, what is it?'

I glance around the waiting area. There are a couple of other members of the public here, as well as the uniformed officer behind the desk. 'I'd prefer to speak in private,' I say.

Henderson sighs, as if my request is both unreasonable and inconvenient, then turns towards the desk.

'Tash,' he calls out. 'Is interview one free?'

The woman clicks her mouse a few times, eyes scanning the monitor in front of her. 'Yeah, you can have that, sir. It's booked at twelve, but you're good for now.'

Henderson checks his watch. 'That's fine. We won't need long.'

I follow him through the door and down a bland corridor of blue carpet tiles, and white walls dotted with notice boards, containing a range of posters instructing people to watch out for various threats: pickpockets, credit card fraud, Covid-19 scams, terrorism. I spot a flyer about domestic violence; at least someone here is considering that an issue. I doubt it's Henderson; he seems to have already made up his mind that I'm a time-waster, a nosey neighbour to be ignored or placated until I go away.

We enter a tiny, airless room and he invites me to sit down on a plastic chair. He drops heavily into one opposite me on the other side of a small table.

'Okay, go ahead,' he says.

'Where's your colleague?' I ask. 'The young woman. DC... Willis, wasn't it?'

'She's busy.' He lays a meaty hand on the tabletop. 'So, it'll have to be me. Let's crack on, shall we?'

'Right. Well, last Friday, I was in the Crawfords' garden, and I saw a child's shoe and a woman's ring. Just lying on the ground. Then, when I went back—'

'Hang on a second.' Henderson holds up his palm. 'What were you doing in their garden?'

'Oh, I-I mean, I was just—'

'Had Mr Crawford invited you in?'

'No, but, at the back, there's a section where the fence isn't—'

'So, you were trespassing on his property?'

This is bullshit. Not only has he interrupted me three times in a row, but he seems entirely focused on whether I'm the one who's done something wrong. I need to stay calm, though, and get my points across.

'The area at the bottom of our gardens is communal,' I reply. That probably isn't true, but I need to deflect his attention away from me and onto what I found. 'I was exploring. I hadn't been that far back yet.'

'How does this relate to?—'

It's my turn to hold my hand up. 'I haven't finished,' I tell him. I go on to describe the shoe and the ring, as well as the shed and the newly dug area of ground beside it, and the fire pit with its charred remains. Then I repeat the words I overheard today. *You know what she was like… it had to be dealt with… there was no love.*

When I stop speaking, Henderson waits for a moment. 'Is that it?'

'Yes.' I hold his gaze. 'Don't you agree it's suspicious, when you put it all together?'

Henderson rasps a hand over his thick salt-and-pepper stubble. The grey hairs glint in the harsh overhead strip lighting. 'It's potentially interesting, if any of it's connected with his wife and daughter.'

'What do you mean? That's clearly what he was talking about.'

'We can't be sure of that. Did he mention his wife or daughter by name during this call you were eavesdropping on?'

'I wasn't eavesdropping. I was in the room on the other side of—'

'Did he mention them by name?' Another interruption.

'No, but...' I feel my frustration rising, my limbs tensing slightly. I've given him everything and he doesn't think it's even related to his missing persons' case. 'What about the shoe? That's obviously Thea's. And the ring has to be Emily's.'

'What did you do with those items when you found them, Ms Northcott?'

'I...' I recall how I screamed, then heard a sound from the Crawfords' house, and ran. 'I left them.'

'Did you happen to take a photograph while you were there?'

'No.' I hesitate to say more but decide it's best to be open. 'I went back the next day to *try* taking a picture, but, er, they weren't there any more.'

'I see.' His simple reply conveys even more scepticism than Jack. Henderson doesn't believe me, either.

'The patch of ground,' I blurt. 'I'm certain it'd just been dug. Surely that needs to be checked out?'

'Thank you, Ms Northcott, we'll decide on the victim and suspect strategies for our investigations. The main problem here is that we don't know if we have a *victim*. We aren't even sure that we're dealing with a crime. At the moment, this is a missing persons' case. And an inactive one, at that, same as it was the last time you contacted me.' He checks his watch again. We've only got a few minutes before someone else needs the room.

'The data on intimate partner violence,' I say. 'The number of cases where—'

'I'm aware of those figures, I assure you. Now, if there's nothing else...'

'What are you going to do about this?' I demand. 'You haven't even written anything down.'

'I don't need to,' he replies. 'If there was any material you'd provided that could advance our inquiry, I'd ask you to make a full statement. I'll make a note on the file about your observations in the garden. I won't put down that you were *in* the garden at the time.'

He thinks he's doing me a favour, but this isn't good enough – not for me, and certainly not for Emily and Thea. 'Are you at least going to speak to Michael about the phone call?'

'Mr Crawford has co-operated fully with our inquiry. That's all I can tell you, I'm afraid.'

'But—'

There's a knock at the door.

'We need to go.' Henderson stands. 'Thanks for coming in, Miss Northcott.'

'Ms Northcott.'

'Right.'

I'm pissed off that I haven't been taken seriously, but I've made all my points at least twice and he's not interested in any of them. I've run out of things to say, and we walk back down the corridor to the reception area in silence. I have the sense I'm being escorted off the premises. Just as we reach the door, I remember something.

'When you came to our house, two months ago,' I begin.

Henderson pauses, gripping the door handle. 'Yeah?'

'You said you'd need to speak to my fiancé, Jack.'

'That's right.'

'So, did you?'

He purses his lips, looks at me. 'Yes, we did.'

'And, er, did he tell you anything useful?'

Henderson cocks his head as if it's a strange question. Maybe he thinks I should be asking Jack, not him. 'No,' he replies. 'He didn't.'

'Right. Thanks.'

A moment later I'm back out in the daylight, blinking. Part of me feels that it was a waste of time, that there'd have to be a dead body lying in the lobby of the police station before Henderson would bother to do something about it. I get the impulse to go back in, to make a complaint, perhaps, or tell the desk officer to write everything down. But I know that won't achieve anything.

What I do know is that if Michael is involved in the disappearance of his wife and daughter – or worse, their murders – then I might be the only one fighting to make sure they're not forgotten. I could be their only chance for justice. And I'm going to do something about it.

I turn my back on the police station and march off with a greater sense of purpose than I've had in a long time.

CHAPTER SIXTEEN

Thursday, 23 September

This morning, it's me who's up and out of bed first. By the time Jack comes downstairs, hair still wet from the shower, I've nearly finished making breakfast. It's the first time that's happened in months, and he can't hide his surprise.

'What're you doing up so early?' he asks, pausing for a second to stare at me before crossing to the coffee machine and pressing buttons that bring it to life.

I shrug. 'Got things to do. Want some porridge?'

'Sure. Thanks.'

He's not used to this, so I have to ask. 'Can you make me a coffee, then?'

'Yeah, course.'

'Flat white, please.'

While I spoon the porridge into bowls and add some toppings, Jack sets about the drinks.

'So, what stuff?' he half-shouts over the noise of the machine.

'Huh?'

'What things have you got on?'

'Oh.' I flap a hand. 'Just research.'

'Documentary stuff?'

'Yeah.' I stop there. I don't want to tell Jack what my research project is: *the disappearance of Emily and Thea Crawford*. Technically, it could turn into a documentary; there are plenty of shows like that. But that's not why I'm doing it. I'm doing it to find out what happened to my friend, to her daughter, and who's responsible for their disappearance, perhaps their murder. Maybe I can stop the same thing happening to someone else.

My plan has two parts: one, find out more background on the Crawfords; and two, make a public appeal for information. I need Michael's help with both; the only problem is, he doesn't seem to want to talk to me. But I've made half a dozen documentaries and I've dealt with reluctant, even hostile sources before. I can do this.

The machine stops whirring and Jack hands me a cup as we sit down. 'Are you feeling okay?' he says.

'I feel great.' It's true, I do. The coffee smells amazing. I take a sip and let the warmth of it spread inside me.

He nods, as though he doesn't quite believe me, like he thinks something strange is going on. But he doesn't say any more. Just picks up his spoon and gets stuck into his porridge.

'By the way,' he says, 'I've got a meeting with the other consultants tonight. We couldn't find a time everyone was free in the day, so we've had to schedule it after hours. I might be back late.'

'All right. I'll get my own dinner then. And if you could swing by the supermarket on your way home, that'd be awesome. I'll text you a list of the stuff we need.'

He frowns slightly and opens his mouth, as if to protest or tell me that's *my* job, since I'm barely employed, but he doesn't say anything, perhaps because I delivered the request so confidently.

'Yeah?' I give him another chance to dissent.

'Er, okay, fine,' he says.

I get the feeling that things are going to start changing around here.

At exactly one p.m., I'm standing outside the Crawfords' front door, clutching a small parcel neatly wrapped in kitchen paper.

Eventually, Michael answers. He grunts in recognition but doesn't say hello, and I don't expect him to. He stares at me. He looks tired, run-down. A lot like Henderson, in fact.

'Brought you some lunch,' I say, holding it out to him.

'Why?'

'Because I'm your neighbour, and I thought you might like to eat something.'

He eyes the paper warily. 'What is it?'

'Sandwich,' I reply. 'Ham and cheese. With pickle. On sourdough bread.'

'Sourdough?' His tone brightens slightly.

'Yup. From the nice bakery down the road.'

That seems to do the trick. He reaches out and takes it, opens the paper, sniffs at it. 'Cheers,' he says and takes a step back, begins shutting the door.

'Wait, Michael.' I put a hand on the door firmly enough to stop its movement. 'There's something I wanted to ask you.'

He blinks. 'I'm pretty busy.'

I stand firm. 'It won't take long.'

He sighs. 'Go on, then.'

I turn towards the house where the curtain-twitchers were watching us last time. There are no faces, no movement, but that doesn't mean they're not there. 'It'd be easier in private,' I say.

When I turn back, Michael's looking at the window across the street, too. He takes a moment to consider, then says: 'Fine. But I've got to get back to work, so it'll have to be very quick.'

'It will be.' I step inside and past him, hearing the door shut behind me. This is the first time I've been in here since Emily and Thea went missing and the place feels different. Devoid of the usual movement, noise and warmth. It's darker, too; Michael must have closed some blinds. Perhaps he's trying to shut out the world, for some reason, or maybe this is just his natural state without Emily and Thea here. There's a smell of something organic that might be male body odour; I can't tell. A chill runs through me.

'What is it?'

I spin round to face Michael. He's looming over me, his expression blank, eyes dark. He's standing between me and the front door. I suddenly realise that no one knows I'm here. I didn't even tell Jack I was coming over. The first twinge of panic hits and I try to take a deep breath. Reassure myself that I've got my phone with me, in the pocket of my jeans, if I need it. I have my suspicions of Michael, but I've got to get closer to him if I want to stand a chance of finding out what's happened. That's the risk I have to take.

'I'm, ah, I was thinking of setting up a webpage for Emily and Thea. Maybe a group on social media.'

'What for?'

'I'm worried about them,' I say. 'And I don't think the police have done enough to find them.'

'They're looking.'

'Are they?'

Michael doesn't reply.

'I want them to do more,' I continue. 'It's not in the papers, now, like it was when they first went missing. You know what the press is like, they get bored and move on. I'm sorry, but they do. We need to raise the profile of it, and I think our best chance is to ask the public. Someone might've seen them or know something about where they are. We can keep Emily and Thea in people's minds. Who knows, maybe Emily will see it and get in touch?'

He's still standing there in silence, and I wonder if I've gone too far. Intruded too much. I think he's involved, somehow, but I need to tread very carefully.

'I'll do all the work, deal with the messages, keep it updated and everything,' I add. 'I just wanted to check it was okay with you. Because you'll want to find them more than anyone, obviously.'

I try to meet his gaze, but he's not looking at me. He's looking past me, over my shoulder – just like with the nosey neighbours – and as I turn, I see he's focused on a door. It's closed.

I recall walking through here, one time, with Emily, and asking about that door. She said it led to the cellar. *Michael's man-cave,* she called it. And I remember her next words. *We're not allowed in there.* She laughed about it, but I knew she was serious. As I study the door again, I notice something new. There's an electronic keypad on it. It wasn't there last time I visited.

'I need to get back to work.' His voice makes me jump. A shaft of light enters the hallway. He's opened the door and is waiting for me to leave.

'Yeah, of course.' I step back outside, blinking in the sunshine. 'So, is it okay about the page, then? I think it could help.'

He snorts. 'I don't really see the point.'

'You want to find them, don't you, Michael?'

'Yes.'

'Then let's give it a try. What harm can it do?'

He's silent for a few seconds. 'All right,' he concedes eventually. 'If you must.'

'Thanks. And what about you?' I ask. 'How are you doing?'

But he's already shutting the door, and he doesn't answer.

CHAPTER SEVENTEEN

Saturday, 25 September

I'm so absorbed in my laptop screen that I don't notice Jack standing in the doorway of the kitchen until he speaks.

'Do you want to come up and strip with me?'

For a second, I think this is an invitation to sex, but when I look up, he's giving me his lopsided grin and brandishing a wallpaper scraper.

'I've had better offers,' I reply.

'Come on, you know you want to,' he cajoles, still playful. He lifts his sweaty old T-shirt with small, circular movements like a striptease, revealing a stomach that's not quite as flat as it used to be.

'I can't, I'm working.'

He lets the tool drop to his side. 'It's a big job,' he persists. 'There's a shitload of wallpaper and it's a bastard to get it off. I could really do with a second pair of hands.'

'I'll do a bit later on.' I point at the screen. 'I'm into this, now, though.'

His smile evaporates. 'Documentary research? It's the weekend.'

'Just cos you're not working, doesn't mean I can't.'

'We're supposed to do the DIY stuff together,' he says, a trace of irritation in his voice. 'That was our plan.'

'Plans change.'

He knows what I'm referring to and, to his credit, he doesn't push it. He walks across and reads over my shoulder. '*Find Emily and Thea*. What's this?'

'It's a missing persons' page for our neighbours. I made it,' I add proudly.

'This is your research? This is what you've been working on so much the past couple of days?'

'Yup. Look, I've linked articles about them, and uploaded a few photos. There's a picture I had on my phone, and a couple off the web, so their images are out there. She didn't have her own social media accounts. Didn't like it, she said. But I've put together what I can.'

He makes a slight scoffing sound. 'Why?'

'Because, Jack, they've been missing two months, and I seem to be the only one who's still interested in finding them.' I give the kitchen table a slap for emphasis.

'Does Michael know you've done this?'

'Yes. He's happy about it.' Okay, *happy* might be an exaggeration. But I resent Jack implying that I need Michael's permission. 'Anyway, she's my friend.'

'How happy is he that you think he murdered his wife and buried her in the garden? And if that's what you think happened, why are you doing this? It doesn't make sense.'

I don't answer that. Instead, I scroll down the page and show him the comments. 'Look, people are posting on it already. I tagged Thea's school, Emily's old workplace, and her university alumni page, as well as a few local community groups and the national missing persons organisations. They've all shared it.'

Someone called Katie Morgan has put:

> *So very sad to hear about this, Emily's the best. Hope they're found soon*

Beside the words are two emojis: a sad face and a fingers crossed hand. There are a dozen similar messages of support. Shalini Acharya has written:

Hope you guys are safe and well x

Alongside half a dozen clasped hands emojis, Milly Cartwright has put:

Sending love and hugs and prayers

From Poppy Eriksson, there's:

Come home soon, wherever you are xoxo

Beneath that is a photo of a classroom full of children waving, and the lines:

We are missing you very much Thea. Love from everyone at Danesfield Manor

'Danesfield Manor?' queries Jack.
'Thea's school. It's in Walton-on-Thames.'
'Hm.'
'It's great, isn't it? Knowing that these people care as much as I do.'
I recall a moment when Emily and I were hanging out here one evening, back in May. We'd both had a couple of glasses of wine and had got on to talking about love. She'd said that real love was this kind of mythical, elusive thing, that the only time she'd ever truly felt it was from their family dog (and he'd died). When I asked if she was serious, she said no, it was just a joke, but

now I wonder if she really did think she was unloved? If she could see these messages now, though, she'd know that she was wrong.

'People aren't forgetting them,' I add.

'No one said they were forgotten.'

'Well, they're not on the news websites any more, the police are doing nothing, and you haven't mentioned it for, like, six weeks.' I twist my neck to look at him.

'Oh, you're keeping track, are you?'

'I'm just saying, Jack, they're your neighbours too.'

He stands up straight, fists on hips, the metal scraping tool sticking out to one side like a strange prosthesis. 'She was your friend,' he replies defensively.

'Was?' I glare at him. 'She still is. Until we know otherwise.'

He shakes his head silently, as if I've gone mad.

'You didn't tell me the police had asked you about it,' I say after a brief silence.

His eyes narrow. 'There was nothing to say. What could I tell them? I was at work when they went missing, and I didn't even really know them.'

A clear picture forms in my mind of Jack's face the first time he saw Emily. Or, I should say, the first I saw him see Emily. Because it didn't look like the first time ever that he'd seen her.

'You could've mentioned it,' I say.

'You – we – had other things on. How'd you know, anyway?'

'Henderson told me,' I reply.

'The detective? You spoke to him?'

'Yeah.'

'You didn't go and tell him about the shoe and the ring, did you?' Jack groans. 'Or that bloody patch of earth?'

I hesitate. 'Actually, I did.'

'Freya. Was that sensible?' It's that tone again, the judgemental one, as though I'm a naughty child or a patient who isn't following his medical advice. But I'm neither, so I don't have to take it.

'Don't patronise me. And, since you're asking, he ignored all of it. Which is why I'm doing this.' I tap the screen with my fingernail.

'You're wasting your time,' he huffs, then holds up the scraper. 'I'm going back to this. And I need your help, if you can spare a moment.' There's an edge of sarcasm to those final words, and no more jokes about stripping. He stomps out of the kitchen and up the stairs with heavy, angry feet.

Jack's reaction is the polar opposite to my therapist's. When I told him about this project in our session yesterday, he didn't judge me or dismiss my efforts – he encouraged me. Asked me questions about what it was that interested me in it, reflected back to me that it seemed to be something that really motivated me. And praised me for finding another meaningful activity to add to my routine alongside the gardening (which I'm still doing every day).

I'm already looking forward to our next session, on Tuesday, when I can tell Laurence about the lovely comments people have posted, and the sense of connection they've given me. The knowledge that Emily and Thea are real people, with real lives out there in the real world, and that there are others besides me who care about them and want to find them – whatever happened to them.

I know my therapist will validate those feelings. There's a sense of safety around him with expressing my thoughts that I don't have right now with Jack. And, I have to admit, with the way Jack's been acting recently, I'd almost rather spend time with Laurence than with my fiancé. I'd like to have a conversation with him about *his* life, not just mine, but I know that's not why we're meeting, and it wouldn't be appropriate. He isn't there to be a friend. He's there to help me recover from a major personal trauma.

I remind myself that I still have friends; I just haven't seen much of them since moving here. There are WhatsApp groups where uni mates or school friends or a netball team I used to play in share memes and links to articles or podcasts. That can be good for a laugh, but when I want to have a deeper conversation, I need to see people face to face. Even speaking by phone's not the same. And the problem is that my best friends are two hours away, now, on the other side of London. It's another small reason to resent Jack; moving here for his job has caused that separation from my friends. But maybe it's me who should be making more effort to go and see them.

I realise I've gone down a negative little rabbit hole and try to refocus on the page for Emily and Thea. I'm considering a post to thank everyone for their kind messages and to remind them to share any information they think might be of use, when I notice that there's a direct message that's been sent to me, as host. I've enabled the private communication feature on the page, in case people want to pass on something sensitive or confidential, and this is the first contact.

I click into the inbox. The message has just been sent, literally this minute. It's sitting there, unopened, on its own in the folder. The sender is johnsmith12643 and has one of those blank-face profile icons, which means they haven't uploaded a picture.

I open it with a slight sense of unease. And I can't believe what I see. Is this some sort of sick joke? Who would write this?

I can feel my mouth going dry as I stare at the screen. And a shudder goes through me as I read the words, again.

Stop what you're doing or you'll be next.

CHAPTER EIGHTEEN

I should have known it was too good to be true. That it couldn't be as simple and perfect as I'd first hoped. I'd been finding out about you for some time, my happiness growing as all the pieces of our future life together fitted into place. But, if I'd thought logically about it – which is something I normally do well – then I could easily have predicted our first obstacle: a rival for your affection.

It's understandable, of course, that someone as attractive as you would have others in the picture. Those who would want to give their love to you, pushing themselves into your world, trying to get close. And there were plenty of them, as I discovered. But I was prepared for that; I wasn't naïve enough to think you existed in a vacuum. In some ways, the presence of those individuals and their desires was proof of how special you were. I watched as you were polite to them, tolerated their adoration, their gestures of devotion, but ultimately you brushed them off. That was fine; it was the other group I couldn't deal with.

The ones you might love back.

That second, smaller group of people was a different thing entirely. I quickly came to see them as a collective threat, a pack of scavenging hyenas waiting in the darkness with glinting eyes, ready to drag you away and have their fill of you. To me, that was unacceptable. The potential for any one of them to derail what I believed we were destined to have together was intolerable. They had to be stopped.

You must understand that I wasn't trying to control you. I'd never do that, because I'm not some sort of tyrant or monster, and love isn't one-sided in that way. It's an equal, mutual thing, and that's part of its beauty. The problem was that those others might trick you into doing something you'd regret. So, you see, I had no choice but to protect you from them and the possibility that they might take advantage of your good nature. I had to protect you from yourself.

   I only ever wanted what was best for you. I never wanted this. Everything I did, I had to do for our sake, for our future. Ultimately, it was you who made me do it.

CHAPTER NINETEEN

Monday, 27 September

Cathy's front door is open even wider than usual this morning, and I know why. I've been listening to her going in and out, mowing the lawn and using other garden machinery for the past hour or so. When the whirring and buzzing stopped, I thought that was probably a good moment to call on her for a cup of tea and another chat. I haven't dropped in to see her since I lost my baby and, each being alone in our own ways, I'm sure we'd both appreciate the company.

But that's not all. I also want to know what she knows about the Crawfords. The problem isn't her willingness to speak, it's my ability to make sense of her snippets and stories. So far, the things she's told me have been intriguing – alarming, even – but frustratingly vague and inconsistent, like pieces taken from different jigsaws and jumbled together.

Seeing her door completely open like this, an invitation to anyone walking by to come in, I feel a sense of worry at the possibility of someone taking advantage of her trusting nature. It's accompanied by a sadness that, one day, this could be me. Living by myself, without Jack or anyone else, leaving my door open, vulnerable to predators.

But these thoughts vanish in an instant as Cathy appears from the garden, wielding a strimmer in her sinewy arms like it's a flamethrower. Are trust and fearlessness two sides of the same coin, I wonder? Have I mistaken her independence for loneliness?

When she sees me, her face creases into a big smile, a hundred wrinkles of joy. 'Hello, Freya, love. I was just about to have a break. You want a cuppa?'

'Perfect,' I say.

I marvel at Cathy's ritual of making tea: warming the pot, adding the loose leaves, letting it brew properly before pouring, milk already in the china cups, sitting on their little matching saucers. It's like winding the clock back to a time when things didn't have to be done at a hundred miles an hour, and I find it comforting.

'I've got some cake here, too, if you like?' she offers.

'I'd love some, please.'

She cuts two large pieces of a dense, dark fruit cake topped with almonds and places one in front of me. 'Here you go.'

'Amazing. Thanks, Cathy.'

Her cat, Archie, saunters into the kitchen and walks right past me, rubbing himself against my leg, turning and repeating the movement a few times, making small miaowing sounds. He appears to have long forgotten our first encounter, when he launched himself at me in an aerial attack, and definitely gave me an evil glare.

'He likes you,' Cathy observes. 'Don't you, darling? Yes.'

I reach down to give him a scratch under the chin, but all I get is my finger nipped. I gasp and withdraw it.

'You have to watch out. He does that sometimes,' says Cathy, taking a bite of cake and brushing crumbs off her shirt. 'So, how are you, dear? You haven't come by for a while. I expect you've been very busy. You look different.'

'I…' I'm not sure what to tell her. I could say something glib about having loads to do, house and work. Then I remember one of the conversations from my last therapy session. I don't want to hide what's happened to me; I'm not ashamed of it. I decide to tell her. 'I had a miscarriage.'

Her eyes widen in sympathy as I recount the events and their aftermath. She reaches out and lays a gnarled but strong hand over mine. 'I'm so sorry.'

'So, it's not been the easiest time,' I conclude. It's one of those ridiculous British understatements, and I can feel myself welling up even as I say it.

'I can imagine. It wasn't for me, either.'

'Really? You?…'

Cathy nods. 'Mm. I had two. One of them nearly killed me, I was bleeding so much.'

'Oh my god. What happened?'

'Well, that one was actually an ectopic pregnancy, but I didn't even know I was pregnant until I started getting these awful pains…' She clutches her ribs and shudders. 'Henry saved me. He got me to the hospital just in time.'

'Wow.'

'We tried again, after a while, for a long time, but we just couldn't make it happen. Henry and I both wanted children so much. Seemed it wasn't meant to be.'

Now it's my turn to squeeze her hand.

'Things were never quite the same between us after that,' she adds.

'Between you and Henry?'

'Yes. He never said it in so many words, but I always got the sense that he sort of blamed me for it, as though there was something wrong with me.' Her eyes lose focus a moment.

'How could it be your fault?'

'Well, exactly. But I'm not sure Henry saw it that way.'

I'm tempted to tell Cathy: *screw him, then*, as I get a fleeting reminder of Jack's unhelpful, almost mechanical reaction to my miscarriage. But instead, I try a question I've wanted to ask her for months.

'What's happened to Henry?'

'Sorry, love?'

'Henry,' I repeat. 'Is he, still, um?…'

'He's gone,' she says flatly.

'Gone?'

'Yes.'

'Where?'

She waves a hand around her in a gesture that could mean almost anything. Then she takes a long drink of tea and sighs.

'Cathy?' I urge gently.

There's a long silence before she speaks. 'No news about the girls, then?'

'Emily and Thea?'

'Mm.'

'Well, there are a few things, actually.' I tell Cathy about straying into the Crawfords' garden, finding the shoe and the ring. I describe the fire pit and the patch of dug earth, the size of a human grave. I tell her about Michael's conversation that I heard from the other side of the wall, and how the police dismissed everything and treated me like a fantasist. She listens, rapt, shaking her head frequently. Finally, I let her know about the webpage I've created to try to gather support and, if possible, new leads. Her expression lights up at the mention of it.

'You made that?' she exclaims. 'I've seen it online.'

'You have?'

'Yes, *Find Emily and Thea*. It's marvellous.' She points at me, a friendly warning. 'Just because I'm old, doesn't mean I don't know what's going on. I am on social media.'

I lean back, impressed. Cathy's full of surprises.

'I'm hoping people can offer information. Maybe someone's seen them or knows something that relates to their disappearance.'

'Well, like I said before' – Cathy tilts her head down, her expression serious once more – 'it's got to be him.'

'Michael?'

'Who else?' She tops up our teas.

'You thought he was involved before any of the stuff I've told you about.'

'That's right.'

'Just because of his temper? You said you used to hear him shouting.'

'I did.' Cathy fixes me with a level stare. 'But it wasn't just shouting. I heard things breaking, too.'

'Inside the house?'

'Mm. There was violence going on, that's for sure.'

I decide not to ask how she could've heard that, for now. 'Did you ever speak to Emily about it, or call the police?'

Cathy shakes her head slowly. 'I asked her, once. She laughed about it, said everything was fine. Told me not to worry, that they'd had a couple of accidents, the dog had knocked some things over, that was all.'

I'm not sure I believe that, although their dog was pretty massive.

'But if she wouldn't open up to me,' Cathy goes on, 'she certainly wouldn't tell the police. So, I didn't go to them, either. When you know something's not right, though, you know.'

I consider this. I lived next door to Michael and Emily for four months before she and Thea went missing, and I had no inkling of it at all. I never heard so much as a door slam.

'I did call them once, though,' she adds.

'The police?'

'Yes.' Cathy breaks off a piece of fruit cake with her long fingers. 'Don't know that they did anything, mind.'

I sit forward, hanging off her words. 'What for?'

She shivers. 'I can remember that sound as clearly as if it was happening right now.'

'What sound?'

'Screaming. A female voice.'

'Oh my god.' I blink. 'From inside the house?'

'No, from outside.' She holds my gaze. 'In the shed.'

Hours later, I still can't shake the scene that Cathy's words conjured up in my imagination. A piercing scream coming from within that old, crumbling shed. Emily or Thea – it had to be one of them – in deep distress, perhaps physical pain, too, but locked inside by Michael and unable to escape. Did they hope that their cries would bring help? But did that, in fact, only cause them more suffering if Michael was listening, too?

Cathy wasn't able to say when this had happened. It's clear she struggles with dates and times. She did say that, when she heard the sound, she went to look, but she couldn't even see inside the shed, let alone open the door, and by then the screaming had stopped. She'd called out, asked if anyone was inside, but she'd been met with silence.

It's a story that chills me, although I can already hear Jack's response, if I were to tell him. He'd be marginally more empathic than Michael, who described Cathy during that first dinner as: *losing her marbles, plain and simple.* I have to retain some scepticism; when I was making documentaries, I never took everything at face value. But why would she lie? And she wasn't confused this morning – she seemed alert and lucid, recounting the traumatic story of her pregnancies. Maybe she was simply mistaken at the time, whenever that was.

On my laptop, I refresh the *Find Emily and Thea* page, and I'm notified that there are a few recent comments. Before I read them, I go back into my messages, but there's nothing new. Yesterday, I replied to the threat from johnsmith12643, who told me to stop what I'm doing, or I'd be next. I simply asked: *who is this?*

I have no idea who John Smith is, and I doubt that's his real name. He might just be a lone nutter, or someone having a laugh at my expense, but it's also possible that the name is an alias for someone connected with the disappearance. Someone who does actually want me to stop looking into it because of what I might find. Someone who might be capable of violence.

I'm still pretty freaked out by that, but I want to see if he responds, or reveals anything else about his identity – perhaps something I can take to Henderson, to get him to investigate. They can't ignore a clear threat, surely, and I'm sure the police have the capability to trace those kinds of messages. I've read about cases where anonymous stalkers and trolls have been unmasked that way.

Returning to the main feed for the page, I check out the new comments. A former colleague of Emily's from the British Museum has posted her wishes for Emily and Thea to be home safely soon. Someone whose account suggests they're a teacher at Thea's school has expressed her sympathy, writing what a positive influence Thea was in their class. When I read the third new post, though, I stop dead.

It's from Alice Hope, whose profile icon is an image of some wildflowers. I stare at the screen, reading and rereading the message. The words are as simple as they are frightening:

> *If he did to her what he did to me, then she's better off getting out and taking her kid with her. I've still got the scars he gave me. I only hope she's alive.*

I can't believe what I'm reading. She must be referring to Michael. But who is Alice Hope, and what does she know about him? Were they in a relationship? Is this the proof that he has an abusive streak? And what scars is she talking about? The effects of psychological trauma, or literal, physical scars, traces of the violence which Cathy is convinced she's heard? Perhaps both... The questions are tumbling out and I can't answer any of them. The only thing that's clear is that I need to know more. I've got to talk to Alice Hope, whoever she is.

I click on her name and begin typing a private message to her.

CHAPTER TWENTY

Tuesday, 28 September

I didn't sleep much last night. My mind was too full, too busy to let me drift into unconsciousness, as though I had to find a solution to Emily and Thea's disappearance there and then, between two and four o'clock in the morning. I could feel a buzz in my abdomen as I lay there, a sensation my therapist will no doubt tell me was my fight-or-flight system kicking in.

The physical symptoms of anxiety, to go alongside my worry, supposedly designed to keep me safe from threats, but in reality just making me feel as though someone's trying to get me. That may not be too far from the truth, though, given the threatening message I received three days ago.

However, my fear of johnsmith12643 is now mixed with a kind of excitement at the prospect of what Alice Hope might be able to tell me. Does she have the missing piece of the puzzle, the key that will tell me where to look, where to point the police so that even Henderson can't miss it?

There's a kind of trepidation at going further, at finding out what she knows, but it's impossible for me to stop now. My imagination has created a hundred little horror movies of poor Emily and Thea, and I have to get to the truth. There's lots of sympathy for them in the community, but I seem to be the only one who's actually investigating, and I can't let it drop.

I won't lose another child.

I try to push away the memories of my miscarriage, for now, and focus on Alice Hope. She's replied to me but, despite my best attempts to persuade her, she doesn't want to meet. She's even cagey about telling me where she is. A google search for Alice Hope brings up so many hits it's impossible to find her, so I guess it's an alias. But I'm not deterred.

I've seen that reluctance to trust before, back when I was making documentaries. Sources whose confidence is hard won, because of what they've been through, who are understandably terrified of the consequences of exposure. I've tried to reassure Alice, but she isn't shifting. Email only, she says. At the moment, I have no choice but to do this on her terms. And her latest message suggests I'm right not to push too hard. It arrived just minutes ago:

Michael and I were together for two years before I escaped, and there's no question in my mind that he's capable of the worst kind of violence. At the beginning, he was charming, in his own arrogant kind of way. And he's good-looking, too. But there's a dark side which I didn't see at first. It only came out later, once we were a couple.

It's what I suspected, what I feared Emily – and perhaps Thea – were being subjected to. An unspoken domestic abuse. But there's worse to come, as I read on:

He has that terrible combination of a temper he can't control and a thirst for alcohol. Each time, he'd say that he was dealing with it, that it wouldn't happen again, that he'd get help. But he never did, and sure enough it happened again, and again. He was careful, though, that he never left any serious marks. He'd throw things, smash them, intimidate. He'd grab me, twist my arm, pull my hair or press the nerve behind my jaw,

and none of it would be visible so much as an hour later. He
knew exactly what he was doing.

Although I've seen Michael's rudeness and irritability first-hand, initially it's hard to square this image of an aggressive, binge-drinking man with the usually well-presented, professional, middle-class neighbour I've known for months. But I realise I've been making assumptions because of how he looks and dresses and speaks, and now I'm seeing him in a new light. He's a large, overbearing guy with minimal empathy and human warmth, and as I read Alice's words, the images of that violence start to come to me all too easily.

Then I remember what Thea said that very first day we met, when she innocently commented on the beer I'd been given by the removal men, saying it was the same drink that her daddy had. I didn't think anything of it at the time, but now it makes an awful kind of sense. One that makes me sick to the stomach: a five-year-old girl being in the home of a large, drunken, angry man. I can see Thea running, hiding, shaking and gasping for breath even as she tries to keep quiet, desperate to avoid his wrath.

I go over Alice's description, again, and I think of the shoe and the ring, the patch of earth and the fire pit. *It had to be dealt with.* I have the strongest sense I've had since their disappearance that Michael did something to them. Did Emily stand up to him? Did she fight back? Perhaps he started to hurt Thea, and a mother's instinct – something which I can now begin to understand, however imperfectly – rose up in her to protect her daughter.

Was it an accident born of violence, where Michael struck her, and she fell, hit her head?… Or was it premeditated? Calculated and carried out with the efficiency of a computer programme executing a command. Was that it – was she *executed*? I feel a coldness in my body at that thought, before I realise that I haven't quite finished reading, yet. There's another couple of lines before her sign-off:

*You asked me if I think Michael is capable of murder. The
answer is yes. Deep down, I think any of us is capable of
anything if the circumstances push us to it – even killing
someone – and Michael is more capable than most, I have
proof of that.*

Do we all have that capacity for violence in us? My younger
self would have disagreed with her. But I've heard too many stories
since then to be so sure.

One that comes to mind is from an interview I did, a couple
of years back, with a woman who had travelled to the UK from
Ukraine, lured on the false promise of a managerial retail job.
When she arrived, the criminal gang that had tricked her forced
her at gunpoint into a brothel, which became her prison. Four
months later, she broke out by stealing a pistol that one of her
captors had left unattended and shooting him twice in the stomach
at close range with trembling hands. She later learned that he'd
bled to death.

Forcing human beings into extreme situations can make
them act in ways they wouldn't have imagined possible, until
the moment arrives and it's a matter of survival. That's what I've
come to believe.

There are still so many questions I want to ask Alice – like
what proof she's referring to at the end of her message – but I
feel that I'm starting to get closer to the truth, now. I just have to
keep going. I interlink my fingers and stretch my arms over my
head, then lean back and rub my eyes. I've been on my laptop
all morning and I need a break from the screen.

Getting up, I walk out to the garden and take a lungful of
fresh air, feeling the sun on my face. I find myself wandering
away from the house, down the path I've cleared, towards the end
where the fences run out. Something is drawing me back towards
the Crawfords' garden and the shed. I remember Cathy's words

yesterday, and the shiver it sent through me when she said she'd heard screaming coming from inside.

I go as far as I dare, getting a partial view of the little outbuilding, but staying on our land because I know Michael is home. I've heard him moving around today, and I haven't seen him go out. I wonder, again, what's in that shed. Whether, if I could get inside it, I'd find something to confirm Cathy's story, or my own instincts. But I can't just force my way in. If Michael is as violent as Alice says, then I have to watch out. Whatever happened to Emily, she wouldn't want me to put myself in danger in search of her.

Despite having more pressing things to think about, I've made myself do a bit of gardening. I want to be able to tell my therapist at our session this afternoon that I'm keeping it up. It's good to get my head away from the disappearance for a while, too, and move around. After a physically intense but satisfying hour of cutting back and pulling up weeds, I go back inside.

As I make coffee, I'm already composing a response to Alice, and by the time I sit down at the kitchen table with a cup (thanks, Jack, for getting that machine), my reply is half-formed. I take a quick look at the *Find Emily and Thea* page, and that's when I see the little red notification that always gets my pulse going. It's the alert for a new message that must have arrived while I was out in the garden. I open the page's inbox and take a quick, shallow breath when I see who it's from: johnsmith12643.

I can read the first line in the display, and I know it's not going to be good. I hesitate for a few seconds, wondering if it's better to leave it unread… but the compulsion to open it is impossible to resist. I click into it and lean forwards, focusing my full attention on the brief few lines as I feel a dread start to grow in my stomach and creep through me as I read.

*It doesn't matter who I am. The most important thing is that
you stop digging. Because you wouldn't want to disappear
like her, would you, Freya?*

It isn't the threat that's making my guts twist and knot. It's
the use of my name. How does John Smith – whoever the fuck
he is – know my name? It's nowhere on the page, and only a few
people know I'm doing this. Michael is one of them. I imagine
him, down in his man-cave, tapping away at his computer and
chuckling to himself as he toys with me. Is the digging a reference
to the grave in his garden? And how real is the danger of—

'You okay?'

Jack's voice sends a bolt of adrenalin through my torso, as if
my chest has been hit with a fully charged defibrillator. He's in
the kitchen.

'Jesus Christ, Jack,' I gasp, leaning back in the chair at the relief
that it's only him. 'Don't creep up on me like that.'

'Like what? I live here, too, you know.' He snorts a laugh.

'What are you even doing here? You're supposed to be at work,
aren't you?'

'Had a session cancelled, so I thought I'd come back for some
lunch with you.'

'You should've let me know you were on your way.'

'Why do I need to do that?' he protests but doesn't wait for
an answer. 'Anyway, I did. I texted.'

I grab my phone, across the table, and tap my PIN. He did
text, I just didn't see it. I give a long breath out. 'Okay, fine.'

I'm obviously on edge from the message, but it scares me even
more how I didn't hear him come in. I must've zoned out with
the laptop, or perhaps he entered while the coffee machine was
doing its noisy thing. Either way, I need to pay more attention
to what's going on around me.

'What is it? You look like you've seen a bloody ghost or something.' He crosses the kitchen, brow drawn in concern, and makes straight for my laptop.

But I slam the lid down before he gets there. 'Nothing.'

'Show me,' he insists.

'No.'

'Why not?' Jack plants his hands on his hips and stares at me, his jaw slack.

'Because it's private.'

I can't explain it, but for some reason I don't want to show Jack the messages from John Smith right now. And it's not just because he's dismissed everything I've told him about Emily and Thea so far as nonsense or a waste of energy. It's also because this is the first time he's come home for lunch since he started his new job, six months ago, and something about it doesn't seem right.

It feels as though he's checking up on me.

CHAPTER TWENTY-ONE

Tuesday, 28 September

'I mean, Detective Henderson can't ignore that, can he?' I say. 'He's got to take it seriously. They have to investigate. He hasn't called me back yet, but…'

Opposite me, Laurence tilts his head slightly to one side, uncrosses his legs and rests his notepad on his thighs. I peer over at the notes, but they're upside down, too small and far away for me to make out. I'd love to know what he writes about me, though. His expression is soft and compassionate.

'There's something I've noticed, Freya.'

'What?' My reply sounds more urgent than I intend.

'It's all right.' He half-raises a reassuring hand. 'It's just an observation I'd like to share with you.'

'About Emily and Thea?'

'No.' He smiles. 'About you.'

'Oh, okay.'

'Well, I'm conscious that we've spent quite a lot of today's session talking about your neighbours, and not very much time talking about you.'

'Have we?'

He nods. 'What do you think about that?'

'I don't know,' I reply. 'I guess… it's just important to me right now.'

'Sure, I can see that it is. And it's great that you have a project that you're involved in, alongside the gardening and all the other parts of daily life, which is giving you meaning and purpose. That's fantastic.' He pauses. 'What I'm just wondering, though, is whether this is the right space for discussing that.'

'Um, well, I-I thought it was...' I tail off, unsure of myself and slightly embarrassed, although I know that's ridiculous, because it's not what Laurence intended and there's no one else here. I remind myself that he isn't judging me; he's trying to help me. But the idea that I've got it wrong still stings a little.

'If we just come back to your goals for a moment, do you remember what it was you wanted to do here?'

I shift in the armchair and pull at a thread on my jumper. 'Recover from my miscarriage, I guess, and, um, be able to move on.'

'That's what you said, yes.' He spreads his hands, angles them towards me. 'We're here to reflect on your thoughts and emotions, and things you can do or maybe not do to help you process the trauma you've been through, and to learn about the meaning of it.'

'Yeah.' I can feel tears prickling at my eyes, and I'm not sure why.

'So, I suppose I was just thinking, listening to you there, that I wondered why Emily and Thea are so important to you at the moment?'

He lets the question hang, and I have a vague feeling he knows the answer but he wants me to say it. That's what Laurence does; he never puts words in my mouth, but it's as if the things he asks are steering me towards something I already know. I called him on it before, and he admitted it was a therapy technique called Socratic questioning.

The answer comes to me in the form of a memory. Emily and I are walking by the river, getting a leg stretch together on a bright, warm day in June, not long before she disappeared. I can still see the sun glinting off the water, her hair appearing to glow golden in the light. She was talking about her devotion to Thea, how a part of her didn't mind not working if it meant she got to spend more time with her daughter. I recall the ferocity with which she described her desire to look after Thea, no matter what the cost. There was something I admired about the way she spoke.

I think that could be why I care so much about them. I want to be the sort of person who loves and protects my family with such passion. I lost the opportunity myself, and now I don't want Emily and Thea to be lost, too.

As I describe all this to Laurence, the weight of those absences brings up a surge of sadness within me, and I start to cry.

'Sorry,' I say.

'There's nothing to be sorry for, Freya,' he replies. 'Take all the time you need. We're here for you.'

'What do you mean, "it's probably nothing"? This person has threatened to make me *disappear*.'

I can't believe this. It's taken me more than two hours to get through to Henderson, but when I tell him about the John Smith threat, he's not interested.

There's a moment of silence before he responds, as if he's waiting for me to calm down. 'That's not exactly what he said, is it? Did he directly threaten to kill you?'

'Well, no… but the meaning was clear enough. If I don't stop digging, I'll disappear like her. It's obvious, isn't it? This is serious.'

'Miss Northcott. We have—'

'Ms Northcott, please.'

'Ms Northcott,' he starts again, 'we have a lot of experience with this kind of thing,' he explains slowly. 'The vast majority of threats made online – direct or indirect – are empty. They're just keyboard warriors, having a bit of fun by trying to scare people.'

'Well, it's worked,' I retort. 'I'm scared.'

'I appreciate that, but we simply don't have the resources to follow up on things like this. I'm sorry.'

'Look,' I insist, 'this guy knows my name. He knows I'm behind the campaign.'

Henderson sighs. 'Perhaps it's linked to the page somehow. Maybe you've inadvertently displayed it somewhere, I don't know. But I'm ninety-nine per cent sure this isn't something to worry about, Ms Northcott.'

'What if I'm in that one per cent, though?'

'Chances are that—'

'Surely there must be something you can do. Can't you trace him?' I demand. 'Find out who johnsmith12643 is? I've already told you who I think it is.' *Michael.*

'It's very difficult to get information out of social media companies,' he says. His calmness is irritating me. It's as if he's already decided that I have nothing of value to give him, and all he needs to do is hold out until I give up. 'It can take weeks for them to respond,' he adds. 'And there might be nothing at the end of it, anyway. Except maybe a twelve-year-old kid in his bedroom, somewhere like the States, who thinks it's funny to screw around with people.'

'So, you're saying you won't do anything about this?' I can feel my face and neck getting hot as I stand in the kitchen, phone clamped to my cheek, staring out into the garden towards the shed I know is there but can't see behind the thick bushes.

'I'm sorry, Ms Northcott,' replies Henderson. 'Unless there's a direct and specific threat to life, we can't act. But, as I said, given the online origin of the message, even if we did investigate, we're unlikely to find anything actionable.'

I clench my jaw. Take a deep breath.

'Was that everything?' he asks.

I want to throw the phone at the wall, but I force myself to chill. 'No, it's not. There's more.'

'Okay.'

I go on to tell him about Alice Hope, about her experiences of abuse at Michael's hands, about her assertion that he's capable of murder. I remind him that johnsmith12643 might be Michael.

'Mr Crawford is not a person of interest in our inquiries,' he says flatly.

'Doesn't this change that?' I protest. 'I mean, here's a witness who can prove he's capable of abuse. Violence.'

'Can she corroborate her claims?'

'I don't know,' I snap back. 'It was years ago. A lot of it would be her word against his.'

'That kind of case is very hard to make. Has she indicated that she wishes to bring charges against him?'

'No, but—'

'Do you even know her real name?'

'I'm not sure, it could be… listen, why don't you ask Michael?'

Henderson makes a sound that could almost be a laugh. 'Ms Northcott, Surrey CID is not equipped to take on historical cases from people of unspecified identity who might not live in the county, or even be talking about events that occurred in our jurisdiction.'

'Jesus fucking Christ,' I exclaim. I realise I'm gripping my skull with my free hand, squeezing it in exasperation.

'Okay, look.' Henderson takes his time, and I have the feeling once more that I'm being spoken to like a child. 'If this Alice Hope is willing to make contact with us, and if she's willing to share her identity with us in a checkable, verifiable form, we would take a statement from her about any allegations she may wish to make and go from there. But she needs to be the one to contact us.'

'She's not going to do that. Don't you get it? She's terrified of Michael. She had to get away from him, presumably because you lot did nothing to help her at the time.'

'Well, I'm afraid that's how it is.'

'This is bullshit,' I tell him.

'Maybe,' he acknowledges, 'but that's how the law works.'

'In that case,' I reply, 'the law's bullshit.'

I hang up.

CHAPTER TWENTY-TWO

I'm still wound up and furious with Henderson when the doorbell goes an hour later. As I pad down the hallway to the front door, I wonder who it could be. I'm not expecting any deliveries, and Jack won't be back from work for a bit longer; even if it was him, he's got keys, unless he left them here when he came home for lunch. I can't see anything because the door has no windows or frosted glass, and we haven't got round to fitting one of those little spyhole viewers yet.

'Hello?' I call out as I reach for the lock. There's no answer.

I open the door and Michael's standing there, tall and tense, a look on his face somewhere between determination and hostility.

'I need to talk to you,' he says, and before I can reply he steps up and inside, brushing past me and into the hallway, where he strides through to the living room.

I catch a strong whiff of alcohol. 'Michael?'

'In private.'

I know what I should do. I should insist that he leaves and that we speak outside, in full view of the street, in case he tries anything. I can recall Alice's words about the combination of his temper and his drinking. Is this the real Michael I'm starting to see, now? Part of me is scared, but I stay where I am. I tell myself that if I leave the door open I have a way out. That if I scream,

Cathy will hear me. And I can't lose sight of my objective, of the plan I made.

If I want to find out what happened to Emily and Thea, I have to get closer to Michael. And he won't speak in the open. If that means taking a few risks, then so be it. I owe that much to the woman and child who've disappeared without trace. I push the door wide and walk calmly through to the living room, where Michael is pacing around. He's taking up a lot of space, his long limbs making sharp movements, and he's obviously agitated.

'What do you want to talk about?' I ask softly, hoping he'll calm down with me, and keeping my distance, with one eye on the door.

'Fucking Alice Hope,' he snarls. 'Posting shit about me on that page of yours for everyone to see.'

I get a tiny stab of adrenalin, because it's confirmation she's for real. 'Who is she?' I ask.

'She's a lunatic, that's who she is.' Michael's still moving around, as though the living room is a cage and he's desperate to break out. 'A crazy bitch. A bunny boiler.'

He isn't drunk enough to be slurring his words, but I can tell he's had a few before coming over. 'Okay,' I reply tentatively. I don't want to make him any angrier, but Michael rarely displays this level of emotion and I need to tap into it. 'Would you like to sit down?'

'No!' he barks.

I hold up my hands. 'All right. Tell me the story, then.'

'I want you to remove her post. I can't have people seeing that. Clients…'

'Sorry?' Is he seriously thinking about his clients?

He jabs a finger in my direction. 'Delete it. Now.'

'I'm not taking anything off the page unless I know why.'

'Because I'm telling you to,' he growls.

I stand firm, holding his unfocused gaze. 'What happened?'

He takes a great breath and snorts it out, flexes his hands. For a second, I think he might come at me. But then he seems to relax a little, and I see some of the tension drop from his shoulders.

'Her name's Alison Templeton. We were together for a couple of years. She was mad about us having kids. She had it all planned out, wanted to start a family before we'd even been going out for a year.'

I nod silently, watching him, taking in the details of his body language. He's not showing any obvious signs of making it up so far, although I know it's hard to be sure about that, especially with someone like Michael, who doesn't give much away at the best of times.

'Well' – he shrugs – 'obviously, I wasn't up for that. It was too much, too soon and I had to get some space. I told her that, she couldn't take it, so I broke up with her.'

'Then what?'

'She went insane. Calling, texting, emailing, every day. I mean, she basically refused to break up with me!' He gives a single, hard laugh, shakes his head. 'Can you believe that?'

No, actually, I want to say, struggling to imagine someone feeling that way about Michael. Then again, Emily was with him for six years. People do strange things when they think they're in love. Or perhaps when they feel they have no other choice.

'She put old photos of us on social media,' he continues, 'as if we were still together and out doing things. She'd turn up at my flat a few times each week, wanting to come in.'

'And then you got together with Emily?'

'Yeah, three months later.' He rubs his face. 'That's when things really started to get out of hand.'

'What do you mean?'

'Well, she hated Emily, obviously. Felt that she'd taken her place. When she discovered Emily was pregnant, a few months later, that tipped her over the edge. Alison threatened to kill her.'

'Wow.' I'm wondering now about Michael's attitude to children; he didn't want them so quickly with his ex, but when he started seeing Emily, it happened almost immediately.

'Emily was terrified,' he continues. 'We had to go to the police in the end, get a restraining order.'

'Shit.'

There's a silence, and I decide to push him a bit more.

'Did things ever become... violent, you know, between you and Alice – Alison?'

There's a split-second delay before he replies. 'What? No. Of course not.'

'Are you sure about that? Because she mentioned scars in her post.'

He looks at me as if I'm an idiot. 'She'll say anything to get what she wants.'

'Hm.'

'Listen, I don't want you talking to her. You need to ignore her. And you need to delete that post.'

'It's a public page,' I tell him.

'Take it down!' There's a look of fury on his face, and he comes a step closer. I've still got one eye on the open door, just down the hallway.

I have no intention of stopping my contact with Alice, and I'm certainly not going to be told what to do by this loud, arrogant man. But I might be able to use his demand to my advantage. 'All right, take it easy. I might – *might* – take it down, if you can help me.'

He sighs, like Henderson and Jack when I make requests of them. 'With what?'

'Can you trace someone?'

His eyes narrow. 'What are you on about?'

'I received a threat, on the private messages of the *Emily and Thea* page.' I watch him closely. 'From a guy called john-smith12643,' I add.

Michael looks at me blankly.

'Does that username mean anything to you?'

'Why would it?'

'I don't know.'

He looks away. 'What did this John Smith say, then?' he asks.

'Told me to stop *digging*, or I'd end up like her. Like Emily.'

Michael nods slowly, as if such a threat is perfectly normal and understandable.

'So, can you help?' I ask. 'Can you find out who he is? Or where he is, at least?'

He considers this. 'Possibly.'

'Okay.'

'If you take the post down, and don't speak to her.'

'Deal.' I'm crossing my fingers in my pocket, so it doesn't count, but he can't see that.

'Fine.' Michael gives me his email address. 'Send me what you have on John Smith.'

'I'll do it right now,' I reply. 'Thanks.'

He grunts at me, then sweeps past in another cloud of alcohol before stomping down the hallway and out. I hear him treading heavily in the gravel at the front of his house, before his door slams shut. It's only when I close my own front door and lock it that I realise how much I'm shaking.

CHAPTER TWENTY-THREE

Friday, 1 October

Maybe I'm only noticing it because September is over, but the nights are definitely closing in sooner, now. It's early evening, but as I gaze out of the back window, I can see the darkness already starting to fall. It's cloaking the outside world in a gloom that matches my mood. Instead of being out at the start of the weekend and having fun, I'm alone in the kitchen on my laptop.

I had a plan to travel across town to Hackney and meet up with my friend Bea for a drink. But she called late this afternoon to tell me that her kid was poorly and needed her at home, so we postponed. Then Jack texted to say he'd be late back, too, because his appointments in the clinic were overrunning. Not that I'm especially bothered about spending the evening with him.

This afternoon, I talked to my therapist about Jack. I explained that I didn't think he was supporting me in my recovery. How I felt that he hadn't been there for me since the miscarriage. When asked why I thought that and, after some more questions, I reflected that it was probably because he didn't want our baby. We hadn't planned it, it was the wrong time, he was just setting up in his new job and we were supposed to be renovating the house – rather than celebrating, these were his reactions to the news of my pregnancy.

'It's typical of him,' I said in the session. 'He can be so closed-minded like that. When something doesn't go his way or fit exactly with his schedule, he just can't deal with it. And it's impossible to change his mind.'

Laurence, being the professional that he is, sat there calmly while I worked myself up about Jack, slagging him off and generally venting. Then he tried to get me to take Jack's perspective, asking why he might feel that way. My initial response was a catastrophic, black-and-white one, built on self-blame: he doesn't want to be with me any more, he thinks I'm useless and he regrets buying a house with me and asking me to marry him. We explored those thoughts and the anger, sadness and anxiety that went along with them, and I managed to come up with some alternatives.

Perhaps Jack is feeling the loss of our baby himself, too, but he doesn't know how to express it, and with the stress he's under at work, his response is to ignore it, to back away. He's a practical man who's trained to fix problems but, when the problem can't be fixed, he's the one that feels impotent and disconnected. My therapist gently suggested talking to Jack about it, perhaps even asking him to come along to a session. That'll never happen, but an honest conversation about what we're each experiencing might help. The only problem is that, to have one of those, he's got to actually be here. Not just at work the whole bloody time.

At least I have my project to keep me occupied. It's more than that, of course; it's about finding Emily and Thea. I'm doing it for them. But I have to admit – as therapy has led me to realise – I'm partly doing it for *me*, too. It's something I can really get stuck into, as a way of keeping occupied while I recover, giving me new purpose in life now that I've lost the purpose I thought I had, at least for the time being.

A large glass of wine later, I'm still on the *Find Emily and Thea* webpage. I've followed up with friends, old colleagues, school mates and well-wishers to see if any of them can help. I know from my work on documentaries that sometimes you – the investigator – can be the only person who sees the whole picture. There might be a snippet of information which someone else thinks is meaningless or irrelevant, but to you it can be the key that unlocks the whole story. There are no new leads so far, though.

Among the private messages that I've been sent nestle the two threads I think about more than all the others. First, there's my chat with Alice Hope about Michael, which held all sorts of promise at the beginning of this week but has since, unfortunately, run aground. I asked her what proof she has that Michael is 'more capable than most' of killing someone. But her terse reply ignored my question. *Why did you take it down?* she wrote. I told her that I needed Michael's support for the page, that he didn't like her post and he'd asked me to remove it. *Well fuck him, then*, was her response. *The world needs to see what a bastard he is, and you need to show them.* I implored her yesterday to *help me show them*, but she hasn't replied.

I can't understand why Alice is playing games… although I remember what Michael said about her. The alternative story of Alice Hope, also known as Alison Templeton, sociopathic ex-girlfriend-slash-stalker. I've googled her real name and found a good candidate: a recruitment consultant from Wimbledon. I wonder if I should contact her via her LinkedIn page or work email, too, but I know our messages are sensitive and I resolve to keep it in the private chat of our social media. Maybe she just needs some time to chill. She'll reply to me when she's ready.

The other thing I'm thinking about is, of course, the threat from johnsmith12643. I simply sent him a message saying: *I'm not scared of you.* His reply was even shorter: *You should be.* It's frightening, sure, but I can't be deterred. I'm hoping Michael will give me something to go on, at least so I know whether or not

John Smith presents any real danger to me. I knocked on Michael's door earlier today – taking him another sandwich and a bottle of beer to keep him sweet – and asked whether he'd found anything. He said he hadn't. I'm not sure whether I believe him, though.

I get to my feet, pick up my wine and begin walking as I start to piece together what I know. I recall Cathy's mention of a 'fancy man' who used to visit the house when Michael was out. What if Michael discovered that Emily was seeing someone and cheating on him, could that have been the start of all this?

I feel as though things might be starting to make sense: Michael behaves violently towards Emily, the same as he did with Alice, aka Alison. Emily chooses to stay with him despite the abuse, perhaps because she's scared, or she's financially dependent on him, or simply for Thea's sake. But her revenge is to conduct an affair with a handsome (as Cathy described him) mystery man in their home: a symbolic act to reclaim her power, and perhaps to find the intimacy that her relationship with Michael lacks.

One day, their conflict reaches a tipping point: he discovers her affair and flies into a rage. This time, though, she stands up to his aggression, and he retaliates with such brutality that she sustains a fatal injury. A head wound, maybe, from impact on stone or metal as she fell after being pushed or struck. I read somewhere that those secondary injuries are the ones that kill.

The tragic story fits together, and I can picture all of it clearly, watching each chapter unfold in my mind. But can I prove what I believe to have happened? What did he do with her body? And where's Thea?

I become aware that, without even realising it, I've walked upstairs and into the second bedroom. The one Jack and I decorated together for the baby we lost. I start to think about our little unborn girl, and a deep sense of loneliness washes over me. I remember the moment when those cramps first started to hit me, just before the realisation that something was very wrong. I see the image of blood on the toilet paper. I wish – as I've wished ever since that day – that things could have been different.

My legs begin to weaken, and I reach out to the wall for support. Stepping closer, I turn my back and lean against it, grateful for how solid it feels behind me. My knees bend and I start to sink gradually, lower and lower, until I'm sitting on the floor. I haven't even switched the light on, and the green-grey paint we chose looks almost black, bar the area in a small pool of light spilling through the open door from the hallway.

I take another gulp of wine, put the glass down beside me and close my eyes.

When I open my eyes, I have no idea how long I've been sitting like this. I was walking, thinking... and then I found myself here, remembering my baby and feeling as though I was being enveloped in sadness. The rest is a blank. I'm not wearing a watch, and my phone is downstairs, so I don't even know what time it is. I do know that I need to get out of this room, though, and away from these memories for a while. Not that I seem to have much control over when or where they come to me.

Beside me, my wine glass is empty. I decide to head back down for a refill, and to check the *Find Emily and Thea* page, again. The thought of more wine cheers me up a bit, and I know that's absurd, but I don't care. I reach the bottom of the stairs and walk through into the kitchen. Then I freeze.

My laptop's not where I left it. I swear it's been moved across the table. As I hurry over to it, I feel the breath of air on my skin. I look up. And any shadow of doubt I had about my computer having been touched vanishes when I see the back door.

It's slightly open.

I stop where I am, listening for any sound. But there's nothing beyond the nocturnal noises of the town: the occasional car, a dog bark, a distant aeroplane overhead.

I put the wine glass down on the table and, heart thumping, cross to the back door. I pick up the garden secateurs that Jack bought me from the little shelf where I keep them. Their curved blades glint in the ceiling lights, hard and cold, and I briefly imagine how easily they could pierce someone's body.

I hold them out in front of me in a firm grip and push the back door wide open. I stand, staring into the dark void beyond the kitchen, ready to defend myself despite my trembling limbs.

'Is anyone there?' I call out.

But there's no reply.

CHAPTER TWENTY-FOUR

Love is often linked with madness. Turn on the radio or a streaming app and you'll hear every other singer going on about being crazy for someone or love driving them insane or whatever. I read a book once which suggested that love itself was actually a kind of madness; a temporary, obsessional state we enter into, where all we can think about is the other person. We go gooey over the smallest thing they do, while turning a blind eye to all of their shortcomings and irritating habits. We're built that way, argued the author, to create a bond for producing children. After a while, though, the madness subsides and many of us are left staring at our partners, scratching our heads and thinking: what have I done?

Not me, though.

For me, there was never a moment when my feelings tipped into obsession, or my behaviour became that of a crazy person. Everything I felt for you was accompanied by a razor-sharp clarity and indisputable logic. Yes, of course, I was acting on a biological impulse to procreate with you. It was perhaps the strongest feeling I've ever experienced. But at no point did I lose my mind. I knew exactly what I needed to do, for us. And, like a machine performing the task for which it was designed, I did it.

My objective was simple: to be with you, and to eliminate anything that might stop that from happening. Those rivals for your affection were the problem. So, I came up with a three-step plan to solve it. Step one: I had to persuade you that the others weren't worthy of your love, that they didn't deserve you, that there was something seriously wrong with them. However, if I couldn't do that, then I'd move to step two: get rid of those rivals. That was a more extreme course of action, but one which became sadly necessary. I'd hoped step two was all that was required, because step three really was the last resort.

What was step three? Well, think about it. If I can't convince you not to love others, and I can't make them disappear, either, then there would only be one rational thing left to do. I'd have to make you disappear. My reasoning was simple: if I couldn't have you, then no one could.

You can understand that, can't you, my love?

CHAPTER TWENTY-FIVE

Monday, 4 October

I decided to buy a doorbell camera that same night that I discovered the back door open. It took me a bit of googling, but eventually I found a decent one: motion-activated, with a direct feed to an app on your phone that alerts you when the sensor's triggered. A courier delivered it the following day, and by Sunday, I had installed it. After the experience of Friday night, I was somewhat happier and reassured. But Jack didn't share my feelings.

He protested that we didn't need the thing, that it was a waste of £150. More precisely: a waste of *his* £150. His single objection managed to pack a double sting: not only was it another reminder of the new financial power imbalance in our relationship, but it also demonstrated that he didn't believe me about what had happened. It was the same scepticism he expressed when I tried to show him the shoe and ring in the Crawfords' garden, only to discover they weren't there.

You must've moved the laptop, he'd said, when I told him after he came home on Friday, *and left the back door open*. I was incensed that he wasn't taking me seriously, and still so scared that I almost considered calling Henderson, but in the end, I just took another big glass of wine upstairs and rang my mum. She's about the only person at the moment – other than my therapist – who seems to be listening to me. But I could detect a trace of scepticism, even in her voice, as I told her about everything that'd been going on recently.

Now, as I work on my laptop, checking and replying to messages on the *Find Emily and Thea* page, my phone pings next to me. I pick it up and tap the PIN, just as the letterbox clatters open and shut again, a slew of mail cascading to the mat in the hallway. My doorbell camera app plays a clip of footage: a wide-angle shot of the postman approaching, extracting envelopes from his bag and dropping them through the door. It's pretty much real-time; there's a delay of maybe ten seconds with the feed to my phone. Satisfied, I return my attention to the computer screen.

I've just posted another request for any information (*no matter how small or old – please share*) that might shed light on what happened to Emily and Thea. The page's audience is growing – we're nearly at a thousand followers, now – and it's surely just a matter of time before someone comes forward with something useful. For the past two hours I've been reading comments, replying to supporters and composing an email to the local newspaper with an idea for a story about the disappearance. I decide it's time for a break. There's something I want to do.

I haven't ventured into the loft, yet, since we moved in, and Jack told me that he hasn't, either. If I'm being honest, I'm scared of what might be up there. But I don't want any part of my home to be off limits. I once interviewed a woman who was attacked in her house by an intruder and couldn't go into her living room any more because it gave her flashbacks and panic attacks. I refuse to feel like that. I want to face up to the fear and conquer it – that's what my therapist would encourage me to do. In any case, we're supposed to be converting it at some point, so I might as well check it out now.

Unfolding the stepladder beneath the loft trapdoor, I climb up, slightly shaky as my raised hands get closer to the ceiling. From the corner of my eye, I can see the stairs dropping away from the landing on the other side of the bannisters, and a wave of vertigo washes over me, the stepladder rocking side to side slightly. My hands drop to its metal frame to steady myself. I'm anxious as hell. But I don't climb down. Instead, I shut my eyes, take a deep breath, straighten my wobbly legs and try again.

Watching my footing as I reach up, I feel my fingertips make contact with the trapdoor overhead. I press against the wood, but it's solid, unyielding. I push harder, but still it doesn't budge. It's as though someone has sealed it shut with industrial-strength glue. Then I have an idea. I fetch the broom and, standing below the door, take aim before thrusting its wooden handle straight up. It bangs into the trapdoor, but nothing moves. I go again, with more power, and a third time. On the fourth blow, accompanied by a growl of effort, it unsticks a fraction.

When I've finally got it loose, I climb up again, push it through and heave it over to one side. I fumble at the floorboards around the trapdoor's edge in search of a light switch, but I can't find anything. Whispering obscenities to myself, I take two more steps up until I'm standing on the top of the stepladder, get my elbows over the edge of the trapdoor, and haul myself up and into the attic.

Inside, it's dark and cold and has a musty, decaying smell. It sounds ridiculous, but I feel as though the loft has started breathing, like it's a giant beast I've disturbed from the deep slumber of hibernation. I take out my phone and play its torch beam around me. Scanning the interior of the pitched roof, I see a light fitting, but there's no bulb in it. Holding my phone torch ahead of me like a talisman, I begin to explore.

There are large stretches of bare floorboards, rough and splintered, and I'm glad to have my shoes on as I walk across them. The wide gaps between the pieces of wood reveal a layer of fibrous insulation beneath that reminds me of looking out of an aeroplane window once you're above the clouds. The previous owners (an elderly couple we never met) were obviously reluctant to throw things out. There's an ironing board, lying on its side, wreathed in cobwebs. Behind it, some old plastic bags are stuffed full of clothes. Beside them stands the empty box that once housed a vacuum cleaner, its cover depicting a smiling woman (typical patriarchy, assuming we'll do the housework) whose eighties' dress sleeves are so puffy I laugh out loud.

Everything is covered in a thick layer of dust, and as I sweep the beam around me, I can see other collections of items, boxes and a few pieces of furniture. There are some objects I can't identify because they're covered in sheets. Advancing cautiously towards one pile of stuff, my foot makes contact with something uneven. Instinctively, I draw my weight back, but not before there's a sickening crunch. I angle my phone down and my breath catches.

It's a bird.

Or, more precisely, what's left of one. It's lying on its back, the long, thin bones of its wings spread as if it's been crucified. The head is angled to one side, its large beak curving to a sharp tip that reminds me of my secateurs. Its legs are almost pathetically thin. Around its wings I see the traces of feathers, sloughed off and decomposed to nothing more than a stain on the wood beneath it. I wonder how long it's been dead. And, perhaps more importantly, how it got in here in the first place. Is there an opening somewhere?

I keep moving, towards one of the sheets. It's covering a collection of tall, unrecognisable things. As I get closer, I can see enough detail in the pool of light to guess it's a stack of chairs and a coat stand. With my free hand, I reach out and take hold of the thin material shrouding it. Then, in one swift movement, I yank it down and away. The fabric has barely slithered off the top when there's a blur and something flies at me in a burst of chattering, piercing screeches.

I throw both hands up to protect my face and feel something leathery brush my arms before it's gone. I turn the torch beam and see a dark shape swooping and whirling with dizzying speed, around and around, like a mad thing, before it disappears. A bat.

'Christ,' I exclaim, and only now do I realise that my anxiety has spiked.

Once I've taken a moment to chill and tell myself I'm okay, it occurs to me that perhaps both creatures came in the same way. But from where? I use the torch to get my bearings. I'm facing the back of the building, I think, so the Crawfords' house is to my right.

Stepping carefully to avoid contact with any more animals – dead or alive – I reach a few flimsy plywood boards that must be the boundary between our house and theirs. But they don't even run as high as the rafters, and I can see that the lofts of our properties are connected. That definitely wasn't in the floor plan when we bought the place, but I recall the estate agent couldn't open the trapdoor during the viewing. He obviously didn't know, either.

When I shine the torch beam along the boards, I notice that one of them is missing. Approaching the gap slowly, I light up the area. But what catches my eye isn't the three-foot gap I could simply step through to get into Michael and Emily's attic. It's the object lying next to it, on our side of the makeshift wall.

A beer bottle, identical to the one I gave Michael yesterday.

As I realise it almost certainly *is* the one I gave him, a shudder as powerful as an electric shock runs through me. Was he in our loft, walking around, snooping? If he was doing that last night, drinking the beer I'd given him, how many other times has he been up here, listening to us?

I'm repulsed by the thought of Michael being directly above our bedroom, just on the other side of the ceiling. I have a sudden urge to get out of this dingy, mouldy place and take a shower, to wash off the icky feeling spreading over my skin. I leave the bottle where it is and, with a final glance at the bird carcass, lower myself back down and onto the stepladder, replacing the trapdoor as I go.

Returning to the kitchen, the attic already feels like some other world that I almost might have imagined, if it weren't for the dust and grime smeared into my hands. Even after washing them, I swear I can still smell the fusty odour of the place on me.

Waking up my laptop, I'm surprised to see that nearly an hour has passed since I was online. How did that happen? The question vanishes, though, when I see the new private message I've been sent. It's from Olivia Burgess-was-Johnson, whose profile icon shows a smiling woman who looks slightly older than me, posing with two little children. I click into the message and read:

> *Hi, sorry to have only just seen all this – I've been off here for a bit. Haven't had much contact with Emily in last few years, but we were at uni together and one thing does stick in my mind. There was this guy who basically stalked her all of the first year. I know it's probably nothing because it's so many years later now – but he was obsessed with her. I can try to get some more details, but I remember his first name…*

I blink at the screen in disbelief as I read the next word.

> *Jack.*

CHAPTER TWENTY-SIX

Tuesday, 5 October

I know it's crazy even to think it. There's no way that the stalker who harassed Emily during her first year at university was *Jack* – my fiancé, Jack. My brain has just made a leap, linking the names, but it's completely irrational. There must be thousands of Jacks in the country. Tens of thousands, perhaps. And I know that they studied at different places, anyway: Emily was at Nottingham, while Jack did his medical training at King's College, London. So, the chance of them being the same Jack is – what? – almost zero.

Almost zero.

I recall how Jack looked at Emily that very first day that we moved in. As if he'd seen her before or something. I don't think I imagined that… I remember how weird and distant he was when we went round to their house for dinner a week later. Is it possible he knew her, from years back? That he stalked her, even? They're the same age, give or take. My mind starts to run away with the idea: did Jack engineer our move here? It was me who convinced him that we could take on the fixer-upper project. I was the one who imagined the home we could create. But, now I recollect, it was Jack who found the place online. Could he have?—

No way. It's preposterous. Emily would've realised; she would've said something. Wouldn't she? I remember her telling me, as we ate takeaway bagels together in the park one lunchtime, that men think they have a right to own you, to possess you, to touch you, just because you're a woman. She was speaking passionately, in response to me talking about my documentary on gender-based violence, and it seemed a natural comment at the time. But might this have been an oblique reference to her personal experiences at uni; perhaps to her stalker, Jack?

Try as I might, I can't shift the tiny niggle of doubt. I have to be sure. I write back to Olivia Burgess-was-Johnson to ask if she can find out the guy's last name. If it isn't Brown – my Jack's surname – then I'll be certain. It's terrible of me even to consider the possibility that it could be him. But it's true that he's been different ever since we got here, and that can't all be down to the stress of his new job. What is he hiding?

An hour later, I'm out in the garden, weeding and clearing. I felt as though I needed to leave the house, to get away from my laptop and the rabbit hole I'd gone down, stupidly googling Jack and looking for connections to Emily (there weren't any). I had to take a break from my mind and just use my body instead. The weeding is tough, physical work and I've got a bit of a sweat on. I've come right to the bottom of the garden, as close as I dare to the shed at the end of the Crawfords' plot. I can make out the rotting wooden exterior through the ivy that appears to be smothering and choking it, and once again I get the urge to find out what's inside.

I glance up at Michael's back windows, but I can't see any sign of him in the house. I guess he's probably in his man-cave. Maybe he'll surface at some point for food, maybe he won't. I wonder whether he's made any progress on locating johnsmith12643. I'm tempted to make him another sandwich just as an excuse to go round and ask. Then I remember the beer bottle in the loft, and the scene I've pictured of Michael lying on his belly just feet above us, pressing his ear to the floorboards as he eavesdrops on our conversations, comes all too readily. I'll speak to him another time, when the thought of it doesn't immediately make me feel nauseous.

I've just switched to clearing some brambles (I'm toying with the idea of making some raised beds for vegetables) when my phone pings. It's the doorbell camera. I haven't heard a knock or a bell, and I'm not expecting any deliveries… although Jack might've ordered something. I take my gloves off, pull my phone from my pocket and check the footage.

At first, I think there must be some kind of mistake. There's a movement from the side, a dark shape lurches across the camera, obscuring its view completely for a couple of seconds, then disappears out of frame. Was it an animal – Archie the cat from next door, maybe? I take the footage back, slow it down, watch it again. Pause. And that's when the dread starts to pool in my stomach, cold and heavy, when I catch the end of the shadow's motion. My mouth tastes of wet metal. There, unmistakably captured on my phone screen is a human arm.

It's not Archie – it's a person. But why haven't they rung the buzzer or tapped on the door? Maybe I can't hear it from here. And why did they approach from the side, rather than the front, up the path? It's almost as if they were trying to avoid appearing on camera. As if they knew it was there. Then I realise this happened at least thirty seconds ago, now. The adrenalin pumps through me again, and I'm back on high alert. I run the footage on, hoping – praying – that it's just someone messing around, that I'll see them walking away. But there's nothing more recorded. Which means one thing.

Whoever came to the front door hasn't left. Either they're right against the door, just out of the lens's range, or… oh, God.

They're in the house.

Shit.

I tap out of the camera app and call Jack. He doesn't pick up. I try him once more. Again, there's no response.

I've got to stay calm. Breathe. Think logically: if the person's inside the house, they must have keys. Only Jack and I have keys to our house. And I'm out here, at the end of the garden. So, it must be Jack. Maybe he's back home for lunch. Perhaps he's just left his phone on silent. That's all this is.

It's now at least two minutes since the original alert from the doorbell camera. Maybe slightly longer, I'm not sure. I pull up the app again and activate a live feed. There's no one there. I call Jack once more. His voicemail kicks in and, this time, I gabble a message for him.

'Jack, there's, um, I think there's someone in the house. Something – I mean, someone, a person, came past the camera, and it pinged on my phone, but I can't see, and – they might be in the house. Is it you? Please answer, or call me. I need to know if it's you.'

I hang up without a goodbye, pocket the phone again and pick up my secateurs. Then I make my way slowly towards the house. I'm aware of every leaf and twig snapping underfoot, every swipe of a branch or bramble I need to push aside to get through. I'm holding out the secateurs like a dagger as I reach the back door. It's open – as I left it – but I can't spot anyone in the kitchen.

'Hello?' I call out, but I'm met with silence. 'Jack, is that you?'

I step inside, two hands on the gardening tool pointing ahead. The blades are so sharp, they're almost daring someone to be there, to show themselves and see what happens. I twist right, then left.

But there's no one.

'Who is it?' I yell, moving down the hallway. 'Who's here?'

I'm halfway to the front door when I realise it's open. Only a fraction, but it's off the latch. I pause and turn, looking up the stairs. Then I step forward, grab the front door handle and yank it open.

'Hello, love.'

Cathy's standing on the path. She's wearing a dark outfit of sweater and loose-fitting trousers. There's a look of concern etched on her face.

'I stepped out and I heard you shouting,' she says. 'So, I thought I'd come and check, just to make sure you were okay. And I saw that the door was open.'

'It was open?' I ask.

'Mm. Just a crack, but…' She flashes me an awkward little smile. 'You're getting like me.'

'Oh.' I stare at the door, as if it'll give me answers. 'I must've forgotten…'

'You want to be careful with those things,' she adds, pointing to the secateurs I'm still gripping. 'You'll have someone's eye out.'

'Yeah.' I start to relax. It was a false alarm; just Cathy, approaching from her front garden and triggering the camera sensor late because of the angle. That was all. I feel the tension start to melt from my neck and shoulders.

'Are you all right, love?'

'Uh-huh.' I take a step back. 'Would you like a cup of tea?'

Cathy beams back at me. 'I never say no to tea. Even if you make it in the mug with a bag.' She winks.

Perhaps it's Cathy's playful response. Maybe it's the relief that everything's fine, that there wasn't someone in the house. Or the reassurance that now I have some human company. Whatever it is, I start to laugh. Big, hearty chuckles, rising from my belly and bursting out of my mouth.

'Come in, then!' I cheerfully cry, once I've got a hold of myself.

As we walk down the hallway, I'm babbling on about the gardening and my idea for raised vegetable beds and whether she's ever thought of putting some in her garden. But I stop talking the second we enter the kitchen. Because my laptop is on the counter, open. And I'm certain I left it on the table, closed. Then something occurs to me. Cathy said that she came over *after* she heard me shouting. And that was about two minutes after the figure appeared on the doorbell camera.

It wasn't her.

CHAPTER TWENTY-SEVEN

Tuesday, 5 October

It's happening once more. I'm lying in the six-foot-deep hole in the earth, dark soil walls rising straight up beside me. I can't move and terror is enveloping my body. A figure I can't make out is standing on the ground above, as before, but this time I can't even tell if it's a man or a woman. There's a noise, as if their spade is hitting metal – *tap* – and again – *tap* – louder, and then it's as if my viewpoint is rising up and out of the grave. As I reach the surface, I think I'm about to see the figure's face, but then I'm awake, blinking and rubbing my eyes. My neck hurts from where I've fallen asleep awkwardly on the sofa. But the noise hasn't stopped.

Tap-tap-tap.

I realise it's the front door. I haul myself off the couch and pad down the hallway.

'Who is it?' My question is now an instinctive refrain where I once just opened the door, confident that I could deal with whoever was there. But I don't feel like that any more.

'Laurence,' comes the response.

Oh my god. I fish my phone out of my pocket and look at the clock. Our session ended an hour ago. Shit. And there are missed calls from him, too, as well as a notification from the doorbell camera app just now. I hastily tidy my hair and wrench the front door open. My therapist is there, a good step or two back on the path, hands in his pockets. He's wearing a tweed jacket, collared shirt, navy chinos and brown suede ankle boots. It's basically his uniform. He looks cute in it. There's relief on his face when he sees me.

'Hi,' I say. 'I'm so sorry. I've just realised... I didn't turn up today.'

'That's okay,' he replies. 'I hope I didn't startle you.'

'No,' I lie. 'I was...' I gesture back inside the house, as if that will mean something to him. 'I nodded off on the couch. I haven't been sleeping all that well, as you know, so...'

'It happens.' He gives a brief, friendly smile. 'Apologies for turning up unannounced,' he adds. 'I tried to call. It's just that, well, when a client doesn't attend, and they're not answering their phone, and, you know, they've been feeling a bit low, then we just need to make sure that person's all right. It's a duty of care thing.'

'I understand,' I say. 'Jack's a doctor, so it's similar.'

'Right.'

'Do you want to come in?' I ask.

'Ah, no, thank you,' he says. 'I appreciate the offer, but I shouldn't. Boundaries, you know.'

'Oh, of course.' I smile at him.

'So, er, I was just checking everything was okay.'

'Yeah, thanks. Apart from falling asleep when I was supposed to be in our session, but hey.'

'It used to be that local NHS would do these checks, to make sure people were safe and well,' he explains, 'but with the cutbacks, the system's changed.'

Without warning, an image pops into my mind: I'm grabbing Laurence by the arm, pulling him into the hallway of our house, shutting the door and kissing him. I'm startled by it, and obviously I can't hide that.

'Freya? Are you?...'

'Yes.' I laugh for a second and shake the picture away. 'I'm fine.'

'Great.' He nods. 'So, see you for our session on Friday, then?'

'Sure,' I reply. 'Looking forward to it.' I don't know why I say that. Maybe because it's the truth; I am. Because he's one of the only people who seems to give a shit about me at the moment, and I like talking to him.

We say goodbye and I close the door. I check the doorbell camera footage of my therapist walking up the path, a couple of minutes ago, holding his little man-bag. The last thing I can remember before the nightmare from which he roused me was Cathy leaving, a couple of hours ago. And I realise I have no memory even of falling asleep.

'It was weird as hell,' I tell Jack as we sit at the table with the dinner I've made. 'Something must've set the camera off.'

'This is amazing,' he says, mouth half-full, jabbing his fork at the plate. 'I never would've thought prawns and feta would be such a great combo.'

'Yeah. Thanks.' I wait until he looks up and I know I've got his attention again. 'I mean, the door was open, Jack. Are you sure you closed it properly when you went to work?'

'Of course,' he snorts. 'I always give it a good slam, then a push to be sure.'

'Right.' That's true; his robust door-closing method has woken me up on more than one morning, but perhaps I should've been up by then, anyway.

'It's not that app of yours, is it?' He waves the fork in the direction of my phone, over on the counter. 'Did you press something that opened the door? It can't do that, can it?'

'I don't know. I don't think so. It's not connected to the door itself.'

'Good, well that's something, then.'

We eat in silence for a moment.

'Doesn't it bother you that someone might've been in our home?' I ask.

Jack shrugs. 'Well, it would, but there's no evidence that's what happened, is there?'

'There's my laptop.'

He groans. 'Are you sure you didn't move it?'

'Yes!' I exclaim, though I'm actually not sure, now. I have been experiencing little lapses of concentration. 'And what about the person?'

'Probably Cathy, from what you said,' he replies casually.

'She said she only came when she heard me.'

'Come on.' Jack gives me a sceptical look. 'She's not exactly… reliable, is she?'

'You're judging her without knowing her,' I counter. 'She's pretty switched on.'

Jack shakes his head and shovels in another forkful of food.

I sigh. 'Let me show you.' I get up, grab my phone and select the app. I tap, scroll, go forward and back. But the footage isn't there.

'Okay, then.' Jack shuffles his chair around slightly. 'Let's have a look.'

'I can't find it,' I say, tapping out and back in again, refreshing, scrolling. 'It should be here.'

Jack waits impassively, his arms folded across his chest in a display that says: *I stopped eating my dinner for this, and you're wasting my time.* He might as well tell me that out loud.

'Are you looking in the right folder?' he asks eventually.

'Yes, I'm looking in the right folder,' I snap back at him. 'It's just not bloody here.'

He picks up his fork and goes back to his food. 'Maybe you were mistaken,' he offers.

'Excuse me?' I stop searching; clearly the clip isn't there any more. But part of me is now wondering if I deleted it by accident.

Perhaps I should check the settings, in case I've changed something to stop it storing footage…

'I'm just saying.' Jack's tone is almost apologetic. 'Is it possible that, you know, you might've imagined it? You've been under a lot of stress lately, and—'

'I know what I saw, okay?' I feel the anger rising up through my body, flushing my neck and face.

'All right.' He holds up his hands in one of those *calm down, love* gestures. And if he says those patronising words, I swear I'll punch him.

'You don't believe me, do you?' I stare at him, my jaw clenched.

'Freya…'

'You don't!' I bang my fist down on the table.

'It's not that I *don't*, I just… could it have been a malfunction with the camera, or the app?' His tone is conciliatory now, but the damage has been done.

'You're meant to be on my side!' I scream, and I know I'm losing control. 'You're my fucking fiancé!'

'I *am* on your side,' he says soothingly and, again, I have the feeling that I'm one of his patients, being gently given the bad news that there's something wrong with me.

'How can you say that?' I demand. 'You obviously think I'm hallucinating.'

'That's not what I said—'

'Do you think I'm mad? Is that it? Crazy miscarriage lady, seeing and hearing things.'

'Freya.' He reaches out to me, but I pull away. 'I'm trying to help,' he adds plaintively.

'Well, you can start by trusting me.'

'I do. It's just…'

'Forget it.' I don't want to have this conversation any more. I get up, still clutching my phone. 'Laurence would believe me,'

I hiss, before ripping open the back door and storming out into the garden.

'Freya!' Jack calls after me, but I ignore him.

It's dark outside, but there's something about the solitude and the night air that starts to calm me down. Jack has stayed in the kitchen, and I glance back to see him helping himself to another plateful of dinner. I consider what I've just told him. I may have blurted it in a moment of fury and frustration, but I stand by it. My therapist *would* believe me, instead of doubting me.

He'd acknowledge that what happened today was frightening, validate my experience, ask intelligent questions about it and offer emotional support. The difference is even starker when I recall what Jack just said about it and, not for the first time in the past few weeks, I find myself wondering whether I'm with the right man. I briefly recall the little fantasy of kissing Laurence that flashed into my head earlier. Is my subconscious trying to tell me something?

I shut my eyes and wipe both hands over my face. When I open them again, a few seconds later, I happen to look up at the back windows. I give a small gasp as I see Michael's there. He's watching me, his face completely expressionless. And his window is open. He's heard everything Jack and I have just said, I'm sure of it.

Michael lifts a beer bottle to his lips, takes a long swig, and continues to stare at me. I'm instantly reminded of what I found in our attic: the bottle I gave him, discarded in our section of the loft. Suddenly, the air feels a lot colder out here.

CHAPTER TWENTY-EIGHT

Tuesday, 5 October

Later that evening, there's an uneasy truce between me and Jack. Our argument over dinner sits like a third person in the room; an uninvited guest who's outstayed their welcome but won't leave. There was no resolution to it. We just stopped speaking. I know that's not good, that it's better to talk things through. Never go to sleep on an argument and all that. I'm still hurt, though, and I'm not going to be the one to reach out to him after what he said.

We're at opposite ends of the living room, now, each of us hunched over our laptops, as if we exist in two separate universes. Jack is on the sofa, headphones on, engrossed in something. His concentration is entirely on his screen (which I can't see), punctuated by the occasional flurry of typing or mouthful of beer.

Curled up in an armchair, I'm doing the same, except that I have wine. I've already drunk a couple of large glasses of the stuff, and I'm definitely feeling the effects of it. At least it's taken the edge off my nerves and anger, although it's replaced them with a sense of sadness, almost emptiness. I'm trying (and failing) to take my mind off that with the *Find Emily and Thea* page.

Olivia Burgess-was-Johnson has commented on it earlier today. She's sent me a little holding message, privately, to say that she's still trying to find out Emily's stalker's full name; she's waiting on someone else to email her back. Then she's posted publicly to express her sympathy, before making reference to the fact that

Emily had more than one person with an unhealthy interest in her, asking: *as women, when are we ever safe?* Her post has received a number of affirmative replies, but my attention drifts away as I read them, back to my own situation. I can't help but wonder: am I safe? And I don't just mean from Michael.

I used to feel secure with Jack. Now, he's treating me like some sort of mad woman. Why would he do that? If it was the other way around, I'd support him to find out what was going on, not doubt his sanity. Perhaps he's just not the partner I thought he'd be, or that I want him to be. I glance up at him, but he doesn't register it. I watch as he takes a big gulp of beer, rinses it round his mouth and swallows, all while glued to the little glowing screen in front of him.

I'm topping up my wine and planning what I'll say about all this in my therapy session on Friday when the notification pops up on my screen: *New post from Alice Hope.*

A post, not a private message? Perhaps it's not surprising, given that Alice has been ignoring me since I took down her public comment which as good as accused Michael of intimate partner violence. I scroll down and there it is, just below Olivia Burgess-was-Johnson's post. Alice writes:

> *Everyone knows that Emily's husband Michael Crawford is an evil man with a sadistic streak and a history of violence, who cannot be trusted. But we should also be asking Emily what she was hiding. She's not the innocent everyone thinks she is.*

I take a large sip of wine and read it once more. Alice is shit-stirring, for sure, perhaps trying to get a reaction from Michael or others. But is she for real? Does she have any solid proof of this violence by Michael? Or, indeed, of anything about Emily that might be relevant to her disappearance? I think again about my theory of what happened, and about the 'fancy man' visitor Cathy described.

Either way, I know Michael's not going to be happy about this and – suspicious as I am of him – I need to keep him onside. I remember his version of events with Alice Hope. Then I picture him, watching me from his back window earlier and, before I know it, I'm recalling the row that Jack and I had shortly before that.

I'm not sure how many minutes pass before the private message arrives from johnsmith12643. Its effect on me is immediate. My heart rate starts to speed up, I feel a constriction in my chest and my mouth becomes so dry I automatically reach for my wine and drink some more. I notice there's a tiny tremor in my hand as I click into his email.

I've already told you to stop Freya but you've ignored me. You need to understand I'm not joking. All this digging is only going to produce one thing – your own grave. Stop now while you still can. Take this page down and STOP looking for her. I won't ask again. You have been warned.

Despite the wine numbing my senses, my anxiety starts to grow, pulsing within me, as if someone's running an electrical charge through my guts. I begin to feel restless, one knee jiggling, and I just want to get away from my laptop, slam it shut and run upstairs, as if that'll protect me.

It's not just the threat – that horrible sense that someone out there wants to do me harm – it's how specific it is to *me*: John Smith knows about the grave, about my nightmare, and there's only one person I told about that dream this afternoon.

Jack.

I look up at him, my leg still shaking in the armchair as if I'm not in control of it. Did he just type that message? Is he johnsmith12643? He's still absorbed in his screen; the light from it giving his face a ghostly pallor. Eventually, he senses something and raises his head, meets my gaze. His expression is unreadable and, for the first time I can remember, I have literally no idea what he's thinking.

'What?' he says. There's a coldness in his voice that hasn't been there before.

I down the rest of my wine, snatch up my laptop and leave the room.

I don't even want to sleep in the same bed as him tonight.

CHAPTER TWENTY-NINE

Wednesday, 6 October

I hardly slept again last night, worrying about Jack, about Michael and about this johnsmith who's determined to stop me looking for Emily and Thea. I caught perhaps a couple of hours of fitful rest, with vivid dreams that – according to my friend, Bea – are a sign of not sleeping very deeply, in my case because my body seems to be on constant alert.

There's the anxiety around whom I can trust, and who might wish me actual physical harm. But there's also a sense of regret underlying it all, the feeling that I've made some bad choices whose undoing will take more than I can manage.

Moving into this house was supposed to be the start of the family I'd always dreamed of having, but now it feels as though the home I'd wanted so dearly isn't somewhere I'm happy to be. The restlessness that came on last night after the new, threatening email from johnsmith is still there, fuelled by the belief that Jack isn't being straight with me.

Part of me wants to run away from all this, to leave and go back to my old housemates in Hackney, or to get on a train up north and stay with my mum. To stop searching for Emily and Thea. But I know I can't do that.

I have to stay, to face up to this, to fight the person or people who've made my neighbour and her daughter disappear and who want to frighten me into silence. My days of documentary making taught me that having the courage and determination to make your voice heard is the only way to stand up to the bastards who want to crush anyone who's an obstacle to them. Who want to exploit, humiliate and hurt others and who believe they're above the law. I won't be bullied by them.

I remember a day back in May, when Emily took me along to her yoga studio for the first time. She'd been practising for years and, losing my balance on the mat beside her as she held headstands and all sorts, I felt uncoordinated, clumsy and weak. Over coffee and pastries afterwards, I told her how strong I thought she was. She laughed and thanked me but said that she always wished she was stronger. I realised she didn't mean yoga or physical strength.

She went on to explain to me that she wasn't strong with people, that she never stood up for herself. It was something she was trying to deal with in therapy (among other stuff, she said), but it went all the way back to childhood. To overbearing, pushy parents who didn't tolerate discussion, let alone dissent. Lots of people thought she was successful, but underneath it all she felt fragile. She told me that, sometimes, she even felt like a fraud, an imposter.

I wonder, now, who was making her feel that way in her adult life. Michael, Alice Hope, johnsmith, or – God forbid – Jack? Was she reaching out to me, but I didn't see it, didn't correctly interpret her veiled request for help? Well, I'm not going to ignore her now, not when she needs me. I'm going to be the strength that she never thought she had. Starting now.

I knock on Michael's door, loud and clear, with confidence. I'm still convinced that he knows much more than he's letting on about why his wife and daughter have gone missing. Whether that extends to murdering them and burying them in the back garden, I'm not certain. There are other possibilities: he paid someone else to do it, or he's keeping them in the basement, perhaps.

I've been down into our cellar a couple of times to check if there's any connection to their house, but there was nothing. Just a dark, empty pit of concrete (whose damp-proofing represents another complex, expensive task on the renovation to-do list). I have no way of telling whether Emily and Thea are imprisoned on the other side of those thick walls, and drilling through them would be impossible. So, whatever Michael is hiding, I need to keep in contact with him if I'm to stand any chance of finding out what it is.

He answers quicker than before and, this time, it's my turn to walk straight in and past him. I stand in the middle of the hallway as if I have every right to be there. I can see that the door to his man-cave is shut, the electronic keypad holding its secrets. Whether it's in response to my show of authority, or whether it's plain shock at my audacity, he doesn't say anything, as if he's waiting for me to take the lead.

'I deleted it,' I tell him.

He nods. He knows what I'm talking about.

'Alice Hope's post yesterday,' I confirm.

'I saw.' He coughs. 'Er, thanks for doing that.'

'I thought you, and your *clients*, might appreciate that.'

He shoves his hands in his pockets. 'Yeah.'

'What I want to know, now, is what you can tell me about johnsmith12643?'

'Ah,' he scratches the back of his head. I've caught him by surprise and he's clearly not sure what to say. 'Well…'

'Have you found out where he is?'

'Yes.'

'Where?' I demand.

'Iceland.'

A sense of relief spreads through me. John Smith is nothing to do with this. He's only a troll, overseas, hours away by aeroplane, who can't get to me. 'Good,' I reply.

'But,' he adds, 'they're using a VPN.'

'A virtual private network.' I don't want him to think I'm some woman who knows nothing about tech.

'Right.' He looks slightly surprised. 'So, if you know what a VPN is, you'll know that Iceland is just where John Smith wants you to *think* he is.'

'Okay.'

'But, in reality, he could be anywhere, and you wouldn't know. He might even be next door to you,' he adds with a chuckle.

'That's not funny.' I put my hands on my hips. 'Is it you, Michael?'

'No!'

I hold eye contact with him, undaunted by his height. 'Now would be the time to fess up, if it is,' I tell him.

'It's not me.'

'If it was a practical joke, or something, because you were pissed off with me, better to just say so…'

'It isn't me.' His voice is lower now, gravelly, and his insistence is tinged with aggression.

'Did you find out anything else about him?'

He pushes out his lips. 'Only that the account was first active on the fourteenth of July.'

I think back. 'Two days after Emily and Thea disappeared.'

'Um, yeah.'

'And when were you planning on sharing this with me?'

'Soon… I was still looking into it.'

'Right.' There's a brief silence. 'So, can you find out the true location?'

An expression of anguish distorts his face. 'It's not as straightforward as—'

'You can't do it, then.' I've learned from experience that the best way to get a man to do something for you is to suggest that he's not capable of doing it – his ego will immediately kick in.

'I never said that,' he replies defensively. 'There are some tools I could try.'

'Okay, great. I'll carry on managing the message board and keeping Alice Hope at arm's length for you, and you find john-smith12643 for me. Deal?'

He blinks. 'Fine,' he says slowly. 'But I can't promise a result.'

I turn to leave but pause when I reach the front door. I look back at Michael, who's waiting by the door to his man-cave, hand on the keypad. I notice that his index finger is on the number 3.

'By the way,' I ask, keeping my tone casual, 'did Emily have any photographs from her time at university?'

Michael sniffs. 'Why?'

'Because I want to be able to trace people who were there with her, who might've...' I choose my words carefully, 'had an interest in her.'

'An interest?'

'Yeah. You know, mapping her network a bit, seeing who she might still be in touch with.'

Michael takes his hand away from the keypad and scratches his jaw. 'You think someone from her uni – what – abducted her?'

'I think we need to keep all possibilities in mind, especially as the police are doing nothing.'

He grunts.

'So, have you got any photos?'

That pained expression again. *Oh, the effort of helping someone else look for your missing wife!* I want to shout at him or slap him, but I wait.

'Emily did keep some, but they're up in the loft.'

'Can you get them?'

He blows out his cheeks. 'Maybe.'

I nod, then open the front door and step out into the daylight. The encounter went better than expected. I actually got some useful information from Michael. The only problem is that, rather than reassuring me, it's made me more worried about this John Smith. The fact he's going to the trouble of using a VPN to disguise his location indicates he's got something to hide. But what? His role in Emily and Thea's disappearance?

Michael was adamant that he wasn't johnsmith12643. Well, he would say that, wouldn't he? Maybe it's the truth. Perhaps John Smith is another person with something to hide about Emily, whatever that could be. I think again of Jack…

But I can't let Michael off the hook, just because he did something helpful and we've had one conversation where he didn't treat me like an idiot. There's still the locked shed, the patch of dug earth, the vanishing ring and shoe, his snatches of conversation where he must have been talking about Emily and the refuse sacks he was so determined for me not to open. He's got to be covering up something, and I'll be damned if I let him keep whatever it is to himself.

This evening, Jack and I are even more distant from one another than we were last night. But I refuse to feel bad about that. He clearly doesn't believe or trust me about what's been going on, and that hurts.

Today, for the first time in a while, I didn't cook him dinner. I didn't make anything for myself, either, because I wasn't hungry. When he realised he'd have to make his own meal, his disappointment was almost comical; as obvious as a child denied sweets. But he couldn't protest – I don't *owe* him dinner. Me cooking for him was just a pattern we fell into because he's working and I'm… not. Now, he seems to think he's entitled to it every night, like I'm some kind of housewife in the 1950s whose main purpose is to serve him.

Hopefully I won't have to spell out the link between his behaviour and my reaction. Even Jack, with his limited emotional intelligence, should get that. I know we need to talk, but right now I don't want to be the one to initiate the conversation. I'm worried that, if I do, it'll open up so much more that's been bubbling away under the surface for months, including since before my miscarriage. I'm scared that might be the beginning of the end.

So, we've spent the past few hours, since he got in from his shift at the hospital, apart. Avoiding one another. Jack is upstairs, 'sorting some stuff out' (whatever that means), while I'm in the living room on my laptop. I've been reading about cases of missing women and children and how, more often than not, it's a partner or ex-partner who's responsible. If they haven't fled abuse, they're likely to have been the victims of intimate partner violence.

The stat I found a couple of weeks ago comes instantly to mind: sixty-two per cent of the 1,500 women murdered in this country over the past decade were killed by someone with whom they were, or had been, in a relationship.

Sixty-two per cent.

I do the calculations. That's one every four days, consistently, for ten years. It makes me sick thinking about it. The idea that someone you trust – or trusted – more than almost anyone else could turn on you and end your life is terrifying. And, by contrast, what proportion of men were killed by their partner or ex? One per cent. The gender asymmetry is disgusting and, looking at the stats, I feel myself tensing with anger. I can't help but imagine the worst with Michael and Emily, and then, of course, in my own home, there's—

'Freya.' Jack enters the living room, his expression serious. I hadn't even heard him come down the stairs. He's silent for a moment. Then, in a sombre tone, he says: 'When were you going to tell me about this?'

At first, I have no idea what he's talking about. Once I see the document in his hand, though, it dawns on me. A horrible, nauseating realisation. He's been going through my stuff. And he's just found proof of the one thing about my past I haven't shared with him. The only thing about me I didn't want him to know. I wanted to forget it myself. I know I should have thrown the letter away. But I kept it because of what it symbolised.

And now Jack knows my secret.

CHAPTER THIRTY

I understood that getting rid of my rivals for your affection wouldn't be easy. It'd be a course of action with significant risks involved and high potential losses. But, like a long-odds gamble, the pay-off I stood to gain was huge. You, basically, all to myself.

I don't really believe in gambling. The very word itself suggests a level of uncertainty and unpredictability with which I'm not comfortable. It evokes wild throws of the dice, spins of a roulette wheel, the turn of cards or outcome of a sports match over which you have literally no control. It makes me think of superstition, of absurd rituals, of lucky socks and sweaty palms clutching charms. Of the 'house' inevitably winning, and making hapless punters look like fools. And that isn't me at all. I work on data: empirical, irrefutable evidence. Nothing less. Naturally, with something as important as you, I refused to gamble. So why did I still play the game?

Simple. Because I rigged the outcome in my favour. In our favour, I should say, because we're in this together, you and me.

The most important thing in improving my odds of success was finding out your secret. Once I knew that, it changed everything. I knew how vulnerable you were. How dependent you were on others. How easily you could be manipulated. I realise that probably makes me sound like a bad person. Of course, I'm not. I know that you know that. Deep down, you trust me, which is why you let me find out so much about you, intentionally or otherwise. I like to think that you did that because you knew I'd make the right decision for you.

That's why the gamble of what I did wasn't really a gamble. It'd cause some short-term pain for you and some others close to you, obviously. But, in the long run – when we were together – I was confident you'd thank me. So, with my risk-reward calculation made, I did what I had to do. I don't get very emotional, but it was sad seeing the effect that had on you. I wish that could've been the end of it and the beginning of our new life as one, as it was meant to be.

But it wasn't. There was a whole lot more pain to come.

And you brought that on yourself, darling.

You left me with no choice.

CHAPTER THIRTY-ONE

Wednesday, 6 October

'I would've told you when the time was right,' I say.

Jack's facial muscles tighten, his jaw clenches. His eyes flick down to the paper and back up to me. 'This is really serious,' he says. 'Why didn't you tell me?'

'I wasn't ready to talk about it.'

'Freya, this…' he gasps, waves the letter at me. 'I mean, it's—'

'It was a long time ago.' I can feel my leg jiggling, my toes tapping out a staccato beat on the floorboard. I press my foot into the ground to help me keep still.

He shakes his head. 'I can't believe this. We've been together four years.'

'I'm not ashamed of it,' I tell him.

He exhales through his nostrils, slow and steady, like he's trying to control himself.

'Anyway,' I continue, 'why were you going through my stuff?'

'It's *our* stuff,' he replies.

'Not the box that was in.' I point to the letter. 'That's my private box.'

'I must've made a mistake,' he says. 'There's so many bloody boxes up there.'

'My name's on the outside. And it's on that letter too. Which was in its original envelope, addressed to me. Not you. And not *us*.'

He shrugs, and I'm reminded of Michael. That masculine indifference. Not giving a shit.

'Why were you looking in the box?' I demand.

'Never mind that.' Jack waves the letter. 'Are you going to explain this to me?'

I put my laptop to one side and stand. 'Not until you tell me why you were opening letters addressed to me.'

He gives a sigh of irritation. 'Oh, I don't know, because you're my fiancée, and I'm worried about you, that's why!'

'You're worried about me?' I can hear my voice getting louder, feel the blood flowing to my face.

'Yes.'

'Well, that's nice, isn't it?' I stare at him for a few seconds. 'You're never here, you've pretty much ignored the fact that our baby died inside me, you—'

'I didn't *ignore* it, I've—'

'I'm not finished.' I hold up a finger of warning. 'You obviously just want me to hurry up and get back to earning money, but in the meantime, you treat me like a live-in housemaid, and *now* you're fucking worried about me? Thanks very much for your concern.'

'That's not fair.'

'Isn't it?'

'No,' he protests. 'I care about you. I love you.' He doesn't quite sound as though he means it.

'And so, instead of actually trusting me, your way of showing it is by going through my private stuff?'

'Okay. Maybe I shouldn't have done that,' he concedes, his voice dropping in volume. 'But I did. And now I've seen it, I want to know what happened.'

'Give me that.' I reach out and snatch the letter back off him. I hold it in front of me and look at it again for the first time in years. I hope Jack can't see the paper shaking in my hands.

'Freya? Tell me what happened.'

'You've obviously read it already, so why are you asking?'

'I want to hear it from you,' he says.

My eyes run over the names and addresses at the top. It's a letter from one middle-aged male doctor to another. More precisely, from one consultant psychiatrist to another. It's entirely about me, but I'm not addressed personally. I'm just cc'd at the end of it, along with my regular doctor at the GP surgery near where I used to live. It was written eight years ago.

Subject: Freya Marie Northcott, D.o.B. 17/01/1986

I'm a *subject*. Like something in an experiment. I read on.

Dear Ahmed,

I hope this letter finds you well.

I am writing to confirm that I will be discharging the above-mentioned patient from the unit and back into your care...

How lovely – the chummy doctors, who call each other by their first names, getting in touch to discuss the latest subject of their treatment. The newest problem they've tried to solve. The most recent mad woman they've had to deal with. And to confirm which one of them will be caring for me because I'm incapable of looking after myself. I skip the rest of the admin crap and get to the reasons for me being there in the first place:

Risk: *As you know, Miss Northcott was brought to our unit by the Metropolitan Police under Section 136 of the Mental Health Act following an incident in which she attacked a member of the public with a kitchen knife. The victim was* *not known to Miss Northcott (though see 'Delusions' below) and, although moderately wounded, he was treated in emergency surgery and recovered. Following my assessment, and on the advice of the police in view of Miss Northcott's mental health, the victim did not seek to press charges. However, despite this record of violent behaviour, I do not consider Miss Northcott currently to be a risk to others or to herself, so long as she continues to comply fully with her medication regimen...*

A film plays in my mind of me brandishing the blade, walking up to the man outside his house in broad daylight and, without saying a word, stabbing him. A single, hard thrust, in and out. Blood blooms at his ribs, soaking into the thick blue wool of his jacket, turning it black, while he just stares at me, open-mouthed, paralysed with shock, until he starts to bellow with pain, gripping the wound before he staggers and collapses, and then there's shouting and people rushing... I feel panic rising, here and now, but I tell myself to be calm. It's not a real memory. It's just what I've imagined, based on what the police and the doctors told me afterwards.

The truth is that I have no recollection of the event. The psychiatrist believes that I 'dissociated' while it was happening. Or, in normal speak, I had no idea what I was doing. I skim down the discharge letter, my mind beginning to race as fragments that I do remember come back, pieces here and there, sparked by the psychiatrist's summary:

Delusions: *The motive for Miss Northcott's knife attack appears to have been a strong delusional belief that she developed about a couple who lived opposite her, but whom she did not know. Over a period of time, and in the context of other life stresses (see 'Background'), Miss Northcott came* *to believe that the man in the couple was responsible for domestically abusing his partner, whom Miss Northcott claimed she was protecting by carrying out her knife attack. She also held a vaguer belief about the couple having stolen a child, which at times she thought was hers, whom they were keeping in their home and hiding from her. However, there is no evidence that any of this is true and, indeed, Miss Northcott does not have any children…*

'Freya.'

I snap out of the memory. Suddenly, I'm feeling overwhelmed. There are all sorts of emotions coming up. Sadness, at how that could have happened to me – a normal young woman, more or less, living a normal life. Anxiety, at the lack of detail I possess, which is one reason why I kept this letter. Anger, at the way I was treated by these men in their positions of power, doctors drugging me up to keep me under control. Embarrassment, at the way I behaved, at what I believed, but which I now know not to have been correct. Guilt, at my actions, this violence that was so out of character, yet for which I alone was responsible. I know there are positives, too, strengths that came out of those hellish experiences, but I can't label them right now.

'It's happening again, isn't it?' Jack has tilted his head down, his brow furrowed. For a moment, I just stare at those folds of skin above his eyebrows, as if I've never noticed them before.

'All this…' Jack continues, gesturing towards the garden, then out to the street, then next door to the Crawfords' house. 'The stuff you suspect about Michael doing something to Emily, the shoe and the ring in the garden, the doors being open, things being moved, the video clip that wasn't there. None of it's… real, is it?'

I return my gaze to the letter, as if it'll tell me the answer, but I can't even focus on the text. 'It's…' I begin, but the words don't come. I just feel like crying.

'I know that was eight years ago,' Jack says, 'but this situation's pretty similar, isn't it?'

'No… Emily was my friend,' I protest, but my voice sounds quiet, weak.

'I think you might be having a relapse, another episode,' he suggests. 'Obviously, it must be tough to hear that, but—'

'I'm fine.'

'I don't think you are.' Jack steps towards me, his arms outstretched, but I back away.

'I said I'm fine.'

'Look, I know this is hard, Freya. But you've been through a lot the past two or three months. And you need to know when to ask for help, before things get out of hand.'

'I don't need help,' I counter. 'What I need is to find Emily and Thea, because—'

'That's the point.' Jack's tone is harder, now, his expression even less sympathetic. 'Whatever's happened to them, it's turned into an obsession for you. Like the couple in the letter, there.' He leans in. 'And the child you imagined.'

'Well, I haven't imagined Emily and Thea. They're real, and so is their disappearance.'

He takes a deep breath. 'This is a difficult thing to ask, but given what's in that letter, is there something you're not telling me about them? About your relationship with them? Something you did?…'

'No! You know all about it. How the police have been ignoring me, how people who knew them have been trying to help, and—'

'Freya.' Jack comes forward again, and I realise he's backed me into the corner of the living room. 'You've got to sort this… this obsession out. Before anyone gets hurt.'

He opens his arms again, and suddenly I feel trapped, as if I'm a patient being held against my will and he's a doctor rather than my partner. His next words confirm it:

'I think you need some medication.'

At that, something flares inside me. I stride forward and push his arms away. 'No fucking way,' I tell him as I walk past him towards the door. 'I'm not taking any more pills.'

'Freya…'

I stop in the doorway and turn back to him. 'I may have hidden this from you,' I say, holding up the letter. 'But I'm not going crazy. Something has happened to Emily and Thea, and I won't let it drop until I get answers.'

'Listen to me—'

'And you know what else? I'm not the only one around here hiding things. Am I, Jack?'

CHAPTER THIRTY-TWO

Friday, 8 October

'It's just such a massive betrayal.' I open my eyes and look at my therapist.

He nods, his expression full of concern. 'I can see why you would feel that way.'

'Don't you agree?' I ask.

He jots a note, shifts in his chair. 'Well, I appreciate you asking for my opinion, Freya, but whether I agree or not isn't relevant, here,' he says gently. 'It's about how you feel.'

'Hm.' I guess he's right.

'And the important thing is that you consider Jack having gone through your personal things, which you kept in a private box, as a breach of trust.'

'Yes, I do. I mean, it *is*.' I realise that I've made a fist with one hand, and I'm squeezing it hard. I let it relax.

'So, how did you leave it with one another?'

I roll my eyes. I can't help it; I'm still furious with Jack. 'He wants me to see a psychiatrist and get back on some medication straightaway. He thinks I'm going to have some sort of, like, meltdown and do something mad. Or dangerous.' I snort a laugh, but Laurence remains impassive.

'He wants you to get an assessment for psychiatric medication,' he says.

'Yeah.'

Laurence tilts his head to one side. 'And how do you feel about that?'

'About as good as I felt being given those pills in hospital eight years ago. And having to carry on taking them for another year after that or risk being locked up again. Shit, in other words. I don't want to be back in that system. I don't even want to be near it.'

'Mm-hm.'

'When you're sectioned,' I carry on, 'you lose your independence. They say it's your decision to take the meds, but the reality is you have no choice. If you refuse, some men hold you down and inject you in the arse. That happened once, and I'll never let it happen again.'

'It sounds as though that was an incredibly difficult time.'

There's a brief silence. 'I should've told you about it before,' I say. 'I'm sorry.'

'I can see why you might have chosen not to,' he replies evenly. 'An episode of psychosis is often a very frightening thing to go through, and lots of people wouldn't want to bring up those memories. But, now that I know, are you okay with us talking about it? The events that led up to it, for example.'

I pick at a small food stain that I've just noticed on my cuff. 'Er, do we have to?'

'No, of course not. But, it might help to put your experiences today in context, draw out some strengths to help you in the present, perhaps give us ideas for coping techniques that worked. Support you on your recovery journey now, basically.'

'Am I going nuts?' I ask him. 'All the stuff I've told you about Emily and Thea, about things happening in the house… Have I made it all up? I mean, is Jack right?'

Laurence holds my gaze and, with absolute sincerity, says: 'No, I don't think so.'

'Okay.' A sense of relief flows over me, like a warm breeze. He believes me.

'There are one or two things you've described which we're not able to confirm as having actually taken place,' he adds. 'We've discussed those things. You know, stuff where there could be more than one explanation for what happened.'

'Where maybe I jumped to conclusions about something, like why the door was open. I might have done it, but not remembered if I was really distracted.'

'Exactly. But the key point is that, in those moments, what you're feeling is very real for you. If you believe someone entered your home, for instance, then your emotion of fear is genuine, whether or not there was anyone in the house.'

'That two theories thing you were talking about. A and B.'

'Right.' He gives a brief smile, and I can see he's pleased that I've recalled it.

'Theory A is that there was someone in the house,' I continue. 'If that's true, I need to call the police, get somewhere safe, potentially defend myself or be ready to escape.'

'Yes. And what's theory B, in that situation?'

'It's that I *think* there's someone in the house, but no one's really there. It's not an intruder or a security problem. It's an anxiety problem.'

'Exactly. So, what would you do in that instance?'

'Calm myself down,' I reply. 'Maybe do a breathing exercise. Or a quick grounding thing, like a mindfulness check-in or whatever.'

'Sure. Great.'

There's a pause while Laurence writes a couple of notes and I drink some water. Then I throw the question at him that I've been waiting to ask ever since Jack suggested it.

'Do *you* think I need medication?' I watch his response closely.

'You know I'm not qualified to prescribe—'

'I know, you're a counselling psychologist. Not a psychiatrist. I want to know what you think, though.'

He considers this for a few seconds. 'Why would it be important for you to know?'

Early on, these kinds of questions might have annoyed me. But now I know why my therapist asks them; he wants me to challenge my own automatic patterns of thought and emotional reactions.

'Because I care about your opinion,' I say.

'Why?'

'Well, because I trust you. Jack wants me to take anti-anxiety medication. He thinks I'm too stressed and I need to calm down. He's my fiancé, and he's a doctor…'

'But?'

'But, right now, I don't trust him.'

Laurence nods slowly. 'It sounds as though you're not sure he has your best interests at heart.'

'That's it. I don't.'

'Why not?'

'Because…' I need to be honest with him about this. 'Because I think he's hiding something from me.'

'What do you think he's hiding?'

If I tell my therapist, there's no going back. At the moment, though, he's the only man who actually seems to be listening to me, so I decide to go for it.

'I'm not certain,' I begin, 'but – apart from going through my private stuff – I think he might have known Emily. Before we moved in.'

Laurence frowns, his pen poised mid-air. 'As in, the missing woman, Emily?'

'Yeah.'

'What makes you say that?'

'I mean, I don't have any proof… just, little things.'

'Such as?'

'The first time Jack saw her, he looked as though he recognised her. He reacted… you know, like she was familiar. I mean, I don't think I imagined that.'

'Mm-hm.'

'And then, I got a message via the page from a university friend of Emily, who said she had a stalker when she was at university, who was called Jack. They're the same age… it's possible.'

He scribbles something down. 'So, they were at university together?'

'I don't know. I accused him of it, of knowing her or whatever. He denied it, obviously, told me they were at different universities, but…'

'You don't trust him.'

'Right.' I meet Laurence's gaze. 'I'm following up on it with the friend, though. I know there are thousands of Jacks, but even so.'

He lays his notepad on his leg. 'I'm sorry to have to ask you this, Freya. But do you believe you might be at risk from your fiancé?'

'I…' A few months ago, I would've laughed at this question. But for the first time, now, I'm actually considering whether my own partner poses a threat to me, like those women in the statistics I was reading. I recall the hard set of his features, the tension in his body as he advanced towards me the other night, trapping me in the corner of our living room. 'I'm not sure.'

'Has he ever hurt or threatened you physically or verbally?'

'No.'

Laurence asks a few more questions about Jack. Does he force me to have sex when I don't want to? Does he try to control what I do, who I see, or my access to money? Does he undermine my confidence and put me down? Is he monitoring me or my communication with others? There's a niggling doubt in some of my answers, given the past few days, but even after the occasional hesitation, I have to respond in the negative to all of them.

'I see.' My therapist taps his pen against the notepad. 'I know those are difficult things to think about. Thank you for sharing that with me.'

I sink a little deeper into the chair, let my eyes close and allow some of the tension to drop from my body. And, as if I have no power over it, the image comes to me. It's vivid, multisensory, almost real. I'm with Laurence, but this time we're in bed together. I savour the fantasy for a moment.

Then I open my eyes, look at him and smile. He smiles back.

He has no idea what I've just been imagining.

CHAPTER THIRTY-THREE

Friday, 8 October

It's the end of the most difficult week I've had with Jack since we met, the lowest point of our relationship. So, it's perhaps fitting that he's not even here, because he's decided to meet someone for a drink after work. An 'old mate', he said in a text that arrived just after six p.m., once it was already too late for me to make other plans. He didn't know when he'd be home.

Well, I've got an old mate, too. A lovely bottle of wine, here with me on the kitchen table, and I'm halfway through it already. I might call Mum or Bea later for a chat, but I know I'll just rehash everything that's happened with Jack when I do, and probably end up crying and feeling worse, which I don't need right now. So, for the moment, I decide to focus on Emily and Thea instead.

I've had a reply back from the local newspaper to say they'd be interested in a short piece ('500 words, max') about the continued campaign to share information that might help to find the missing pair, and how people who knew Emily and Thea are supporting one another online ('focus on the community angle,' they told me). They want to publish it on their website to mark the three-month anniversary of their disappearance, next Tuesday. I'm starting to write it now, but I'm distracted, flicking back and forth between my draft and the inbox of the *Find Emily and Thea* page.

Earlier today, I reached out to Alice Hope again. I know I told Michael I wouldn't (I did have my fingers crossed at the time), and it would piss him off if he found out, but I have to take that chance. In her second post on the page, she hinted that Emily had a secret, that she wasn't *the innocent everyone thinks she is*. I need to know what she meant by that, and whether it might hold the key to what happened to her and Thea. Could it be a reference to the affair which Cathy believed Emily was having?

So, I wrote Alice a private message, explaining why I had to delete her post, apologising, and asking if she wanted to meet and talk. I keep refreshing the page to see if she's replied, but there's nothing yet. It's frustrating to think I may have lost contact with her, and everything she knows along with it.

I remind myself what Michael said about her, though. That there are always two sides to every story, and I can't necessarily trust anything she does tell me – same as I can't trust Michael. The thought even flashes through my mind that Alice might've done something to Emily if, as Michael claims, she was obsessed with him and thought that Emily had somehow supplanted her in his affections. It's not impossible.

I'm writing and drinking, drinking and writing, when the alert pops up: *new message*. Immediately, I switch tabs to the *Find Emily and Thea* inbox. But the message isn't from Alice Hope. It's from Olivia Burgess-was-Johnson. I try to click into it so fast that my cursor actually misses her message and I open the most recent one from johnsmith12643, just below it, instead. A shiver runs through me as I see those words about digging my own grave. I click again, this time opening Olivia's email. I read it once, twice. Then I release the breath I didn't even realise I'd been holding.

> *The guy who stalked Emily at uni was called Jack Watkins. Don't know if that helps. No one in our group has any photos of him – probably a good thing! Let me know if you need anything else. O*

Watkins. It wasn't Jack. Not *my* Jack, I mean – Jack *Brown.* Thank God. But the relief is soon replaced with an uncomfortable sense of guilt. I've as good as accused him of sexual harassment and lying. I've even talked about it in therapy. I feel awful.

I shouldn't have doubted Jack, and I should have trusted my own judgement that I wouldn't get together with a man who had been a stalker. That I'd see – something – signs of it in him, that I'd hear little alarm bells going off, warning me. My guilt quickly turns to sadness at the mistake I made. I pour the remainder of the wine bottle into my glass and trudge upstairs.

Without really knowing why, I wander into the spare bedroom, where my private box of things sits among a collection of other unopened containers. I know what's in them: books, mostly, plus some photo frames and ornaments to go on shelves we haven't made yet. We've been here nearly seven months and the shelving hasn't happened. I remember a conversation, early on, Jack and I both full of enthusiasm for it, talking about sourcing the wood, cutting and painting it ourselves.

Looking at my cardboard box of personal items, I recall how angry I was with Jack two nights ago, when he marched in holding that discharge summary from my psychiatrist. Part of me is still pissed off about that, and hurt, but perhaps better that it's out there. And, now, that rage is slightly tempered by the realisation that Jack wasn't Emily's stalker, that I was crazy even to think it.

I take a large slug of wine and stand there, staring at the box. Maybe Jack's right, and my anxiety is getting the better of me. Perhaps I do need help – medical help that my therapist can't give me – to get on top of it. I imagine patching things up with Jack when he comes in, apologising, holding one another in a warm embrace, both of us softened by a couple of drinks. Resetting and moving forwards. I picture his lopsided grin, his little jokes, his calmness in a crisis. I start to remember the Jack I fell in love with, long before we came here, the man who—

Rrreeeaaa.

The sound comes from directly above me, loud and clear. It's a floorboard creaking. I freeze, listening. It comes again, more softly, then the unmistakable noise of footsteps.

Thum, thum, thum…

Someone's walking in our attic.

Bang.

The wine glass slips from my hand in reaction to the hard sound of something dropping overhead. The glass shatters and red wine explodes over the carpet. My mind starts to race. It's Michael, above me, now. He's the real threat. It was always Michael who posed the risk to Emily and Thea, not Jack – never Jack – and I should've stuck with my first instincts about that. The statistic flashes through my mind. Sixty-two per cent of female murder victims killed by a partner or an ex.

I'm breathing quickly now because I'm certain that he's coming. He's going to open the trapdoor and slide through, holding god-knows-what kind of weapon. I picture him pursuing me through the house, yanking doors open, sniffing the air for any trace of me. Hunting me down.

I pull my phone from my pocket and call Jack. He doesn't pick up. I don't leave a voicemail.

Instead, I hang up and call the next person who comes to mind. Someone who can help.

'Hello?'

'Is that, um, Detective Henderson?' I swallow, mouth dry as my eyes dart over the ceiling, trying to pinpoint the movement. I can still hear floorboards shifting under the weight of heavy steps.

'Yes. Who's this?'

'There's somebody here,' I blurt.

'Sorry, who is this?'

'Freya – Freya Northcott. You know, er – Emily's neighbour. From Sunningdale Road,' I add.

'Right, okay,' says Henderson. 'And what's happening?'

'There's someone in the loft,' I say, suddenly remembering to lower my voice. 'I can hear them above me. I-I think they might be coming down.'

'In your loft? An intruder?'

'Yes.'

'Are you in danger?' he says, his voice suddenly switching gear, his tone more serious.

'I don't know. Maybe. Yes. Oh God… Please just help me.'

This time, there's no scepticism, no sighing or derisive snorts. 'All right. Listen carefully to me. I'm going to put a call to a local patrol car to divert to your address. It'll be quicker than a 999 dispatch, now you've called me.'

'Um, okay.' I've pressed my back to the wall, and I'm scared to move.

'Is there somewhere in the house you can lock yourself away, like a bathroom or a toilet?'

'Yes.' My pulse is pounding in my ear, as loud as the movement going on above me.

'Right, go there, lock the door, and we'll have a car with you soon.'

'Thank you,' I whisper. 'Please hurry.'

'It's going to be okay, Ms Northcott. I just need you to stay calm for me and get yourself somewhere safe. I'm going to hang up now, and I'll call you back in two minutes.'

Suddenly, there's a kind of growling from the loft and I picture Michael in the same kind of rage as when he attacked Emily, just as I'd originally thought. The steps are moving towards the trapdoor.

'Please,' I say, 'they're coming closer.'

The activity outside the house makes quite a scene. A police patrol car – its powerful swirling lights turning the whole street deep blue – sits alongside Henderson's unmarked vehicle. Unsurprisingly, all the neighbours are looking. Some of them are silhouettes behind curtains, as usual, but others aren't trying to hide their interest, standing by open windows, and a handful have even come out into the road. They're watching as I wait on the front path with Henderson. One observer, a teenager I don't know, is filming on a smartphone. I'm not sure whether they're expecting someone – Michael – to be led out in handcuffs or whatever. And I don't care. All that matters right now is that I feel safe.

'How much have you had to drink this evening, Miss North-cott?' Henderson studies me. Ironically, he's the one who looks like he's been on the booze, with his loose tie, unshaven jaw and deep purple bags under his eyes. I want to tell him that, but I manage to control the impulse.

'For the last time, it's *Ms*. Not Miss,' I say, exasperated. 'And I've had a glass of wine.'

He raises his eyebrows.

'I'm not drunk,' I tell him. 'I know what I heard.' There's a breeze in the air and I hug myself to keep warm. I should've grabbed my jacket as I came out, but there was no time. That urgency seems silly now.

He doesn't reply, but the silence between us is broken as two uniformed officers emerge through the front door. The older one who leads shakes her head.

'Nothing in the loft, sir,' she announces as she approaches us.

Henderson nods. 'All clear, then?'

'Yeah. Although the attics are connected across the properties.' She sweeps a hand over our building, from Michael and Emily's house, past ours, and over to Cathy's. As I follow the officer's movement, I see Cathy standing at the side of her house, arms folded. She's regarding Henderson with a stern expression, but he doesn't seem to notice.

'I see.' Henderson nods, as if it all makes sense, now. 'So, you were in a room next to the neighbour's house, you said. You'd been drinking, and you heard some movement above you.'

'No… well, yes, but it was definitely footsteps overhead.'

Henderson exchanges a look with the officers. 'I'd say it was probably just a neighbour, then. Up in their part of the loft, but it *sounded*… threatening. Just a mistake about the location, easily made.'

'No. They were right above me. And they were moving towards the trapdoor. I swear.'

Henderson doesn't respond.

'I was really scared,' I say.

'I'm sure you were,' he replies.

I point towards the house. 'Aren't you going to go and ask Michael what he was doing?'

Henderson follows my gesture and stares at the Crawfords' place for a while. Then it's as if he snaps out of a trance and he turns back to me, shakes his head.

'I don't see any need to bother Mr Crawford about this,' he says. His voice sounds strangely detached.

'But—'

'Next time, *Ms* Northcott, best to call 999 rather than ringing me.' He's back to his usual brusque tone. 'But please only do so if it's a genuine emergency and you believe you're at risk, having checked that what you think is an intruder isn't actually just your neighbour, in their own home.'

I don't protest any more. I'm just pleased that Michael wasn't there, that no one attacked me.

'I'd advise you to consider sealing off your attic from the neighbouring properties at some point, too,' he adds. 'Just for peace of mind.'

'Right.'

'We'll leave you to it, then, Ms Northcott.' Henderson shoves his hands in his coat pockets. 'Oh, by the way – any particular reason you didn't call 999?'

I glance at the uniformed officers. A movie starts in my head: the chaotic scene I've mentally reconstructed of cops coming to arrest me after I attacked that man with a knife. I'm still holding the bloodied blade, and I don't know what's going on. They're shouting at me, making threats with batons and pepper spray and tasers. Then there's grabbing, twisting, pulling, forcing to the ground, handcuffs…

'I, ah, I didn't want them to take me away,' I mumble.

'Take you away?' Henderson frowns, gives a small chuckle. 'Why would they do that? You haven't committed a crime. Have you?'

CHAPTER THIRTY-FOUR

Saturday, 9 October

By the time Jack got home from the drink with his 'old mate' last night, it was as if nothing had happened. The police had gone, the neighbours had returned to their houses and I was back inside, alone again.

Jack found me on my hands and knees in the spare bedroom, clumsily picking shards of glass out of the carpet while simultaneously trying to salt and blot the red wine stains all over it. I'd cut my finger without realising, and he led me to the bathroom, washed and dried the wound, then covered it with a sticking plaster.

I remember crying and apologising and telling him what happened. Promising him that I wasn't imagining it or making it up. That I really had been scared and that was why I'd called Henderson. Jack spoke softly and stroked my hair while he held me, and for the first time in a while I felt connected to him and that he genuinely cared about me. That we were closer than we'd been for months. He tucked me into bed, and I remember feeling safe as I drifted into a deep, dreamless sleep.

This morning, though, all that changed.

Things started off okay; we were drinking some great coffee that Jack had made and getting stuck into a hangover-cure brunch of scrambled eggs on toast with bacon and avocado. I was building up to say sorry for suggesting that he'd been hiding something from me – how I'd been wrong about it, how it was stupid of me to think that he had known Emily before we moved here. I was testing out some phrases in my head, and after a couple of minutes I was ready.

Then Jack told me who his old mate was.

Conall O'Leary. The name didn't mean anything to me. He's a friend from med school, Jack explained. *Dr* Conall O'Leary. A psychiatrist. I still didn't know who he was, but with the mention of that one-word job title, I understood what was going on.

'It wasn't a social catch-up, then, was it?'

Jack clears his throat, gabbles something about meaning to meet up with him anyway.

'Don't bullshit me,' I tell him. 'Two nights ago, you tell me I need psychiatric help, medication or whatever, and then you meet up with a friend you've never mentioned who just happens to be a psychiatrist?' I frame the statement as a question, a challenge.

'He's worried about you. And so am I,' he adds hastily. 'We both just want you to be… well. Conall thinks that, given your history, a course of benzodiazepines in the first instance would help to calm things down a bit, you know, and—'

'You don't care about me being *well*, Jack. You and this Conall guy, whoever the fuck he is, just want to give me some pills to shut me up. Don't you?'

'It's not like that, Freya. I promise.' He spreads his hands, palms up, as if that somehow proves his honesty.

'Isn't it?' I scoff. I saw off a piece of toast and bite down on it hard. 'Am I embarrassing you, is that it? Is my mental health an *inconvenience* for you?'

'No, of course it's not. It's just about, um, helping bring your anxiety down a bit. Conall said it's quite common, after, you know…'

'What, after your baby dies? Jesus Christ.'

'After a trauma, like that.' Jack's voice is soft, and again I have the impression I'm a patient he's trying to placate, to medicate. For a second, I have a horrible flashback of being locked up: take your pills, like a good girl, or they'll be given to you, one way or another.

'I don't want anything. I'm fine, okay?'

'I did you the prescription myself,' he persists. 'Swung by the hospital on my way home last night and picked it up from the pharmacy.'

I glare at him. I can't believe this man who's trying to force drugs on me now was the same person I was feeling guilty about letting down last night, with whom I wanted to make amends and start over.

'They're very effective at combating anxiety,' Jack continues. 'We've used them in the clinic with some of our cardiac patients who've suffered with panic attacks.'

'Good for them.'

'I've seen them work really well.'

'Aren't they massively addictive?' I pick up my phone and type in 'benzos'. When the search hits appear, I scroll down, shaking my head. 'I knew it. Valium. Xanax. "Mother's Little Helpers",' I say, reading the snippets.

'Some people do develop problem use of them, yes, but Conall's suggested the right dose. If you stick to that, you'll be fine. I'll help. I've put the tub in the bathroom cabinet for you.'

I toss my phone on the kitchen table. 'This is fucking unbeliev-able,' I say, jabbing my finger at him. 'Our neighbour and her daughter have disappeared. No one's looking for them except me. The missing woman's weird, sociopathic husband, who spends all his time in a locked basement, is walking around in our loft. People are threatening me, and your solution to all that is to get me hooked on sedatives?'

There's a moment's silence before Jack replies. 'Who's threatening you?'

I blink. I haven't told him about johnsmith12643. 'Just someone online,' I reply.

'What's it about?' he demands. 'What kind of threats?'

'Oh, now you're taking this seriously?' I grab my phone, shove my chair back and march out.

'Freya!' he calls after me. But he's too late. I snatch my jacket off the peg, kick on my shoes and slam the front door behind me on the way out.

I've walked up and back along the towpath beside the River Thames for more than an hour, trying to calm myself down. I'd sooner do that than pop some addictive, tranquilising happy pill any day. When I was discharged from the secure psychiatric unit years ago, it was fresh air, nature, exercise, friends and absorbing, meaningful work that supported my recovery.

Medication might help some people, but for me it only made things worse, distorting how I saw the world while creating a dependency that was hard to shift. I'm determined not to let Jack force that on me now, with or without the so-called expert opinion of a shrink I've never met. Screw both of them.

Yes, I've been through a trauma. Yes, I'm anxious, most of the time. Yes, I get sad. But that's as far as it goes. This isn't the same as my episode eight years ago, where I believed things that weren't true, imagined stuff that wasn't real. I know what I've seen and heard, and I'm not going to let a group of men shut me up by pumping me full of sedatives and ignoring me. I need to fight back.

As I turn into Sunningdale Road, I automatically walk towards the house. But then I stop. I don't want to speak to Jack right now. Instead, I walk up the path of number eleven and down the side of the building. As always, Cathy's front door is ajar. I knock, push and enter.

'You did entirely the right thing, love,' Cathy says. She reaches out and lays a large hand over mine on the table. I can feel the strength in her long fingers.

'If you thought that nasty man was going to come into your house and attack you,' she continues, 'then the first thing to do was call for help.' She pats my knuckles and withdraws her hand.

'Thanks, Cathy.' I take a big bite of cake, glad of the reassurance.

'I've never trusted David.' She shakes her head emphatically. 'Never liked the look of him.'

'David? Don't you mean Michael?'

'Who?' Cathy's lips turn down in confusion.

'Emily's husband, Michael. Michael Crawford. Thea's dad.'

'Mm.'

'Cathy?'

'What?'

I don't know how to handle this. She's not quite making sense. It's not the first name this morning she's jumbled things up, asking me earlier how 'Peter' was doing. It took several minutes to convince her of my fiancé's name. I remember what both Michael and Jack have said, uncharitably but perhaps accurately, about the state of her memory. I try a different tack.

'Do you ever go up there?' I ask.

'Where?'

'The loft. I had no idea they were connected across the three houses.'

A shadow passes over Cathy's expression. She doesn't answer, her face frozen in a rictus, her eyes wide.

'Cathy? Are you okay?' I extend my hand gently towards her, but she abruptly rises and strides off, muttering something I can't decipher. I've upset her, somehow, by mentioning the attic. I hear her climbing the stairs and moving around the room above me. Suddenly, I feel incredibly awkward in her home, as though I shouldn't be there. I'm not sure whether to stay or leave, whether to sit still or follow her upstairs and check if she's all right.

I get up and walk out of the kitchen, but taking the stairs feels like even more of an intrusion, so I just stand in the hallway, looking around me. I'm drawn to the old photographs, to these people from decades long gone, preserved in black and white.

I take a step towards the gloomy living room to examine a framed portrait on a bookshelf, which I guess must be Cathy and Henry. It's dark, so it's hard to make out the details, but there's something familiar about the man that I can't quite place. I pick up the frame to inspect his image more closely. And that's when I see the keys.

Three of them on a fob. They'd been lying behind the frame on the shelf. There's a long, barrel-shaped one with teeth at the end. Then a medium-sized, flat one for a smaller lock. And, finally, a little, thin one that barely looks strong enough to secure a suitcase. Curious, I slip my finger through the fob and lift them towards the light. A plastic tag twists to reveal a tiny paper sticker with a number on it: 13.

Could these be?... I recall Michael's throwaway line at the dinner party, that first time we went round to the Crawfords' for dinner: *we should get our spare keys back off her… she can't be trusted.* Perhaps these are the keys, and he's forgotten to collect them. Still holding the bunch, my eyes flick back to the photograph. My breath catches in my throat as I realise what's familiar about it. It's Henry.

He looks like Jack.

I remember how Cathy called Jack by the name Henry when she discovered us in her kitchen, the day we moved in. Now I know why. Their hairstyles are different, of course, and Henry has a moustache, but there's a similarity in the shape of the jaw, the nose, the ridge of the brow. And the eyes. As I stare at Henry's eyes in the photo, I start to imagine that—

'Put that down.'

Cathy's voice from behind me sends a blast of adrenalin through my abdomen.

'Christ, Cathy. Sorry.' I gently return the frame to the shelf, my heart hammering against my ribs. I've still got the keys in my other hand, shielded from Cathy by my body. I hesitate, briefly considering where it might lead if I take them, and whether I want to go there. But I know that I can't miss this opportunity. I slip them into my pocket.

'Thank you,' she says.

'He's a handsome fellow, your Henry.' I nod towards the photograph. 'That's the two of you, isn't it?'

'Yes.'

'Looks a bit like Jack,' I venture.

'Who?'

'Jack. You know, my fiancé.'

Cathy doesn't respond. Instead, she turns and walks back towards the kitchen. 'Do you want some tea, love?' she shouts over her shoulder.

I follow her through. I can feel the keys jangling in my pocket. I know I shouldn't steal them, that it's betraying Cathy's trust as well as Michael's. I tell myself I'm doing it for Emily, though, and for Thea. It could be the breakthrough I've been hoping for.

In the kitchen, Cathy stops and stares at the teapot, hands on hips. I sit back down at the table, and, after a long moment, she lays a hand on the pot, as if testing its temperature. She frowns, as if she can't remember that we were just in here, drinking it together. She picks up the pot and crosses to the sink, tips the contents away.

'He came back,' she says almost absent-mindedly.

'Who did?'

'Her man.'

'Sorry, Cathy – whose man?'

She pulls a wad of wet tea leaves out of the pot and scrutinises them, as if she's about to tell my fortune.

'Emily's fancy man,' she states without looking up. 'He came back.'

CHAPTER THIRTY-FIVE

Saturday, 9 October

Long after I've left Cathy's house, I can't shake her words: *Emily's fancy man*. I mull it over, turning and testing the idea, like when you rotate a piece of a jigsaw to see if it fits the space you're trying to fill. And I'm pretty sure it does.

Cathy was out there, last night, staring at Henderson as he patronised me in front of the whole street after his officers had found the house empty. I recall how he appeared to lose concentration for a few moments as he gazed at Michael and Emily's place. Then, today, Cathy says that the guy Emily had been seeing discreetly had come back. *Quite a handsome fella*, she'd said, the first time she mentioned this man. Okay, that might be a stretch, but Henderson isn't bad looking, and I can see him scrubbing up all right.

I asked Cathy if Emily's visitor was a detective named Paul Henderson, but she said she didn't know the man's name. When I told her he was the man from last night, she couldn't remember exactly what had happened last night. I'd obviously caught her on a difficult day, so I let it drop.

Nevertheless, it's given me enough to go on, and I think I've got it: what if Henderson is the man whom Emily was seeing? Michael discovers the affair, although maybe without knowing Henderson's identity. Then he punishes Emily for her infidelity, perhaps making her pay the ultimate price. The theory works, but what I need now is confirmation.

I fire up my laptop and write another message to Alice Hope. I don't want to put words into her mouth, so I keep it simple:

Does the name Paul Henderson mean anything to you?

I've already apologised to her for taking down her post, so I don't rehash any of that. She might continue to sulk, of course, and not reply, but I'm gambling on the fact that – if she does know anything about Henderson – she won't be able to resist answering my question. If she was stalking the Crawfords, as Michael claims, then she may be able to confirm my new suspicions. And if Alice knows about Henderson, is that what she was accusing Emily of hiding?

I'm gazing at the screen, on the off chance that I'll get an instant reply, when my fingers brush against the small bunch of keys inside my jeans pocket. I remove them and examine them once more. I feel a strange mixture of guilt and excitement at having taken them. Guilt, because I hate the thought of Cathy going to look for the keys and being confused about where they've gone, or Michael marching round and demanding them back, berating Cathy for her forgetfulness when she can't produce the bunch, because I've stolen it. And excitement, because I know these keys might just be what I need to finally work out what happened to Emily and Thea.

I rotate and study each key in turn, imagining what I might find if I were to let myself into the house one day when Michael is out. The secrets he's keeping at number thirteen. Clues Emily might have left. Then I remember his man-cave: the basement with its electronic lock, and I realise that the keys wouldn't get me in there. I'm hit with a moment of doubt. Perhaps there's nothing to which they'd give me access; maybe it was pointless taking them and I should just return them to Cathy.

I start to wonder if I could let myself into their home through the loft, instead. But, a few moments later, I catch myself. Am I seriously thinking about trespassing and snooping around inside my neighbour's home? Henderson would have a field day if I was caught doing that. Of course, if Michael found me wandering around his place, I hate to think what he might do. *He's capable of the worst kind of violence*, that's what Alice Hope wrote to me. I need to slow down and think this through.

Looking at the keys, the smallest one captures my attention. It doesn't seem as though it's made for a door lock. So, what does it open? A locked drawer, box or cabinet somewhere in the house? My gaze drifts out of the window, towards the garden, as I think. And then it hits me.

The shed.

This afternoon, I'm in the garden. I've been out here for a couple of hours, weeding, chopping and clearing. But I'm not losing myself in the activity, as usual. I'm waiting for my opportunity.

Jack went out to the DIY superstore about half an hour ago, to get some stuff for making shelves. Before he left, he came out to find me ruthlessly cutting and stabbing with the secateurs and, for a moment, he looked almost frightened as I turned to him, gripping them in my closed fist. Maybe he was thinking about what it said in that discharge letter. What I'd done eight years ago to a man I believed had kidnapped my non-existent baby.

Jack asked me about the threats I'd received online. Had I told anyone about them? Did I have any information about who it might be? I dismissed his concerns, told him I could handle it. I didn't let on that I'm still scared about how much johnsmith12643 knows about me. And I didn't mention that the thought had even crossed my mind at one point that it could be Jack.

As he stood in front of me, clearly uncomfortable after my reaction to him trying to push psychiatric medication on me, I thought about how similar he looked to Cathy's husband, Henry, when he was younger, and how strange that was. But I can't be sure I wasn't mistaken, that it wasn't just the low lighting and the poor quality of the photo.

My speculation about any connection between Jack and Henry evaporates as I hear the car engine. It's the loud, deep purring of Michael's Range Rover, rising and then fading into the distance. He's left.

I have to take my chance, now.

With a deep breath, and my body already tingling with anticipation at the illegal act I'm about to commit, I make my way through to the back of the garden and across onto the Crawfords' land.

I duck the larger branches and push the smaller ones aside, the brushwood crackling underfoot as I step slowly and carefully towards the shed. The air is still and silent, except for the sounds of my movement, the rustle of my jeans as I walk, the swiping of leaves against my jumper. Somewhere in a nearby tree, a crow caws.

I creep around the back of the shed. I'm struck again by its state of decay, as if the dead wood from which it's made is being gradually eaten by ivy, moss and lichens. On the other side of it, I see the patch of bare earth. It's the proportions of a human grave, and nothing is growing on it, as if that rectangle of soil is poisoned.

I wonder what's beneath its surface and, for a horrible moment, that nightmare image comes to mind. I'm lying on my back in the grave, looking up at a figure shovelling soil in on top of me, and I can't move. I can't even breathe. I don't know who this person is because it's too dark to see their face. I only know that they want to kill me.

The crow caws again and I snap out of the vision. My breathing is fast and shallow, and I force myself to take a big lungful of air and let it out slowly. I repeat this a few times, but I know I can't stay here long. Michael or Jack could be back at any minute.

Stepping to the front of the shed, I find the door locked on the outside, as usual. For the first time, it strikes me how incongruous the large, shiny new padlock is, compared to the old, dilapidated structure it's sealing shut.

I take the bunch of keys I stole from Cathy out of my pocket and select the smallest one. I glance over my shoulder, just to be sure, but the windows of the Crawfords' house are empty. I'm exposed here, but no one seems to be watching me. I need to do it now.

The key slides smoothly into the padlock, and it clicks open. I remove it from the hasp and pull the door open. It sticks, the wood groaning as the door separates from the lintel, while the hinges screech as if in pain. I'm sure someone must have heard me. With a final look over my shoulder, I hang the open padlock back on the hasp and step inside, pulling the door closed behind me to avoid being seen.

The interior is almost pitch-black. What little light there is has been filtered through the cobwebs and mould coating the inside of the tiny, smeary window. I take out my phone and switch on its torch.

The first thing I see are more cobwebs, and I'm temporarily paralysed with fear as I clock the number of them, lying as thick as wads of cotton wool in the corners. My torch beam picks out a handful of huge, fat spiders, motionless, as if they're waiting to attack me. I know it's ridiculous to be frightened of them, that they won't hurt me. I tell myself that out loud and remind myself why I'm here: to find out what happened to Emily and Thea.

I sweep the beam around the edges of the space. It's full of junk. I see big sacks of compost, plant pots, folded garden chairs and tools. None of it looks as though it has been used in years, and part of me wonders if this is a wild goose chase, and whether

Michael and Emily haven't even set foot in this place the whole
time they've lived here.

But I remember the shoe and the ring I discovered outside.
And the brand-new padlock that must've been put on the door
for a reason. As I shine the beam down to the floor, I freeze. I
think I've found that reason.

Blood.

I stoop to take a closer look. There's no doubt about it – it's
blood. There's dark red staining over the floor, as if someone has
lain here badly wounded. I recall what Cathy said about hearing
screaming coming from the shed once. Could it have been Emily
in here? Thea, even? The thought is almost too much, as I can't help
but picture those images in all the gory detail of a slasher movie.

My throat begins to tighten, and I can feel tears coming to my
eyes. I straighten up to standing, and stumble, suddenly unsteady
on my feet. My toe catches on metal, and there's an almighty
crash as a spade I've kicked falls over, taking several other tools
with it. I curse aloud. Once the ringing sound of metal on metal
stops, that's when I hear it.

The car engine.

Panic starts to rise in my chest, tight and urgent, and I frantically try to stack the tools up where I found them. But it's dark,
and I'm doing it one-handed, still holding my phone to see where
they're supposed to go. The engine noise stops as the vehicle parks.
I hear a car door open and clunk shut again. I wait. The spade
slides over once more, clattering to the floor.

Shit, shit, shit.

Now, I'm sure there are footsteps coming nearer. I switch off
the light on my phone, pull the door tight shut and sit down
inside the shed. I'm inches away from what could be a pool of
Emily's or Thea's blood, there are spiders overhead and my chest
feels as though it's going to explode.

I dare not try to prop the spade up again in case the sound gives me away. If Michael is home, and he's walking through the garden, any noise could alert him to my presence. If he gets close enough, he might even be able to see that the padlock on the shed is open.

The footsteps grow in volume, and I shut my eyes, waiting for the inevitable. For the door to be flung open, for Michael to find me here.

But nothing happens.

I wait some more, keeping as still as possible, hugging my knees to my chest on the floor to avoid knocking over anything else, and to give myself a sense of protection. I can feel warm tears running down my cheeks. I picture Henderson turning up, arresting me for trespass…

But there's only silence.

What seems like an eternity later, I turn the torch back on to light my path out of this little hell-shack. The blade of the shovel I kicked over glints in the beam, but there's something about it that catches my eye.

I direct the beam back onto it, hold it steady. I blink, trying to process what I'm seeing. The taste of bile rises from my throat, and I swallow it back down.

Dried over the metal, streaked and spotted, is the same unmistakable dark red staining as on the floor.

Blood.

CHAPTER THIRTY-SIX

Saturday, 9 October

He's killed them. He must have murdered them and buried them in the garden, beside the shed. Beneath those thick tangles of branches, where he couldn't be observed doing it, and where no one – except me – is looking. It's the only explanation that fits the facts.

I had already imagined the events in grim detail: Michael striking Emily, her falling and hitting her head, Thea screaming as she watched her daddy attacking her mummy. Now, there's an extra scene in that movie, where I see Michael coldly and mechanically digging a grave for his family at the back of their land. And he thinks he's got away with it.

He's wrong.

I know that having found the bloodied spade – and the evidence that someone was lying on the bare, splintered floor of that shed, bleeding to death – I should call the police. But the memories of being dismissed by them are still fresh in my mind. Henderson's scepticism at whatever I say, casting me as the crazy woman, the nuisance who keeps wasting his time. Especially now that the one time he took my panic seriously it turned out to be nothing. Then there's his lack of willingness to investigate Michael, and the possibility that *he* might have been seeing Emily. What's his agenda in all this?

I want to tell someone what's in the shed. But right now, I know that they wouldn't pay attention to me. Even if I contacted an officer who wasn't Henderson, the inquiry would go to him. This is Surrey; it's not London's 40,000-strong Metropolitan Police. It's a small force, with only a handful of detectives in the area working on these kinds of crimes, and Henderson's in charge of them. I know, I've checked. So, if I go to them, I need cast-iron proof. Something that Henderson can't ignore or ridicule.

I need to see what's buried in the ground.

The thought of digging in that patch of earth – surely the same one I've dreamt about lying in while a faceless figure heaps soil on me from above – is absolutely terrifying. It scares the hell out of me to think of what I might find there. I can feel a tremor in my hands, and sweat is prickling my palms and face as I picture it.

But, if this was Emily's fate, and perhaps Thea's too, then I need to confront that fear. And I have to do it myself because, at the moment, I don't know if I can trust anyone else.

My phone pings next to me on the kitchen table. It's the doorbell app. Suddenly, I'm aware of my surroundings again. I must've drifted into a daydream, and I'm not sure how long I've been sitting like this. I pick up my phone to check the app but then there's a key in the lock and I hear the familiar voice cry *Hiya* as Jack comes through. I watch as he stacks a handful of long wooden boards against the wall in the hallway and walks into the kitchen.

'All right?' he asks. There's a friendliness to his tone, as if he wants to try again after our argument over brunch (the one he started by trying to medicate me).

'Hey,' I reply.

'Freya, are you – are you okay?' He steps closer, his expression clouding with concern.

'Yeah, fine.'

'You're shaking,' he says, laying a hand on my shoulder. He touches the back of his fingers to my brow – the instinctive response of his medical training. 'Your temperature's normal,' he states. 'How are you feeling?'

It's good of him to ask that, now. After so many opportunities that he's missed. But I know that what he wants isn't an outpouring of the emotions which have felt recently as if they're going to engulf me – sadness, anxiety, full-blown terror, frustration tipping into anger, guilt and shame. He wants medical facts, one-word answers, to let him diagnose and treat. I want to blurt out everything: what Cathy said about Henderson and Emily, how I stole the keys from Cathy's house, what I found in the shed.

What I think Michael did to his family.

But something holds me back. I don't think Jack will listen to me, either.

'I'm fine,' I tell him again.

'You look terrible,' he says.

'Thanks a lot.'

'Come on, I don't mean it like that.' He takes a step back. 'You're pale, you're shaking and you've obviously been crying. What's going on?'

'Nothing.'

Jack stands there, hands on hips. Even with his limited emotional intelligence, he knows I'm keeping something from him. But, faced with the complexity of everything I've been going through, his reaction is to default to clinical mode.

'Have you started taking that medication yet?' he asks briskly.

'No,' I reply. 'I told you, I don't want it.'

He exhales slowly. 'Look, I'm not a psychiatrist, but I've seen enough panic attacks in the cardiac ward to be pretty confident that what you're experiencing now is acute anxiety. And the benzodiazepine will really help you with that. Trust me.'

'What, because you're a doctor?'

'Well, yeah. I am.'

The problem is, I don't trust him, now. Not since he read my letter and talked about me to his shrink friend behind my back. I may have been wrong about him and Emily, but those other betrayals still stand.

'I don't need any pills,' I say. 'I know I have some issues with anxiety, and I'm working on them with my therapist. I want a proper, long-term fix for those problems, not a sticking plaster. That takes time. It's not going to happen overnight.' Those are Laurence's words to characterise the difference between therapy and psychiatric drugs, and the process of his treatment, but it seems appropriate to borrow them now.

'Mm. I wanted to talk to you about that.' Jack's voice is harder. 'I don't think it's working.'

'What's not working?'

'You, and… your therapist,' he says.

'What do you mean?'

'Well, I'm paying two hundred and sixty pounds a week to that guy to sort you out, but things are just getting worse.'

'*Sort me out?*' I repeat, incredulous at his language. 'What, am I just some broken object you get a workman in to fix, like a blocked drain or something?'

'You know what I mean.' Jack holds his hands out, as if he's being completely reasonable. 'The point is, those sessions obviously aren't helping.'

'How would you know?' I demand.

He ignores my question. 'Why are you being so stubborn about this?'

'Why is it that women are always called "stubborn" when we stand up for ourselves?' I answer. 'If a man did exactly the same thing, he'd be called self-assured or confident. It's typical bloody patriarchy.'

'This isn't an argument about feminism,' he counters. 'This is about you being... well.'

I'm seething, but I force myself to take a breath. 'Listen, Jack. I'm recovering. By talking to a professional. I'm not taking those pills, and that's final, because—'

'But it's science!' he cries. 'I don't get why you won't just try them. There's grade-A clinical evidence that they work. They've been tested in randomised controlled trials.'

'And they're addictive. I don't want that. So, stop asking me to take them.' I slice a line through the air between us. 'That's it. End of story.'

Jack's face tightens, his lips compressing as he tries to contain his anger. I see his fists clench, and he paces around for a few seconds before he speaks.

'Right, then,' he announces. 'If you won't listen to me, you won't see a psychiatrist, and you won't try the medication I've got for you, then I'm not paying for you to see that guy any more.'

'What?' I exclaim.

'You can call him on Monday and tell him you're done.'

'No.'

Jack scoffs. 'How are you going to pay for it, then?'

'You prick.'

He shrugs. 'That's the way it is. Sometimes you've got to be cruel to be kind. I'm doing you a favour.'

'Bullshit!' I slap the table. 'You're trying to control me. Admit it.'

'I'm not trying to control you, Freya,' he insists. 'I'm trying to help you. Can't you see that? You're obviously in state of severe anxiety, and it's stopping you working, it's stopping you from... I don't know, just doing normal stuff. You spend almost all your time in the house. You hardly ever see your friends, and—'

'That's because they all live so fucking far away, now we've moved here for your job!'

'We made that decision together. We'd already talked about moving to this area, having a bigger place,' he says. '*Then* I got the job.'

'That's not true. It was the other way round.' I'm trying to think back. I know I'm right; that was how it happened... wasn't it?

'Anyway,' he continues, 'there's all that going on. But, most worryingly, you're obsessed with our neighbours. Now that I know what you did eight years ago, when you got some weird ideas into your head about the people in your road, I won't let that happen again.'

'Right, so, you're scared I'm going to stab someone, is that it?' I retort. I want to argue back against everything he's just said, but his last words have evoked a memory for me. The first time I saw the couple over the road from my old place.

The man was tall, well-dressed, good-looking – and I fancied him immediately. The woman was, predictably, even more gorgeous than him. I'd just been through a horrible break up, my stress levels were through the roof and I wasn't sleeping. Right away, my vivid imagination started to picture me together with this guy, instead of the woman. At first, I wanted to be her. Then, I felt the urge to get rid of her, to take her place, to have a family with him in their home.

It's embarrassing to recall how long I spent watching them. Observing from my bedroom window. Walking past the front and back of the house, searching for any little clue as to what their lives were like, how they spent their time. Even – to my shame as I think of it, now, for the first time in years – looking in their bins. I wanted to have a baby with that man. Somehow, I came to believe that they had a child that should've been mine, then that I had a child whom they'd taken. There were moments where it made perfect sense, and other occasions when I felt as though everything was a complete muddle.

Chris Merritt

But this time, today, things are different. Michael and Emily aren't that couple. I know what I'm doing. I'm not crazy. And I'm not going to let Jack tell me otherwise.

He's still talking, trying to reason with me in that heavy-handed way that men do when they can't get what they want, using a mixture of aggression and sulking. But I've zoned out, and I'm not listening to him any more. Because I've just seen a notification on my laptop screen that a new message has arrived from Alice Hope. I pull the machine towards me, click into the message and read the first line:

Oh yes, I know Paul Henderson. I know that two-faced bastard very well.

CHAPTER THIRTY-SEVEN

Saturday, 9 October

'Freya!' barks Jack. 'You're not even listening!'

'I was, I'm just…' My eyes flick up to him and back to the screen.

'Fuck's sake,' he mutters. 'What's so important on there, anyway?' He strides across, rounding the table to take a look at what I'm reading. But I slam the lid shut before he can see.

'It's private,' I say.

He's breathing heavily, trying to keep control. 'What are you hiding?' he demands, staring long and hard at me.

I hold his gaze. 'Nothing you need to worry about,' I reply.

'Well, maybe I should be the judge of that.' He starts pacing again, agitated. 'Let me see,' he demands, pointing at the laptop.

'No.'

His jaw muscles are working again, his fists clenched. He blinks several times. 'This can't go on,' he says. 'You need help.'

'I'm getting help,' I say. 'Or, at least, I was.'

Jack opens his mouth to speak, but just shakes his head and stomps out of the room like a petulant child. He grabs the wooden boards and heaves them upstairs. I hear his footfalls above me, objects banging and clanking as he performs random DIY tasks at a hundred miles an hour to show me how angry he is.

An electric drill whirrs and the walls seem to vibrate. Moments later, there's the hard *bang* of a hammer connecting with something solid. Maybe he can channel his masculine rage into something productive, like putting up shelves. It reminds me of the TV series *Fleabag*, where the eponymous character breaks up with her boyfriend every time she wants the house cleaned. I could almost laugh, if I wasn't still so pissed off with Jack.

I shut my eyes for a moment, take a breath to ground myself, then open the laptop again and read the rest of Alice's message about Henderson:

Is he still playing the good-guy detective, helping the innocent victims? Well, let me tell you – it's all an act. He isn't helping anyone. He's part of the problem. When Michael wanted to stop me exposing his violent and abusive behaviour, he went to the cops and accused me of harassment. Paul Henderson was assigned to investigate, and he took their word for it – he even threatened to arrest me! I know that he made several visits to see Michael and Emily, more than—

I break off a second to process this. Henderson knew Emily before she went missing. He's never told me that, in all of the conversations we've had about her and Thea, since they disappeared. Why would he hide it from me? I finish reading:

…more than was necessary to deal with their complaint against me. And I also know that some of those visits were made when Michael wasn't home. I sometimes kept an eye on them, you see, because I had to make sure that Emily wasn't in danger. I got suspicious, so I kept watching. Eventually, I found out what she was doing – cheating on Michael with that arsehole detective. In some ways, I can't blame her. She was looking for a way out. But I became the victim of that, because Henderson was clearly wrapped around her little finger. He was obsessed with her, doing everything he could

for her, which included making threats against me – even though I was trying to help her. In the end, I had no choice other than to back away, but Henderson kept going to see Emily, I'm sure of it. The question is where that led – because her relationship with the detective wasn't the only thing that Emily was hiding from Michael, you know.

This is the confirmation I've been waiting for. So, Henderson was Emily's 'fancy man', as Cathy put it, and Michael must have found out. I've heard stories before of police entering into inappropriate relationships with victims, or witnesses – sometimes even perpetrators of crime – and that's what seems to have occurred here. It's a clear motive for murder.

But what does she mean by Henderson not being the only thing Emily was hiding? And what about Henderson being *obsessed* with Emily? There are no more details, though, and the message ends abruptly, without a sign-off.

I can almost hear a tiny alarm bell ringing, warning me that there's a small chance I've misunderstood this. But I also need to remember what Michael said about Alice Hope. In his version of events, she stalked them and even threatened to kill Emily. Now, Alice is telling me she was trying to protect Emily. I'm not sure who to believe, but I don't know why Alice would lie about Henderson.

Then the idea comes to me: what if it was Alice who started this whole thing, if she discovered that Emily and Henderson were seeing each other and told Michael? Maybe she wanted to get her revenge on him, or on all of them, and initiated a chain reaction that led to Michael murdering his wife… and perhaps his daughter, too. Could that explain why Henderson hasn't been investigating the disappearance properly, because he doesn't want it to come back to him and cost him his career?

*

After dinner, Jack says he's going to watch TV. It's a statement rather than an invitation, but I decline to join him anyway. I feel a small pang of sadness for the days when we used to snuggle up on the sofa, working our way through a series that we'd chosen to watch together. But I have no desire to do that tonight.

Jack did – unusually – cook the meal this evening (a spaghetti Bolognese, which I have to admit was delicious), but I'm still furious with him for trying to force his medication on me, and for threatening to stop paying for my therapy sessions unless I try those pills. I called him on it, labelling it for what it was: a means of control, disempowering. But he was unapologetic, citing my 'best interests', telling me it was because he cared and rehashing his medical terminology about evidence.

There's a distance between us now that's becoming hard to bridge. Our meal tonight was full of silences, punctuated by admin-type conversations, perfunctory exchanges of information. The music we had on in the background helped to cover some of that awkwardness, and it was almost a relief when we finished and I told Jack I'd load the dishwasher.

By the time I'm done stacking the plates and pans, I can hear the TV coming from the living room – all screeching tyres and gunfire – and I decide that the next hour of my life would be better spent up in the loft.

Or, more accurately, in Michael and Emily's loft.

This time, I feel much more relaxed as I mount the stepladder, push open the trapdoor and clamber up and into the attic. Perhaps it's because I know what to expect. I've taken a proper torch with me this time, an LED headlamp that Jack bought a couple of years ago for a hiking holiday. I'm ready for animals – dead or alive – and whatever Michael's left lying around. In fact, that's exactly what interests me.

I've been thinking about coming back up here ever since I realised that it was possible to access the Crawfords' loft from ours. My desire to return grew when I heard Michael walking around above me the other night, because I'm curious to check whether he's left any trace of what he was doing. Also, I recall him saying that Emily kept some of her stuff up here, including photos, so I want to see if I can find anything that'll support my theory of what happened to her.

I'm poised for a bat to burst out of the gloom and attack me, but nothing happens. The attic is still, quiet and dark – except for the cone of light shining out from my forehead. The stale, musty smell is almost reassuring. I turn to where I remember the dead bird lying, but it's gone. Approaching, I see that its outline is still visible, a stain of death in the floorboards, but the carcass itself has vanished. Did Michael remove it? Maybe I'll ask him, I think, grinning to myself. Put him on the spot.

In contrast to the hammering heartbeat and urgent breathing of my previous visit up here, I'm quite calm as I advance towards the Crawfords' section of the attic. There's almost a sense of… happiness – weird as that sounds – as I slide my body through the gap in the boards that mark the boundary between our properties. Maybe it's because I'm finally getting close to the truth.

I take my first steps, perhaps directly above Michael's head, and feel the boards shift slightly under my weight. I'm trespassing, now, but I actually feel pretty chilled about it. Whatever's brought this on, I could get used to it. For the first time in weeks, my thoughts seem to be moving in a straight line at normal speed, instead of buzzing around in a cloud of noise, like a wasp's nest. And it's great.

I've been searching for Emily's personal things for nearly half an hour. There's a lot to go through: I've found a ton of old computer equipment that I guess belongs to Michael, stacks of furniture that has presumably been superseded by the newer, more expensive stuff downstairs and baby toys for which Thea must have grown too old. Perhaps they were being kept in case another child came along. It brings a lump to my throat as I see them there, and I wonder where Thea is, whether she's still alive. I allow myself a moment, then I keep looking.

In one corner, there's a set of workman's tools, boxes of nails and screws, coils of thin picture wire and a plastic bag filled with offcuts of wood. I shift a folded workbench to get to the cardboard boxes behind it. As I move the bench, my headlamp picks out a solitary letter, written in marker pen, on the side of the largest box: *E*. It must belong to Emily. Personal stuff, in a container marked just for her.

I pause, listening for any sound below me, but there's nothing. Michael is probably three floors down, shut away in his man-cave, coding or whatever. I pull the box towards me and carefully untuck the flaps.

Inside, there's all kinds of random stuff. I pick out some CDs of nineties' music (Destiny's Child, All Saints, Spice Girls) and get sentimental for a minute, imagining Emily attending the same kind of school discos that I did. There are some notebooks, and a quick riffle through the pages suggests they were diaries from her teenage years. Flat against one side of the interior is a graduation portrait of Emily in her gown and mortar board, holding her degree. Behind this is the transcript of her results. As I lift it out, I see a bunch of photos. I gather them up and begin sifting through them.

Holding these images is as nostalgic as finding the music from the nineties. These prints are relics of a pre-digital era when you had to take a camera film to the chemist or print shop and wait a couple of days for it to be developed. The excitement as you picked it up, the moments with friends captured spontaneously, before everything in life went digital, snapped a hundred times then filtered and stage-managed for social media.

One photo is unmistakably Emily as a teenager, pouting at the camera. There's something knowing in her eyes, as if she's already aware of how attractive she is, the effect she has on other people. It's so beguiling that I get out my phone and take a picture of it. Maybe I could use it on the website.

Another print shows a young couple I don't recognise, but who resemble Emily closely enough to be her parents. Then there's a baby. I turn the photo over, to see if there's a clue as to who it is, but the reverse is blank. I'm leafing through some more snaps – parties, sports, holidays – when I hear the sound of steps below. A few photos slip from my hands.

I freeze.

Holding my breath, I put the rest of the images down, switch off the headtorch and crouch in the darkness. There's a heavy footfall, a door slamming and silence. Michael must be just beneath me. I shiver at the thought of our bodies being so close, and I remember how the situations were reversed just last night. I keep absolutely still. This time, I manage not to knock anything over.

A toilet flushes and seconds later footsteps beat a rhythm over the floor, growing in volume before receding into the distance. He's gone. I let the breath out, turn my headlamp back on and stand up, shaking out my stiff legs.

I stoop to gather up the photos, now scattered around me. One has fallen behind the workbench and catches my torch beam. I must've dropped it a minute ago when I heard Michael beneath me. I pluck it from its hiding place and examine it.

At first, I'm not sure what I'm looking at. The picture is poorer quality than the others, as if it's a copy. It's older, but there's no date on it. There's a man in it, standing alone, his face angled down and slightly away from the camera. He's smiling, as if he knew the photo was being taken but he didn't want to pose for it.

I feel my heart rate start to rise, the familiar tingle in my limbs. Because, even though he's a lot younger than he is now, I can still recognise him.

Jack.

I stare at the picture. Check the back, but there's nothing written on it. I recall that moment when Jack saw Emily outside our house, for what I thought was the first time. His expression suggested he knew her. Now, I know I wasn't crazy to think that.

I continue studying the image, taking in the details, trying to match it to what I can recall about Jack's past. There might be something that connects—

'Freya?'

His voice echoes across the loft moments before his torch beam sweeps around in the darkness like a helicopter searchlight picking out a fugitive.

'Where the hell are you?' he calls out, the beam getting stronger, closer.

I put the photo of him to one side, then shove everything else back into the box and close it. I kick it to the wall and cram the workbench up against it just as Jack's torchlight illuminates me, so bright I have to shield my eyes.

'Jesus, Freya!' he explodes. 'What do you think you're doing?'

I look up. Jack is just a dark shape behind the light, and I can't see his face. Which is fitting, because right now, I feel as though I don't know who he really is.

CHAPTER THIRTY-EIGHT

I could have saved you. If only you'd come to me when it all started to unravel. You'd built your life on something that wasn't true, wasn't real. You deceived those closest to you, manipulated them into thinking what you wanted them to think. It would all have emerged someday, anyway, sooner or later, with or without my intervention. That was the risk you took when you wove a tissue of lies and began pulling at the loose threads all by yourself.

You should have trusted me. When it was clear that things were starting to go badly wrong for you, when the events you'd tried to hide were finally exposed, I was ready to be your rock. Not just a shoulder to cry on, or a hand to hold. I was prepared to share my whole life with you, to give you everything, every part of me. Forever.

But you didn't want that.

Instead, you chose that moment – the very point where you needed me more than ever before – to spurn me. I'd never experienced a rejection like it, and I doubt I ever will again, because you are The One. I'm still convinced of that, despite what happened.

Your choice knocked my world off its axis and sent it spinning out of control. I thought about you all the time. I didn't sleep properly, turning over and over what went wrong. Dwelling on what I should have said to change your mind. And on what a terrible mistake you had made by not accepting me – one you would surely come to regret. You destroyed the future which I had planned for us. It was the lowest point of my life.

But you, of all people, should know that the power of my reaction would match the intensity of my feelings for you. Feelings that were so strong, sometimes it seemed as though they were taking over my whole being and giving me no choice but to follow their commands, as if I was no longer in control of my own body. I'll admit that it was scary to feel in the possession of something so powerful that it could make me do things I never imagined doing. Things I doubt you'd ever imagined me doing, either.

That's because you'd only known my passion in its positive form, the purest expression of one human being's desire for another. You hadn't yet seen its dark side.

My plan for us had three steps. The first two had failed. I didn't want to have to use the third because it was the last resort. But it was all I had left.

Making you disappear.

CHAPTER THIRTY-NINE

Sunday, 10 October

As I lay in bed last night, watching Jack sleep peacefully beside me, I thought about what we'd kept from one another. I hadn't told him about being sectioned and the episode of delusional psychosis I'd had, when I stabbed a stranger whom I believed had taken my child. Did Jack have a right to know about that, any more than I had a right to know that he and Emily had crossed paths, at some point in the past? I asked him, after that first time we visited the Crawfords' house for dinner, if he knew her, and he said no. Now that I've found a photo of him in Emily's possession, I know that he lied.

Obviously, Jack went crazy when he caught me in the neighbours' loft. He'd demanded to know what the hell I was doing, ordering me to get out of there immediately. He didn't know that I'd seen the photo. I fought back my desire to show it to him, to compel him to account for it being among Emily's personal stuff. To explain when and how the two of them had known one another, what kind of relationship they'd had… Instead, I breezed past him towards the trapdoor, telling him simply that it wasn't a big deal; I'd just been exploring.

Jack had followed me back downstairs, hissing his incredulity and again raising the issue of me getting help, *before something seriously bad happens*, he'd said. I enjoyed the role reversal of being the one to tell him to calm down and, after a while, he did. When we eventually went to bed, he was visibly more relaxed. He fell asleep easily, leaving me to wonder what Emily had chosen to hide from me during the course of our short friendship.

I remember an evening when she invited me over for a glass of wine. Michael was travelling, off at some tech conference, and Jack was working a late shift. Emily was still putting Thea to bed when I turned up some time around eight, and I got involved in reading the bedtime story as she lay tucked up, under the covers. Thea was impossibly sweet, a gorgeous miniature version of Emily. As we headed down to the kitchen, Emily told me I had the 'magic touch', asking if I planned to have kids of my own. I said yes, for sure, if I could. It can't have been long after then that I got pregnant…

That night, Emily had been in a contemplative mood. We drank a bottle between us, easily, and had ended up talking about truth and what version of events we present to others. She asked how I knew what the truth was, in my work; I replied that I made no claim on it, but simply let the people I interviewed tell their stories and invited viewers to form their own opinions. Of course, I acknowledged that I could be unconsciously biased in terms of who I interview and what material of theirs I kept or cut.

Emily thought that curating an exhibition was pretty similar to editing a documentary; you chose what artifacts to include and what to leave out. History's winners had already determined much of what was available to select. Then you shaped others' perceptions of the truth by what you let them see. You created the narrative around the facts. It was a lot like our lives, she said, and the selves we present to others. And, sometimes, you needed to hide a part of the truth from people you loved in order to protect them. I agreed with her; I still would. I had thought of Jack and of the past I'd kept secret from him.

Back then, her words had struck me as abstract, the musings of someone with a couple of large glasses of red inside them, happy to let the conversation meander. It reminded me of the endless chats I'd have with friends in university halls, when we'd got back in from a student night out and were sat around in the communal kitchen, making tea and toast. At the time, that evening with Emily left me with a warm feeling of connection. Now, as I replay her words in my mind, I wonder if she was also referring to Jack. Maybe I'll never know, unless—

'Freya!' Jack's voice comes from downstairs, friendly once more. 'Breakfast's ready!'

This is the second meal he's done in as many days. It's unprecedented. If it wasn't just some food, which I knew he'd make for himself anyway, I'd be suspicious of his motives. I'm not complaining, of course. After months of me cooking for him, it's about time he returned the favour. Perhaps this is just Jack's way of trying to apologise for his recent behaviour. He's still got a lot of making up to do.

It's mid-afternoon and I'm walking to the park. I feel calmer, again, and my limbs are light, relaxed. I'm not sure where this sensation has come from (my guess is the yoga class I did earlier), but it's quite pleasant, so I'm not going to interrogate it too closely. Jack is off on one of his epic runs along the Thames path, which are too long for me to join him on, so I've taken this chance for an outing of my own.

I see him from a hundred yards away, sitting alone on a bench, looking around. He spots me advancing and gives an awkward little wave. He tugs at the sides of his jacket and begins to stand, but then realises I'm still too far away and sits back down again. His gaze roams around until I'm within ten paces.

'Hi there, Laurence.'

'Hello, Freya.' Now, he gets to his feet, and we shake hands.

'Thanks for agreeing to meet up between sessions.'

'Oh.' He flashes a smile. 'It's no trouble. Your text said it was an emergency, and I'm just around the corner…'

'Shall we walk?'

'Uh, sure,' he replies tentatively. 'So, erm, what's going on? I mean, is-is everything okay?'

Outside of his consulting room, and without a notebook and pen, my therapist seems less sure of himself. Almost slightly nervous, as if he's worried about us being seen together. It doesn't bother me. I think we kind of look like a couple, anyway. It's no less than what I've imagined.

'Jack wants me to stop our sessions,' I say.

'Right. I see. Why?'

'He thinks they're not working. He reckons I'm getting worse, not better. And he's trying to push pills on me. Benzodiazepine. He prescribed them for me.'

'Wow, okay. How do you feel about that?' he asks. Classic therapy question.

I glance sideways at him. 'Pissed off would be an understatement.'

'And, er, when you say "push"… he can't make you take medicine. It doesn't matter that he's a doctor. That can only be done if you're—'

'Locked up, like I was. I know.'

'Yes, of course.' He hesitates. 'Freya, if you feel unsafe, then—'

'I don't.'

'Okay, good. Did you take any of the pills?'

'Nope. I told him to stick them up his arse.'

Laurence emits a small chuckle, but then turns it into a cough, as if he's trying to maintain his professionalism. I couldn't care less about that, though; I'd like him to be less professional, share a bit more of himself with me. It feels as though we've already crossed a boundary by walking together, here, on a Sunday afternoon. It's as if we're friends, now, rather than therapist and patient, and I like it.

'How did he react to that?' he says after regaining his poise.

I shrug. 'He tried to blind me with science, said it was in my best interests. I used that thing you told me about long-term fixes and sticking plasters.'

'Ah, you remembered that.'

'Yeah.' I give him a smile, then turn back to the path.

'That all sounds as if it's been quite stressful,' he observes. 'It's difficult when a person's partner doesn't support them in their therapy.'

'That's exactly the problem,' I say, 'because he's the one paying for our sessions. And he says he's going to stop.'

'Oh.' Laurence sounds crestfallen. For a moment I have a window into his emotions, and a hint of vulnerability. But he quickly returns to work mode. 'And how did you react?'

'I think I swore at him.'

'That's understandable.' There's no laughter from my therapist this time.

'It's shitty behaviour by Jack, but the main thing is that I don't want our sessions to end. They're really helping. I'm improving, I know I am.'

'I'd agree,' he says. 'I don't think it'd be a good idea to stop now, either.'

'So, um… could we have like a tab, or something? Just until I get some more work, I mean, then I can pay—'

'It's fine.' He gently holds up a palm. 'I'll do it for free.'

'Seriously? Would you?'

He nods. 'It's not actually that uncommon. Therapy can be a long process – even years long, in some cases, though I'm not suggesting you need—'

'It's okay, I know.'

'Right. Yes, so, it can take a while, and people's circumstances change, their finances, jobs or whatever. At the end of the day, though, they're people. Human beings. As an independent therapist, I can choose to keep working with someone if they're at a critical stage, even if they can't pay.'

I stop walking, turn to him. 'Thank you. I appreciate it.'

Laurence stops too, squinting into the sun behind me. 'You're welcome.'

For a second, I think we might kiss. But then he breaks eye contact, shoves his hands in his pockets and we walk on. As we loop around and slowly return to the park gates, I tell him about what I've found recently on Emily and Thea. How I've posted an update on the website (featuring the photo of Emily which I snapped in the attic) calling for any new information. How I think I'm pretty close to finding out what happened.

He listens patiently, and when I'm finished, he cautions me not to place too much of my own emotions into this project. He reminds me that there's an optimal balance for recovery between prioritising my needs and focusing on others, and that mobilising support for Emily and Thea shouldn't become a way of avoiding dealing with my own loss. I hadn't quite thought about it like that, but my therapist might be right; he usually is. I thank him again for his help and tell him I'll see him on Tuesday for our usual session.

As he walks away, I can't help but imagine what it would have been like if we'd kissed.

What it might be like if we did.

When I told my friend Bea about my therapist the other day, she said it sounded as though I was having an emotional affair. She asked whether it was a just reaction to the problems Jack and I have been having since the miscarriage, or if there was something more to it. A sign, perhaps, that Jack isn't the right man for me. I told her I was thinking the same. It's confusing.

My mind is still on that as I turn into my street. But the thoughts vanish as I see Michael outside his home, just feet away from my front door. He has his back to me, and he's stuffing things into the bin. Watching him, I wonder if he knew about his wife's affair with Henderson, her connection to Jack. If he attacked Emily, then he must have discovered something. But did he have the identities of the men she'd been involved with?

'Hello, Michael.' I'm relaxed and confident as I walk over to him, perhaps because of the new power balance I perceive between us, given what I've found.

He straightens up and grunts in reply. He's scruffy and stubbly, his hair sticking up in tufts. He looks like a man who's losing his grip. Is the guilt starting to wear him down, I wonder?

'How are you doing?' I ask him.

'Fine.' He blinks. 'Busy working.' Three words of reply from him isn't bad. That's two more than usual.

'It's Sunday,' I respond cheerily. 'Can't you have a day off?'

'No.'

'Housework, is it? Stuff in the loft?'

'What?' He narrows his eyes.

'Or something you're doing in the garden, maybe?' I study him for any little signal of discomfort. There's nothing. Then again, sociopaths don't show emotions in the same way as normal people.

'It's work-work,' he says eventually. 'Software. I'm patching.'

'What's that?'

Michael exhales hard, as if he's already fed up with talking to me. 'It's a fix you make to resolve a vulnerability.'

'What kind of vulnerability?'

'Security.'

I nod. 'So, there's something you don't want people to discover, but you've just realised they could, so you have to do something about that quickly. Cover it over, hide it or whatever.'

He tilts his head. 'More or less.'

'And what if you don't fit this… patch in time?'

'Then outsiders can gain access to your confidential stuff,' he says. 'And you're in deep shit. But I'm not going to let that happen.'

I hold his gaze, unfazed by our height difference. I want to ask him how long ago we stopped talking about computers.

'You'd better get back to work, then,' I tell him.

He grunts again, shuts the bin lid and strides back into his house, slamming the door behind him. I allow myself a smile as I head towards my own front door. He knows I'm on to him.

I'm woken suddenly by a loud, mechanical grinding noise, and for a second, I have no idea where I am. Then I start to make sense of my surroundings. I'm on the sofa bed, upstairs in the spare bedroom, and the sound is coming from down in the kitchen. It's the coffee machine.

I must have come in here for some reason, felt tired and stretched out for a nap. I don't know how long I was sleeping, but it's long enough for Jack to have come back from his run. I lie still for a moment, massaging my eyes with the heels of my hands. Then I swing my feet onto the carpet and stand up, immediately feeling light-headed. I put a hand on the wall to steady myself.

Downstairs, Jack is on his laptop, sipping a coffee. He's still in his sports gear, although he doesn't look particularly sweaty.

'Good run?' I ask.

'Hm?' He looks up from the screen. 'Oh, yeah.'

'Was it busy by the river?'

'No, just… normal.'

He doesn't ask what I've been doing, and I don't tell him. He doesn't need to know I've met up with my therapist.

I go over to the machine and start making coffee; I need to drag myself out of this zombified state.

'I was thinking of doing a risotto tonight,' Jack offers, once the machine has stopped whirring. 'What do you reckon?'

'Sounds great.'

I drink half the coffee down in one go, grab my laptop and sit opposite him at the kitchen table. I log into the account for *Find Emily and Thea* and check the updates. I'm pleased to see that my latest post is doing well; it's had loads of shares, including some by missing persons' charity accounts with a ton of followers. That should generate some interest. You never know which share will be the one that sparks a reaction for somebody.

I click into the messages. There's nothing back from Alice Hope, yet, in response to my follow-up questions to her. But there is something from johnsmith12643. I shudder when I see his username on my screen, the start of the unread message standing out in bold font. I glance up at Jack to see if he's watching me, but he's absorbed in his own screen. I click and open the email:

Sunningdale Road's a lovely place, isn't it Freya? I wonder, though, do you get lonely spending the days there on your own? Even the safest home can be dangerous when no one's around in the daytime to protect you. Especially when there's plenty of space to bury a body out the back.

I try to contain my fear, but there's too much of it, rising too fast. It feels as though it's enveloping me, suffocating me.

I slam the laptop shut.

And I scream.

CHAPTER FORTY

Monday, 11 October

I'm going to do it now. Jack's at work, I've just heard Michael go out in his car and it's time I stepped up. I need to see what's buried at the bottom of the Crawfords' garden, in the patch of earth beside the shed. The spade, the shed floor and the blood tell me that a living thing has been put in the ground, and I've got to find out what it is.

Who it is.

Henderson isn't investigating, Michael's giving nothing away and it's anyone's guess what Jack thinks about the disappearance of the woman he lied about knowing. In the absence of physical evidence that I can show anyone, my theory would be just another excuse for these men to tell me I need help. Which, for me, is a very good reason to act on my suspicions. Because I'm the only one who realises that something's there: the answer to the question of what happened to Emily and Thea. Nobody else is taking it seriously. It's on me.

The only problem is that I'm absolutely terrified.

I had felt better last night, after a big plateful of Jack's risotto, but this morning my anxiety returned with a vengeance. I slept late, and Jack had already gone to work, but my fight-or-flight system was crackling from the moment I woke.

Perhaps I'd been unconsciously processing John Smith's latest threat and the idea that he knows where I live. That he might come for me, in my own home, when no one's around. I tell myself that the doorbell camera will pick up any would-be intruders. But I'm also carrying the secateurs with me wherever I go, now, just in case.

Jack thought that the threats were nothing to worry about, that it was probably just some online troll or kid trying to show off to his mates, having a laugh. He said it would be easy enough for someone who knew a thing or two about computers to guess the street I was on from the IP address I was using.

He suggested that I show the police, but I told him that I was sure they wouldn't do anything. I can still hear Henderson's words as clearly as if he was here with me now, when I reported to him that someone had said they'd make me disappear: *Did he directly threaten to kill you?* I have a better option than Henderson, anyway – Michael.

I sent the new message on to him this morning. Even though he's still my number one candidate for johnsmith12643, I wanted to show him that I'm not scared, maybe trick him into giving something away about it. If it's not Michael, of course, then his computer skills might be able to tell me some useful information about the guy; hopefully beyond the fact that he probably uses a VPN to pretend he's in Iceland. Whoever's behind it, they're not going to stop me from finding out what happened to Emily and Thea.

It's time to get closer to the truth.

My heart and lungs are already in overdrive as I cross the invisible boundary into the Crawfords' garden. It's an overcast day and, with the leaves starting to turn brown and die, the shed looks even creepier than usual. A steady wind ripples the ivy enveloping its rotting wooden exterior, as if a giant organism is slowly suffocating and swallowing the little outbuilding.

I check the back windows of Michael and Emily's house, just to be sure, but there are no signs of life. I drop my trowel on the ground and use the keys I stole from Cathy to open the padlock on the shed again. I begin to feel nauseous as I prise the door open, just wide enough to check that the blood-spattered spade and deep red stains on the floor are still there. They are. Unbidden, the film of what must've taken place here comes to me.

Emily is lying on the ground, wounded and bleeding. She's clutching a hand to her stomach to stem the flow, screaming – in pain – for help, for Thea, for Michael to release her... for something. Anything. The desperation and anguish I can see on her face is almost too much, and I feel my throat tightening, my lips pressing together and trembling. I release a jagged breath, blink and close the shed door again, clicking the padlock shut once more.

Now comes the real test. I grab my trowel and take the few steps across to the rectangular plot of turned soil beside the shed. The charred remains of something are still sitting in the fire pit a few feet away, and Michael clearly isn't making any effort to get rid of them. I bend, kneel and sweep a few large sycamore leaves away from the surface. Beneath them, I notice that one smaller area of the plot – about a square foot – appears to be even more recently disturbed than the rest of it.

I decide to start there.

Cautiously, I slide the trowel into the earth, moving small sections away. I work gingerly at first, as if there's a living thing there I might hurt if I dig too deeply or quickly. But I know that's ridiculous. There's not going to be anything *alive* down here.

I stab the trowel harder into the ground, taking a bigger scoop of soil and throwing it aside. Then another scoop, and another. About six inches below the surface, I thrust the trowel in again and lift, but it catches and doesn't come out as easily. Something's there.

Gently withdrawing the tool, I use my hands to reach into the dirt, and my fingertips connect with something smooth and hard. The objects are long and thin, and I close my eyes, forcing myself to explore further. My hands search until one palm wraps around a small, bulbous shape. The fingers of my other hand travel in to meet it and find a thicker shape connected to it, tapering to a sharp point.

I gather as much of it as I can and pull upwards. The topsoil parts easily and, even though chunks of damp earth cling to it, I know exactly what I'm holding.

The skeleton of a bird.

Is it the one from the loft, removed by Michael and buried here? It has to be. But why? Is he just a guy who's into dead things? Or was there something symbolic about it for him, related to his family?

I place the bird carefully to the side of the grave-plot and look at it for a moment. I think of its final hours, perhaps days, trapped in the loft. Did it hit its head and die immediately, or was it a slow, agonising demise from starvation and dehydration? I wonder which of those two fates befell Emily in her home. My thoughts flit around – life and death, how fragile our bodies are, how easily the flame that keeps us alive can be snuffed out, how much we take for granted in—

Vrrrrooooom.

The car engine snaps me out of my morbid trance. The noise is coming from the street.

I wait, rooted to the spot.

The sound of the engine rises, peaks and then falls again as the car fades into the distance.

I shut my eyes in relief and breathe. It wasn't Michael. But it's a reminder that I need to keep moving. Steeling myself, I move onto the centre of the plot and start digging again.

This time I work at pace, thrusting the trowel in and heaping soil to right and left. A few minutes later, I've made a crater about a foot deep.

And I've found nothing.

I do a few more trowelfuls of earth and sit back on my heels. I'm still on edge, sweating and shaking from the combination of fear and exertion. But I'm starting to doubt myself. I wonder if I should give up, throw the soil all back, return the bird to its resting place and go home. The idea occurs to me that perhaps there's nothing here beyond that tiny carcass. That it was just a patch of ground Michael dug for vegetables he never got around to planting.

Then I remember the spade. The floor. The blood.

I start digging again with renewed energy, hunched over the grave, shovelling earth, my breath coming in short, audible gasps. The muscles of my forearm are stinging with fatigue, my lower back is aching and my hands and knees are covered in dirt. But I plough on, the crater deepening in front of me. I see earthworms wriggling and writhing, woodlice and beetles scuttling as I invade their home, and I begin to wonder if…

Crack.

My trowel hits something solid. I know it's not the *chink* sound of metal on stone. I stop digging and toss the trowel to one side, clawing at the soil with both hands like a woman possessed.

Seconds later I freeze, because I've exposed enough of the object to see what it is. Off-white, smooth, arcing in a thick band. There's another just like it less than an inch away. I sweep away more earth and see a third, then a fourth. All lined up.

For a moment, I stay absolutely still, kneeling over what I've found. There's a coppery taste in my mouth and a coldness is spreading through my stomach.

I reach one hand tentatively out, my fingers probing the ground beside it, where I already know there'll be a second, identical arrangement, a mirror image of parallel curves. I'd know their form by touch, even if it was pitch-black.

It's a ribcage. About the same size as my own.

And I know I've found her.

What happens next is a blur. I'm standing, stumbling, kicking heaps of soil back into the crater, pulling at my hair and wiping my hands over my face... hands that have just touched Emily's remains.

I only know that I can't be here, that I have to get away from this place, to be back in the safety of my house. I can't see the bones any more. It's just thick, dark ground below me again.

My pulse is pounding in my ears as the pressure in my head grows. I can't take it any longer.

I turn and run home.

CHAPTER FORTY-ONE

I rush through the back door and shut it behind me. Then I lock it and stand with my back against it, trying to calm myself, but I can't. My whole body is shaking. I pace around the kitchen, flexing my muddy hands, gripping my scalp, unable to be still.

I force myself to sit down at the table, just to stop moving for a moment, but I can't focus on what I should do. The only thing I can think of is that ribcage, stained with soil, crawling with worms. The decomposed remains of my neighbour Emily, my friend. Murdered by her husband, Michael, and buried at the bottom of their garden in an unmarked grave.

My mouth is dry, my skin feels clammy and my guts are knotted and twisted. I realise I've never seen a human corpse before. Well, apart from my grandmother's open casket at her funeral when I was a teenager. But her body was intact, and she was dressed, with the appearance of being peaceful and at rest. She'd been ninety-one and passed in her sleep. This is the opposite of that.

A woman in her thirties, full of life, a mother, cut down because she dared to stand up to her abusive husband; her violated body dumped in a shallow grave, dug by her killer, and left to be eaten by bugs. It's that final thought that tips me over the edge.

Gripping the table, I pull myself to my feet and race upstairs. I just make it to the bathroom in time to plant my hands on the toilet seat and put my head over the bowl before I vomit. My stomach heaves, the muscles tightening and pushing everything inside me up and out.

It slows for a few seconds, before another almighty wave rises, and I can't control it, as if my body's trying to purge the horror of what I've seen. My hair's getting caught in my mouth, my eyes are streaming with tears, but still it comes, even though there's nothing left except spit.

When the dry retching is over, I stay sprawled on the bathroom floor, hugging the toilet. Eventually, I reach for the flush and somehow get to my feet, turning and steadying my wobbly legs by leaning on the sink.

I stare at my reflection in the bathroom mirror. My face is streaked with dirt, my eyes are dark and sunken, their whites bloodshot, and my hair is wild and tangled. I barely recognise myself.

The image of what I've become sends a new spike of panic through me, my heart firing with the intensity of a pneumatic drill, hammering at a hundred miles an hour against my ribs. The sensation makes me picture the ribcage once more.

And I know I can't take this. I feel as though it might never end, that I might suffocate or that my heart will stop and I'll die. I imagine desperately calling the ambulance; I see paramedics zapping my chest with a defibrillator before driving me to the hospital, where Jack appears and says, *I told you that you needed help, but you didn't listen.* It's too much.

I have to do something. I remember what Jack said about the pills. I still don't want to take any, but right now I don't think I have a choice. I need them. I snatch open the bathroom cabinet and search frantically for them.

I clear some other bottles and packets out of the way – aspirin, paracetamol, ibuprofen – sending them across the floor or clattering into the sink, but the ones I want – the ones Jack got for me – aren't there. Shit.

My eyes dart around the bathroom, but then I remember the other cabinet beneath the sink. I drop to my knees, grab the little handles and fling the doors wide. Straightaway I see them.

A cardboard packet of Xanax, with the prescription label on the front, my name printed on it in capital letters. I grab the box and rip the flap open, pulling out the first foil-covered sheet of tablets. But then I stop. There's something wrong.

Five of the pills are missing.

It takes a moment for me to realise why.

Now, I know what Jack's been doing.

My memory of the event that led to me being sectioned under the Mental Health Act is piecemeal and hazy. I've imagined most of it from what I've been told. Now, what I remember is the film I've edited in my own mind, rather than the event itself. In some ways, I'm glad I can't remember what it was like to push a knife into another human being's body. However, my recollection of the secure psychiatric unit at the hospital is all too clear.

Nobody was really on the ward by choice. If they said you had a choice, they were lying. The only choice you had was whether you were there voluntarily, or whether they put you there by force. And the moment you set eyes on the psychiatric nurses – the jailers, we called them, because of the big jangling bunches of keys hanging off their thick belts – you knew you didn't want them to do anything to you *by force*.

The same went for your medication. Everyone in the unit was being given something. There were pills to speed you up, pills to calm to you down, pills to keep you stabilised somewhere in the middle of the extremes that a few patients cycled through. Most of us accepted that you needed to take your medication willingly, because the alternative was so much worse.

Occasionally, though, someone tried to fight that system, and their reward for opposing it was to be tackled to the ground by three large, powerful men who spent as much time weightlifting as they did at work. They'd half-drag, half-carry you to the nearest clinic room and push you face down onto a bed. Then you got a syringe in your bum, and the drugs were in your body anyway.

The doctors called this a 'best interests' decision. I even had it done to me, once. But it wasn't always a jab in the arse. Sometimes, when people refused their pills, the staff didn't use brute force. They just waited for the next mealtime and put them in your food. Crumbled, mashed, mixed in with a strong-tasting dish, like chilli or curry, so you wouldn't notice. I saw the nurses doing it.

And I think that's where those five pills have gone.

I should have known that something was up when Jack started cooking. But I didn't question it. I wasn't suspicious enough. I just thanked him and merrily tucked into his spag bol, his porridge, his risotto, marvelling at his sudden change of heart. No wonder I'd been feeling so chilled. My bastard fiancé was medicating me with Xanax.

He barely lifts a finger in the kitchen for months, treating me like his own private chef, then cooks breakfast and dinner for the whole weekend. How could I be so stupid? If I'd been more sceptical, I could've seen it coming. Did he believe he was acting in my *best interests*?

Before now, I thought I might not be able to trust Jack.

Now I know I can't.

CHAPTER FORTY-TWO

I have to keep going. The realisation comes in a moment of clarity as I stand in front of the bathroom mirror, looking my dishevelled, panicked reflection squarely in the eyes. Michael the killer; Henderson the cop, covering his own arse, and my lying fiancé, Jack, might all be determined to stop me. But I owe it to Emily to get justice for her death. And I owe it to Thea, who might be alive somewhere, perhaps even inside the Crawfords' house. I see her trapped in the basement, sobbing, bereft of her mother and terrified of what her father might do to her.

My heart breaks as I imagine that poor, sweet little girl being kept prisoner, but I'm also filled with rage. Anger towards these men who think they can just tell women what to do, and who will use deception or violence to get what they want from us if we don't just meekly accept their demands. I wipe my eyes with the back of my hand, take a single deep breath and go back downstairs. I've got to keep digging.

As I head out into the garden, I can feel the tingle and thrum of anxiety in my body. It never really went away after my panic at finding the ribs; it just receded slightly. Now it's coming back. But I know I've got to face it and stay strong. I use my fury at how I've been treated to drive me on. My own fiancé, crumbling Xanax into my food. Bastard.

As I walk towards Emily's grave, I wonder again about Jack's relationship with her. The photograph of him was old, that's for sure. It was obviously taken years before he and I met, maybe a decade or more. He looked so young, so different.

Had he and Emily known one another at university? Could he have been the Jack Watkins accused of stalking her, who left after his first year, perhaps then changing his name to Brown, to stop the incident ruining his medical career? But, if that was their history together, then why would Emily have kept a photo of him, smiling, as if he meant something to her?

I turn over the possibilities as I approach the Crawfords' side of the garden once more. Might the connection between Jack and Emily have had anything to do with her murder? And, if so, what would that mean for Henderson's role in all this?

I can't make sense of it right now. But I know one thing: I have to unearth Emily's bones again – sickening as that task is – to photograph them and show the world what's happened. I've got to stop Michael destroying the evidence. Then I need to call the police.

I check I have my phone in my pocket, ready to dial. I'm not messing around by going to Henderson. I'll call the emergency number when the moment comes.

I don't waste any time. Striding back to the grave, emboldened and defiant, I push the vegetation out of my way until I'm back by the shed. My trowel is still on the ground next to the plot, where I threw it after I panicked and ran. I pick it up again, drop to my knees and dig.

Before long, I see Emily's ribs begin to protrude through the dark earth. I pause, blinking, as a stream of images flood into my mind's eye, but I push on. Scraping soil away alongside them, I've exposed half of their curved shape, and I can even see some of her spine. I realise that I'm choked up, a hard lump at the top of my throat.

It feels so wrong to be doing this, but I know I must. I've got to tell her story. If I do, perhaps I can stop the same thing happening to other women like her. Maybe I can save lives. That's got to make this worth it. It has to.

As I dig further, I hit another hard object. I use my hands to remove the surrounding dirt. It's a separate bone. This one's long and straight. Emily's upper arm, maybe? It's almost too morbid, too disgusting and terrifying all at once to even think about. As much as I want to keep Emily – the victim – in mind, I have to tune out the personal to get the job done right now.

My hand slides up the smooth surface of the bone until it catches on something hard and thin. I shift the earth above it to one side and wipe it enough to see what it is. Wire. I study it more closely. And I recognise it.

It's the picture wire from Michael's collection of DIY stuff in the attic. It's further proof of what he's done. I follow the wire as it wraps around the contours of the bone, and realise that it's binding another long, slim bone beneath it.

Jesus Christ. He's tied her up with picture wire. Suddenly, I visualise Michael and Emily in their home, years ago. They're hanging a painting on the wall together. She's uncoiling the wire and cutting a length of it for the picture frame, thinking only that it's for decoration, never imagining that her husband would later use it to—

Ping.

I jerk out of the daydream at the alert sound from my phone. It's the doorbell camera app. Instinctively, I drop the trowel and pull the device out, tapping into the feed. I haven't heard a doorbell, but maybe I'm too far away. I'm not expecting anything, or anyone…

The clip loads, and I watch. A dark figure approaches the door, hood up. I can't see his face. Then he vanishes from view, beyond the camera. I notice my pulse rising again. It can't be Jack because he's at work – and why would he be wearing a hood, as if he's trying to hide his identity? It has to be Michael. The camera shot is empty, now. I rewind, watch again, but there are no clues. Then I hear a back door open.

From my position here, right at the end of the long garden, I can't tell which house it is. I glance down at the exposed bones, the picture wire. And I realise I'm in danger.

I leave the trowel where it's lying and scramble to my feet, just as I hear steps from close to the building.

I slip behind the shed, taking care not to tread on any brushwood and give myself away. I shut my eyes for a moment, listening. The footsteps are getting louder. They're heavy, a man's steps, tramping over the garden towards me.

Holding my phone in one hand, I extract the secateurs from the pocket of my jeans and grip them tightly. My belly is bubbling like magma, but my skin is cold and damp with fear.

If Michael finds me, if it's me or him, I'm not going to end up in that grave. I'm going to fight for my life. It won't hurt to have some backup, though. I can't leave it too late. Now's the time to call.

I dial 999 and press the phone to my left ear.

'Emergency, which service?' says a woman's voice.

'Police,' I whisper, glancing over my right shoulder. I can't see anything, and I don't dare move further out from the cover of the shed.

'Stay on the line, please, connecting you now.'

There's a click, and another woman says, 'Surrey Police, what's your emergency?'

'There's… erm, I'm in my neighbour's garden, and he's coming for me…'

'Okay. Is your neighbour threatening to attack you?'

'Yes – well, he will, I know it, if he finds me. I think he'll kill me, like he's killed her.'

'Sorry, are you saying someone's been killed?'

'Yes, it's his wife. She's in the garden.'

'Right, whereabouts are you?' Her response is impossibly calm. 'What's the address?'

I keep my voice as quiet as possible. 'Thirteen Sunningdale Road, Weybridge.'

She repeats the address back to me and asks if that's right. I murmur 'yes', and she starts saying something else, but the noise of Michael approaching is growing and I can't keep talking. I shove the phone back into my pocket and clutch the secateurs tightly in both hands.

The footfall, swishing of branches and crunching of leaves rises, louder, the sounds almost physically pressing in on my skull as I hold my breath and stay absolutely still. The blade of the secateurs is in front of me, my last line of defence. It's as curved and hard and sharp as the beak of the dead bird buried behind me.

I'm looking to my right, but the voice comes from my left.

'Freya, what are you doing?'

It's Jack. He's standing there, watching me. His eyes flick from my face to the secateurs and back up again. 'Are you okay?' he asks.

'Why are you here?' I hiss.

He frowns, shakes his head. 'I just came back for, um, lunch, and—'

'I know what you've been doing,' I tell him.

In that instant, I can see the guilt on his face. He presses his lips tight together, then holds out a hand to me. 'You can put them down,' he says, 'it's all right. No one's going to hurt you.'

I don't know if I should listen to him or not. In those few seconds of indecision, I relax slightly. The noises around me fade out a little.

And that's when it happens.

There's a rapid movement to my right and suddenly my arm is being clamped, a vice around my bicep. I scream and twist and it's Michael and he's towering over me, looking at me as if he's going to kill me.

'You crazy bitch!' he roars.

I take the secateurs in my left fist and extend that arm away from him.

I hear Jack cry, 'No, Freya!' But he's too late.

My torso whips towards Michael.

My arm follows.

Then the blade.

CHAPTER FORTY-THREE

Monday, 11 October

Henderson leans forward in his chair, resting his elbows on his knees and steepling his fingers underneath his chin. He scratches at the perma-stubble.

'So, shall we start from the beginning, Ms Northcott?'

I look up from the sofa, where I've been cradling my head in my hands. Opposite me, Jack is sat beside Henderson, as if they're both jointly interrogating me.

'If you'd been paying attention to what's been going on,' I say, my gesture taking in the neighbour's house and garden, 'then you'd know. But you don't give a shit. You've just been letting him get away with it for months.'

Henderson sighs. 'I assume you're referring to Mr Crawford.'

'Course I'm referring to him, for fuck's sake,' I retort.

'Freya,' says Jack.

'He's murdered his wife and buried her in the garden, and you lot have been blind to it,' I continue, jabbing an accusatory finger at the detective. 'Emily is yet another woman who's a victim of violence by a male partner. But she's just one more statistic for you, right?'

Henderson sits back, glances sideways at Jack. 'There's no evidence at the present time to indicate that Emily Crawford has been the victim of any kind of violence, let alone murder.'

I bark a single laugh. I can't believe this. 'No evidence? What, other than her skeleton lying in a shallow grave out there?' I can hear the volume of my voice growing.

'You mean Seamus?' replies Henderson.

'What?' I blink, stare at him.

'The dog,' he says. 'Mr Crawford explained to us that the family pet, a large dog, had died about two years ago. He buried it in the garden, next to the shed.'

'No, that can't be... it's not – it's Emily, I'm sure.'

'Of course, if we're being picky, he really should've buried it a bit deeper, according to the letter of the law. Two feet, at least. Probably three, to be on the safe side. All depends on the soil composition, you see.' He makes this last comment to Jack, as if only men can understand technical things like that.

'It's not a dog,' I state. 'It's a person.'

'I'm afraid not, Ms Northcott. It's very much a dead dog.'

'He's right, Freya,' says Jack. 'I've seen it. The forensic officer uncovered the rest of the skeleton. It's not human.'

'It's her,' I protest, but I can feel the fight draining from me.

'It's got a tail,' Jack adds.

'But... there was the bird, there, too.'

Henderson plants his hands on his knees and straightens his back. The chair he's on is higher than the sofa, and he's looking down at me.

'Look,' he says, 'we're very lucky that no one was seriously hurt. Mr Crawford's clothing absorbed some of the impact, and the wound he sustained wasn't significant, fortunately for him. Lucky for you, he's not pressing charges.'

Jack's eyes widen with concern. 'Michael needed three stitches, you know. Just under his collarbone.'

'He grabbed me.'

'You were on his property,' Henderson counters.

'He was going to attack me.'

'Mr Crawford says he felt scared.'

'Scared of me?' I scoff. 'Bullshit. Have you seen the size of him?'

Henderson tips his head forward. 'You were holding a weapon.'

'It's a gardening tool.'

There's a brief silence.

'Well,' Henderson shrugs and slaps his hands on his thighs. 'It's not going any further. But what I will say is that this whole incident wouldn't have occurred if you hadn't been trespassing on his land and digging up his garden.'

'He's buried a body there.'

'Like I said, it's a dog. An Irish wolfhound called Seamus. Bloody great big thing, apparently. I can see why you might've thought it was a person.'

'I believe there's a person in that grave.'

Henderson inhales deeply through his nose. 'I would strongly encourage you to seek the assistance of a psychiatrist, Ms Northcott.'

'That's what I've been saying,' Jack offers.

'I don't need a psychiatrist,' I reply immediately.

'With respect, Ms Northcott, perhaps you're not the best person to judge that.' The detective's eyebrows arch, and I want to punch his smug face.

'Anyway, what do *you* know about Emily?' I demand. 'You investigated the allegations of stalking she made against Michael's ex-partner, Alison, years ago, didn't you? And while we are on the subject, have you investigated Alison?'

Henderson looks shocked. But it passes quickly, and he regains his authority. 'I'm the one asking questions today, okay? We could do all this at the station, of course, under caution, if you'd prefer?'

'Maybe we should,' I say. 'Then you'd have to put your relationship with Emily down on record!'

Henderson stares at me. His right eye twitches.

'That won't be necessary, Paul,' Jack says soothingly. He's irritatingly relaxed, given what's happened. And since when were they on first-name terms?

'What about the spade?' I cry. 'The blood on the shed floor? Surely that's evidence…'

'Oh, that.' Henderson runs a hand through his cropped black hair, flecked with silver. 'Yes, it's evidence that he buried his dog with that spade and hasn't used it since. The dog was hit by a car, apparently, and died from its wounds. Michael kept it in the shed to stop his daughter seeing it before he buried it. It bled in there.'

'That's what he told you?' I can hear the scepticism in my own voice.

'We have no reason to question his account.'

'Have you taken a sample of the blood?'

Henderson sighs, again, and I can tell he just wants to leave. I've rattled him with the mention of his contact with Emily. 'Yes, we have,' he says wearily. 'But I fully expect our test to confirm that it belongs to Seamus, not to Mrs Crawford.'

'You'll see,' I respond, though I'm not sure what I mean by it.

Henderson gets up. He hasn't taken his jacket off.

'I'm telling you now, Ms Northcott, not to set foot on the Crawfords' property again,' he says, glancing at Jack, as if to elicit his support in keeping me under control. 'And please see a psychiatrist while you still have a choice about it.'

CHAPTER FORTY-FOUR

Tuesday, 12 October

'You should've seen the way both of them were looking at me,' I say. 'Like I was some sort of crazy woman!'

Cathy laughs and shakes her head, her mane of white hair bouncing around her shoulders. 'I remember Seamus,' she says, raising her teacup to her lips. 'Huge creature, he was. Always very friendly, though. Wouldn't hurt a fly. Shame what happened to him, poor thing.'

'A car hit him, didn't it?'

Cathy tilts her head down and peers at me over the rim of the cup. 'If you believe that…'

'Hang on.' I feel my forehead furrowing. 'You're saying—'

'Mm-hm.' She gives a single, deep nod.

'Michael…'

'Yes.'

'Murdered the dog?'

Her ice-blue eyes widen. 'The day he died, I remember hearing a lot of screaming and shouting. I looked out and saw Michael in the garden. Seamus was on the ground in front of him, his stomach slashed open. A car wouldn't have done that, would it?'

I pause. It's horrible, but I try to picture the impact and the injuries it would cause to a dog. 'I don't really know,' I reply. 'No, I suppose not.'

'A man with a garden spade, on the other hand…'

Suddenly, I can see it. Seamus lying on his back, Michael wielding the tool above him, unemotional. 'Oh God. You're right, that makes a lot more sense.'

'You see?'

'But why would he do that? Apart from the fact that he's probably a psychopath, and they kill animals for fun, don't they? To get a kick out of it or something.' I'm sure I've read that somewhere.

'If you say so, dear. As to why he killed Seamus, though, it's simple. Control. It's what he does to them. He knew Emily and Thea loved that dog. They made him angry somehow, about goodness-knows-what, anything, and that was his revenge.'

'Are you sure?'

'Sure as I know how to make a cake.'

I study the chocolate marble cake she's made (which is delicious) on the plate in front of me. I imagine the cruelty and callousness that it would take to kill an affectionate, loyal family dog with a spade. The kind of monster you'd have to be to do such a terrible thing. There's a brief silence while I ponder this, and Cathy tops up my tea. I watch the leaves catch in the strainer, lost in thought.

'You know there's been a new sighting of them reported,' I say eventually.

'Really? Where?'

'The Isle of Wight. A place called Sandown. Woman in her thirties, with a child, walking by the beach. Someone sent a message to the *Find Emily and Thea* page about it this morning.'

'Do you think it's them?'

I blow out my cheeks and shrug. 'I have no idea. Maybe. Probably not.' It wouldn't be the first false alarm since they went missing. 'I still think Michael killed her,' I add, though I'm less sure why I believe that, now, given that the grave and blood turned out to belong to a dog.

'Oh, I don't doubt it.' Cathy's response is instant.

'What do you reckon he's done with her body, then?' I ask.

Cathy considers this. 'You say that Seamus's skeleton was at the top of the grave?'

'Yes, about a foot below the surface. Wait, what do you mean, "top"?'

'Do you remember the Balkans War in the early nineties?' she asks cryptically.

I think back. I can recall news footage of night-time explosions, families of refugees, ethnic cleansing. All of it happening just on the other side of Italy. 'Not really. I remember some stuff, but I was, like, a kid when it started. Why? What's that got to do with Emily?'

'One of the tactics they used to hide the human graves of genocide victims was to put an animal over the top of the corpses.' Cathy's completely matter-of-fact as she delivers this grisly history lesson, as if she's talking about compost on a vegetable patch. 'Sniffer dogs and inspection teams would come along, pick up a scent, they'd dig down a bit, find a dead farm animal – a horse or a donkey or something – think it was a false alarm and move on without finding the bodies beneath.'

'The bodies beneath,' I repeat. It sounds like a book title. A true-crime domestic horror story. 'So, Emily could be buried underneath Seamus? That's why the plot looked freshly dug, even though Seamus died, what – two years ago?'

'Something like that,' replies Cathy. I can tell she has no idea about the timing of this event. 'Either her body is below the dog,' she continues, 'or it's in the basement. Perhaps that's where he's keeping little Thea.'

'The basement,' I repeat. That's exactly what I'd imagined yesterday.

'These houses were built between the wars,' Cathy explains. 'They made the basements like bomb shelters! You could hide anything down there. Or anyone. Scream as loud as you like, no one could hear you.'

'Oh my god.' I think back to the one visit I made to our basement. The walls were rock-solid, and there was no way in or out except the door at the top of the stairs. Michael's *man-cave* – as Emily used to call it – would be just the same. And its keypad entry system would make it the perfect prison. I berate myself for not giving it enough attention; I was too focused on the garden.

Then I remember that I have the keys to their home. I haven't confessed my thievery to Cathy, even though I'm sure she would've lent them to me anyway. I feel a pang of guilt about that minor betrayal of her trust. But I'm not going to give the keys back to her just yet.

Because I know what I need to do next.

'What comes to mind, now, when you think of that moment? Take your time.' Laurence is calm and relaxed, and it's just what I need to be able to talk about what happened yesterday.

'I… I just felt scared, but I knew I had to defend myself.'

'Sorry to interrupt you for a second there, Freya,' he says. 'But I notice that you've moved your hands up to your chest, almost like you're physically protecting yourself.'

I glance down at my front. He's right, I've crossed my forearms, fists closed, like I'm ready to fight again. 'Oh – I didn't even realise I'd done that. It must've just been automatic. A lot like… you know.'

'When you stabbed Michael?' He leans forward slightly.

'Mm.'

'You mean, you were just acting on instinct?'

'Yeah. Almost as though I didn't have to think about it. Like my body knew that there was this threat, and it just went into action. I don't feel that bad about it, to be honest. He shouldn't have grabbed me when I was holding the secateurs. And I still think he's murdered Emily. You know what?' I give a short laugh. 'I don't regret it. Can I say that?'

'However you feel about it, Freya, those are real feelings.'

That's the therapist's way of saying *yes, you can say that.*

'And I'd do it again if I had to,' I add. 'If a guy who deserved it attacked me, or tried to kill me, I wouldn't hesitate. Now I know I can react like that.'

'And how does *that* possibility make you feel?' he asks.

I think about it for a moment. 'Kind of... strong,' I reply. 'But it's also a bit, you know, scary. To think I'd be capable of that.'

Laurence nods. 'It might seem frightening, but the body has a very reliable way of reacting to keep itself safe. We've evolved over a couple of million years to do that. And it sounds strange, but fear is an incredible catalyst for... well, violence, for want of a better word.'

'Our fight-or-flight system?'

'Right.'

'Only sometimes,' I say, 'it goes a bit out of control, doesn't it? Like when I've been feeling so anxious over the past few months, every little thing setting me off. Thinking someone was coming into the house, or moving my laptop, when it was probably just me, but I couldn't remember doing it.'

'Anxiety can definitely distract us enough not to remember small things we've done, almost on autopilot.'

'Or when,' I continue, 'when I thought that guy in my road had taken my baby, years ago. My mind had distorted the reality, probably due to anxiety. I misinterpreted the facts, and my body was reacting as if there was danger, pushing my anxiety even higher. Like a cycle. A vicious circle or whatever.'

'Exactly.' Laurence seems pleased, and he smiles briefly at me before jotting a note. Despite what we're talking about, a fantasy flashes into my head about me and him. I realise it's been quite a while since Jack and I have been intimate together. Maybe my body is trying to tell me something else, too.

There's a brief silence. 'It's really kind of you to carry on seeing me,' I say.

'Oh.' He blushes. I've caught him off-guard, and he can't find one of his therapist's phrases to hide behind. He looks away and, while he writes a couple more notes, I think about what a dick Jack has been, stopping paying for the therapy. What did he have against Laurence? Could it have been the way I talked about our sessions? Did the idea of me spending so much time alone with another man make him jealous? Was it pure, unreconstructed male vanity on Jack's part?

My therapist and I talk some more about how I've been feeling, and about my discovery that Jack had tried to put pills in my food to sedate me. Laurence is deeply concerned, but I say that I'm not accepting any more food or drink from him, now. I assure him that I'll deal with it properly once I've followed up my next lead on Emily and Thea: trying to corroborate the sighting of them on the Isle of Wight.

Laurence expresses a balance of caution and reassurance, emphasising the need for me to prioritise my own well-being to help my recovery, and not to let Emily and Thea's disappearance have a negative impact on that. As we sit there talking, I think how wonderful it is just to have someone listen to me.

I know my mum would be there for me if I called her, of course, but she has enough on her plate with her health. I don't want to stress her out, leaving her alone in her home, hundreds of miles away, worrying about me.

My best friend Bea doesn't have enough brain space, now, with her new baby; every time I try to speak to her about what I'm going through, there's a baby-related interruption of one

kind or another. I can't begrudge her that; I'm sure I'd be just as
devoted to my own child.

And Cathy's lovely, but she does get a bit confused. Plus, I
don't know her *that* well, and I wouldn't share my most private
thoughts with her. I glance up at my therapist and think how
lucky I am to have him.

I only wish I could say the same about my fiancé.

Michael's departure later that afternoon is signalled to me by the
doorbell camera. He sets off the motion sensor by going to his car,
which is right outside our house. I'd been checking, periodically,
anyway, for the chance to put the first part of my plan into action.

Once the noise of his car engine dies away, I slip out with my
water bottle, a kitchen cloth and the keys. I let myself in through
his front door, shut it behind me and make my way down the
dingy hallway to the keypad outside his basement.

'Thea?' I call out. 'Emily?'

I put my ear to the door and wait, but there's no reply. I repeat
their names, louder, just in case. But, even as I shout, Cathy's
words come to mind: *scream as loud as you like, no one could hear
you.* I switch on Jack's headtorch and shine the beam onto the
keypad, just in case I can see which buttons Michael has been
pressing, but I can't make out any difference between them. So,
it's time for the next step.

I give the bottle a good shake to make sure that the spoonful
of washing powder I've just dropped into it is properly dissolved.
Then I unscrew the top of the bottle and blot some of the foamy
solution (not too much) onto a kitchen cloth. Carefully, I wipe
it over the keypad, angling the light at it to make sure I've coated
each digit. I watch the moisture gradually evaporate, leaving
the surface dry and clear. Then, just as swiftly and quietly as I
entered, I'm gone.

No curtains twitch as I leave and cover the dozen or so steps back home.

Safely back in my own hallway, I breathe a sigh of relief.

For now, at least, I've got away with it.

CHAPTER FORTY-FIVE

Wednesday, 13 October

Just after eleven a.m. the next day, I'm notified by my app as the delivery guy comes up the path. I'm already walking towards the door as the small cardboard packet drops through the letterbox, thudding onto the mat below. I've ripped open the tab and extracted my new tool before I've even got back to the kitchen.

The four-inch-long cylinder of hard black plastic looks much the same as a regular pocket torch. Yet, if this does what it's supposed to, according to the Reddit thread I found (the same one that mentioned the washing powder solution) then it could be as good as having the key to Michael's basement. Because this is a UV blacklight. It can let you see things that would otherwise be invisible. And it might just save Thea's life, or Emily's – if either of them is still… no, I don't want to think about that.

I insert the battery into the top and click it on. A purplish-blue beam, clear and strong, hits the table.

I'm good to go.

It's well past lunchtime when Michael finally leaves the house for the first time today, striding briskly down the road on his long legs until he's out of sight. But it could've been worse; if he'd gone out before the torch arrived, I'd have needed to wait until he left again, which might not have been until tomorrow.

I've been watching for hours, keenly aware of the low thrum of anxiety in my body, anticipating what I might find in his cellar.

Who I might find.

As I walk down our front path, remembering the first day we arrived and met the Crawfords, I happen to glance up at the house opposite. The middle-aged woman who lives there is at the window, looking right at me. I freeze.

For a moment, neither of us moves, our eyes locked on one another. Can I trust her? Is she an ally? I can't say for sure; I've never exchanged anything more than a *hello* with her in six months of living here. I have no idea whether she's a friend of Emily, or Michael, neither, or both. All I know is that this can't wait any longer.

Whatever's in that basement, I'm going to find out right now.

Her gaze follows me as I reach the pavement, turn into the Crawfords' front yard and march up to their front door. It takes me a moment longer to insert the key into the lock this time, because my hands are already shaking.

I don't look round to see if I'm still being observed, though I assume I am. I want my actions to seem natural, as if I'm meant to be there. As if Michael's totally fine with it. By the time I've got inside and shut the door behind me, my heart is already pumping like it's the bass beat of a techno track.

Approaching the keypad, I take a deep breath. I hope my plan has worked. I take out the UV light and click it on. As I direct the purple beam at the numbers, I let out an involuntary gasp.

Five of the digits are lit up, still coated with my washing powder mix. The other five are not. And one of them is '3', the number which I know Michael was about to press, the time I talked my way in here and spoke to him. This is it, then: 0, 2, 3, 7 and 8. These are the five numbers which make up the entry code. The only problem is, other than starting with 3, I don't know which order they go in.

I know from looking this up that each number can only be used once, which means there are twenty-four possible combinations of the remaining four digits. Or permutations, as they're apparently called, when the order matters – which it does.

I begin trying them in turn: *3-0-2-7-8*, *3-0-2-8-7*, *3-0-7-2-8*…

I'm a dozen numbers in, and I've had no luck so far. I can feel my hands getting clammy as I press the buttons again and again. Then I see there's an 'Enter' button at the bottom right. Shit. Was I supposed to press that after each attempt? I don't know.

I feel the panic rise as I realise I need to start again.

3-0-2-7-8-Enter. Nothing.

3-0-2-8-7-Enter. Nope, not that either.

I suddenly wonder if the woman watching has called Michael, or whether he's just taken a ten-minute trip out for milk and could return anytime. My pulse starts to pound in my ears and a tightness creeps behind my eyes. What if he comes back? I've forgotten to bring the secateurs. Oh God. If he finds me here, how will I defend myself, if he?—

I've lost count. Fuck. My concentration wandered off and now I'm not sure where I got to: *3-2-7-0-8*, I think… I know I need to hurry, and that pressure makes the anxiety twice as bad.

Okay, I tell myself, *stay calm. Breathe normally. You're all right. You can do this.* I imagine my therapist, telling me I can cope. I picture Emily's and Thea's faces. And I get back to work.

I'm focused, now, my fingers moving more quickly over the buttons as I fight to keep the nerves at bay.

3-7-8-0-2-Enter. Silence.

3-7-8-2-0-Enter.

Click.

I stare at the keypad in disbelief for a moment, then I reach out and grip the handle. I snatch the door open, but it's heavy, and I have to lean back and drive through my legs to open it.

Inside, the basement is completely dark.

'Emily!' I yell. 'Thea! Is anyone here?'

My voice echoes in the enclosed space, but I can't hear anything beyond a low, whirring, mechanical noise. I fumble around on the wall beside me until I find the light switch and flick it on.

Unpainted plasterwork is illuminated around me. I'm at the top of a set of metal stairs that lead down into the basement. The air is cold and stale, and there's a slight smell of something… human. Sweat, maybe. Then a whiff of food: old stuff that's going off, and the sour tang of booze. A tiny taste of bile comes to the back of my throat, and I swallow it back down.

This could be the moment I find the truth.

Slowly, cautiously, I begin my descent. Each footstep clangs against the ironwork, the harsh sounds reverberating off the walls. At about the halfway point, I hear the door click shut behind me. I wipe sweaty palms on my jeans and keep going down.

I can see the extent of the so-called man-cave before I reach the bottom. It's what I'd imagine the back of a computer shop to look like – not that I've even been in one.

There are machines everywhere. I see shelf upon shelf of black boxes in a tall metal tower, their lights winking green and yellow behind a glass door. There are stacks of old computers, with panels removed, wires and circuit boards sticking out. The floor is littered with beer cans and bottles, pizza boxes and other food packaging.

On one side is a workbench with tools – I spot screwdrivers and a claw hammer – and on the far side, furthest from the door, is a large desk with two keyboards and three monitors. It's covered in documents, and there are more pinned to the wall behind it, though I'm too far away to tell what any of them are. The only thing I can make out on the desk is a little red shoe. It must be the one I found in the garden; Michael's discovered it and brought it in.

'Hello?' I say. But there's no response. Wherever Emily and Thea are, they're not here.

I glance up and behind me at the door, then walk over to the desk. In contrast to the chaos of the floor, everything here is neatly organised. But there's so much information, it's hard to know where to begin. Next to the shoe, I see the gold ring, also no doubt retrieved from the garden.

The shoe and ring are proof that Michael's hiding something, but I need to know what. I need information. My eyes roam over the papers until I alight on one whose form I recognise. It's a bank statement.

The account is in Michael's name, but amid the reams of paper he's printed out – going back almost a year, by the look of it – certain transactions have been highlighted. I leaf through them: chemist, supermarket, some online shopping. There's a yoga subscription, and a payment to a hair salon which is way too much to be a man's haircut. Then it dawns on me. He's highlighted Emily's transactions. The most recent one I can see is Sunday, the eleventh of July. The day before she went missing.

Towards the back of the desk is another, similarly recognisable set of papers: mobile phone records. The name on the account, again, is Michael's. But the number – I check by pulling out my phone and going into the contacts list – is Emily's. As with the bank transactions, he's gone through, picking out a few numbers in fluorescent yellow marker pen. Numbers that repeat. Some of them seem familiar, but I don't have time to check right now. I'll photograph them and do that later. Again, the last call is the eleventh of July.

It's clear what he's been doing: he's been monitoring her. There's another stack of printouts that appear to be social media posts and messages about her, lists of friends and connections. I even see a few maps, probably showing where she's been. Jesus. What a disgusting creep.

I've read about this, heard it from the mouths of women who've experienced it themselves, and now I'm seeing the proof of my friend having been through it too. It's a form of domestic abuse: tracking and surveillance, with the aim of controlling.

I briefly think of Jack and the pills in my food. It all makes me sick with rage, these fucking men who think they can make us their little puppets, too terrified ever to step out of line or do what *we* want.

My anxiety mutates into anger, and I know I have to get evidence of this. It's the only way that Michael will be brought to justice. As I switch my phone to the camera app, I see there's no signal. I must be too far below ground… The realisation that I can't contact anyone sends a jolt of fear through my belly. I try to suppress it by concentrating on what I need to photograph first.

Then something familiar catches my eye: johnsmith12643. I grab the stapled sheaf of papers. There's a load of technical stuff on there, metadata or whatever, but I can pick out a date and time. And I recognise them.

It's when he sent me his most recent threatening message, the one about me being alone in my house on Sunningdale Road. Then there's the IP address, along with a bunch of location data. I flip the page and see a map. But this isn't Iceland, where Michael said johnsmith12643 was based, or wanted the internet to think he was based.

It's a place called Sandown.

The seaside town on the Isle of Wight where the most recent supposed sighting of Emily and Thea occurred.

Is this where the man calling himself John Smith really is? Is it possible that Emily and Thea aren't dead and that he's kidnapped them?

I can't work it out yet, but I know I need to capture this stuff on camera. I begin with the johnsmith12643 document. I focus, tap, then check the image is clear. Turn over and repeat. And again. Got it. Then I move on to the phone records.

I'm so absorbed that I'm not aware of anything else around me until I hear a soft click come from the top of the stairs. I spin around and look up. A pair of shoes come into view, followed by long legs, descending the stairs with slow, heavy steps.

Michael's home.

CHAPTER FORTY-SIX

Wednesday, 13 October

I realise there's no escape. There are no other doors in or out, and Michael's tall frame is blocking the only exit. I'm trapped. I feel my limbs tensing, my fight-or-flight system kicking in and taking over. And flight isn't an option.

I search frantically for something I can use to protect myself. Because I know what's surely coming, now. Then I spot the workbench and lunge towards it, grabbing the claw hammer and backing away towards the desk as Michael's head comes into view.

He's deliberately taken his time coming down the stairs, knowing that I have nowhere to go. He hasn't said a word yet, either, almost as if he expected to find me here. When our eyes finally meet, his gaze is cold and detached. He shakes his head in the way that people do when they're disappointed, when their expectations of being let down are met.

'You just won't listen, will you?' he says with a little smirk.

'Let me leave,' I say calmly, though I can hear a tremor in my voice.

'You've broken into my house.' He takes the final step, surveys the room. 'How the fuck did you get down here, anyway?'

'I'm serious, Michael.' I raise the claw hammer. 'Move aside. Or I'll use this.'

Michael traces his fingertips over his right collarbone, where I stabbed him. Rolls his shoulder. 'Put it down,' he says.

I stand firm. 'No.'

'I said put it down!' he roars, drawing himself up. For a moment, I'm stunned by the sudden burst of aggression, at the way he seems to grow even bigger. I picture Emily and Thea, both terrified of this side of him, and whether they might trigger such an explosion at any moment.

I swallow, my mouth bone dry. My legs are trembling, but I won't be cowed into submission. I keep my grip on the hammer tight. It feels heavy in my hand.

'Listen to me, Michael. I know what all this is.' I gesture vaguely behind me. 'You've been monitoring and controlling Emily for months, maybe years. What you need to do now is confess what you did to her, and to Thea, and where their bodies are. Because I'm not going to stop looking for them.'

For a second, I think his simmering rage is going to erupt at me again. But then he relaxes slightly, blinks a few times as he processes what I've said.

'You're out of your mind,' he snorts. 'You're as barking mad as that senile old woman next door.'

'Now's the time,' I state. 'No more bullshit, no more hiding. Where are they?'

He doesn't reply. Instead, he takes a step towards me. I draw the hammer back, ready to strike. He looks over my shoulder at the documents I've been going through. For a moment, the basement is completely silent, except for the low buzz of machines around us. Then he launches himself at me.

I barely have time to react. I swing the hammer just as his arm shoots out forward and blocks it. He grabs the tool and plucks it from my grip like he's taking a toy from a child.

I'm breathing hard, my gaze flicking from his emotionless face to the claw hammer and back. Is he going to kill me? I feel myself shrinking slightly, my body closing in on itself out of self-preservation. My phone has no signal, and no one will hear me if I scream for help. I need to buy some time.

'The woman across the street knows I'm here,' I blurt. 'She saw me come in. If I don't come out again, she'll call the police.' In truth, I have no idea if she'll do that, or if she literally doesn't care and has gone back to watching daytime TV.

Michael looks at me, his eyes narrowing and jaw clenching. He's deciding whether or not to kill me. His hand flexes on the handle of the hammer. Then I remember what's in my pocket. My fingers creep inside and curl around the handle of the UV flashlight. He hesitates, weighing his chances of getting away with it. And that's when I strike.

In a single movement, I draw the torch from my pocket and thrust it up and forwards. I know I have one chance to get this right.

He tenses and begins to pull his arm back. But he's too late. The end of the barrel connects with his Adam's apple, crunching against the cartilage. He emits a deep choking sound as the hammer falls from his grip, its steel head smacking against the floor.

'Bitch,' he gasps as both hands go to his throat and he stumbles to his knees, catching himself on the ground with one hand and doubling over.

I've incapacitated him for a moment, and now I need to get the hell out of here before he regains his strength. For a second, I look at all the documents, the proof of his coercion, which he will have the chance to destroy. But if I don't escape right now, I might not get another opportunity.

I step around him and make for the stairs, just as he pushes himself up on one arm, the other hand still clutching his neck. I hear him wheeze as I reach the bottom step.

'I didn't… kill them,' he whispers as I mount the stairs two at a time. 'I'm trying t-to find them.'

*

It takes a while before my heart and lungs stop feeling as though they're going to burst. I've double-locked and bolted every door and window in the house in case Michael comes for me. I have my secateurs at the ready. And the large glass of gin I've swallowed neat has helped, too. My mind is still racing, but I try to let my thoughts settle so I can make sense of what's happened.

Twice this week I've tried to get to the bottom of what Michael's hiding. Twice he's caught me, and twice I've ended up assaulting him (in self-defence). I felt so sure that he had murdered or imprisoned his wife and daughter that I scarcely considered any other possibilities.

The documents in the basement seem to be irrefutable proof of his abuse of Emily. Not necessarily physical violence – I never saw any evidence of that – but abuse, all the same: control through monitoring of her activities. And yet, there was something in his admission as I fled that's niggling at me.

Have I got it wrong?

I think back to the time, eight years ago, when severe anxiety and life trauma led me to believe that the couple opposite me had stolen my baby; a baby that didn't even exist. Has the combination of my miscarriage and Emily's disappearance done a similar thing to me here? It's hard to separate out the facts from my interpretation of them. But I try listing what I know:

One, Emily and Thea disappeared on the twelfth of July. Two, prior to then, Michael had some level of control over their lives – financially, if nothing else. Three, unless Cathy's right about her Balkan-grave theory (and I'm not sure she is), neither Emily's nor Thea's body is hidden in their house or garden. Four, both Detective Henderson and my own fiancé, Jack, knew Emily in some capacity. Five, the man who's been threatening me to stop looking for them appears to be located in the same small town on the Isle of Wight, a few hours from London, where Emily and Thea were supposedly seen.

It still doesn't make sense.

Did Emily run off to the island with the man with whom Cathy believed she was having an affair? Is that man Henderson? Or has she been taken there against her will, or by deception, perhaps even kidnapped? Could this John Smith guy be stalking her? Is she in danger?

I don't trust Michael or Henderson enough to share the information of the sighting at Sandown with them. And I can't message johnsmith12643 to let him know that I know, either, because that could put Emily and Thea at even greater risk. The more I consider it, the more I think there's only one thing I can do to help Emily and Thea, to make sure they're okay.

I have to go to the Isle of Wight myself and try to find them.

CHAPTER FORTY-SEVEN

Friday, 15 October

'I can't believe we're doing this,' says Jack, his eyes fixed on the
road ahead as we speed down the A3 towards Portsmouth for the
car ferry to the Isle of Wight. 'I still think we should be calling
the police.'

Beside him, in the passenger seat of our car – *his* car, as he
reminded me – I say nothing. We've been through this already,
twice – yesterday, when I told him what my plan was, and again,
this morning, before I reluctantly said that he could accompany
me. Not that I had much choice in the matter, because he
effectively gave me an ultimatum: let him come too, or he'd call
Henderson and tell him what I was doing. I argued back, swore
at him, but he maintained it was simply to protect me. In the
end, I gave in for Emily's and Thea's sake. He's still pushing the
idea of going to the authorities now, though.

'I mean, if it's really them,' he continues, 'if they're there at all,
and they're genuinely in danger from this John Smith guy, then
surely it's better for the cops to sort it out, right?'

'Nope, no way.' I swivel in my seat to face him. 'Have the
police done anything useful in the past three months, since Emily
and Thea vanished? Like, can you name one thing?'

'We don't know what they've been doing behind the scenes…'

'They haven't done anything.'

'You can't be sure—'

'Jack! It took me digging up a *skeleton* in the garden to get their attention. Before then, all they seemed to care about was stopping me from asking Michael too many difficult questions.'

'Well, he's probably very upset, and didn't want to be—'

'Bullshit! I saw the evidence that he was controlling her with my own eyes. Money, mobile phone, social media, all of it. Monitoring. It's abuse. Don't try and tell me he cares about her. I don't buy it.'

'You can't be certain why he had those documents. And you shouldn't have been in his house, anyway,' he adds.

I ignore his last comment. 'If Michael is trying to find Emily and Thea,' I return, 'then it's only because he wants to get them back under his control. Not because he loves them.'

Jack presses his lips together. He's gripping the steering wheel hard enough to turn his knuckles white. Why is he so tense?

'You okay?' I ask.

'Fine,' he replies.

Since last night, I've been wondering about his motives for coming with me on the trip. If Emily fled and Jack was somehow a factor in that because of their past, could I be putting her in danger by bringing him along to search for her? When I pressed him on why he wanted to come with me, he said it was for *my* safety, given everything that's happened.

Maybe that's true, and I'm just imagining that there's any more to it than that. And perhaps it would be useful to have a man there if I did come face to face with John Smith... Still, though, I've got my eye on Jack. If he's hiding something else from me, this trip might reveal it. Then I'll know for sure what's going on with him.

He also insisted that if we didn't find Emily and Thea, I stop looking for them and move on with my life. I don't want to do that, either; right now, it feels like my main – perhaps only – purpose in life. But a tiny part of me wonders if, despite everything that's happened, Jack is right. My therapist has expressed a similar view – albeit in much more supportive terms – so I should probably consider it.

Next time Laurence and I speak, I'm sure I'll have lots to tell him. I called him yesterday evening to cancel our appointment today and let him know what I was doing. He said he understood, that he knew how important this project was for me.

I continue to sit sideways in the car seat, studying Jack. Something gives me the feeling that this trip will be make or break for us. I think about his strange behaviour these past months. His denial of knowing Emily, before I found a photo of him among her stuff. His lack of support for me after the miscarriage. Going through my things and finding the report from my episode eight years ago. Trying to force his psychiatrist mate and a bunch of Xanax pills on me, to the point of putting them in my food. Attempting to stop me continuing my therapy with a selfish display of financial power. Worst of all, perhaps, his claims that he was acting in my best interests throughout. It's opened a fissure in our relationship, leaving me scared and suspicious.

I wonder if I'm doing the right thing, searching for Emily and Thea with a man I don't completely trust. And if I can't trust him, can we even be together? It's unbearably sad to think I might have made a mistake in committing to a future with him. To see my dream of starting a family with the man I love in our forever home evaporating.

My eyes are hot with tears, and I wipe them with my sleeve.

'You okay?' It's Jack's turn to ask the question, now.

And it's my turn to lie. 'Fine.'

We lapse into silence, and I'm grateful to be alone with my thoughts for a while. I rest my arm on the door and my gaze drifts to the wing mirror next to me, the road falling away behind us as we travel further from London. I wonder if Emily and Thea made the same journey, on this exact road. What it was that drove them away from their home, and what drew them to the Isle of Wight, if that's even where they are?...

I realise that I've been staring at the same vehicle in the mirror for a while. There's something familiar about it. I'm sure I saw it earlier – much earlier, like half an hour ago, when we were coming out of Weybridge. But I can't be sure. It's a grey car, normal size, generic style. Too far away for me to read the number plate. Probably nothing. All the same, though, it sets me on edge, and I feel my thoughts begin to speed up: the very first signs of the fight-or-flight response in my body.

Instinctively, my hand drops to the secateurs that I'm carrying in my pocket. Jack doesn't know I've brought them along, and I want to keep it that way; he'd surely tell me to leave them behind or get rid of them, given what happened with Michael in the garden on Monday.

'Have you seen that car behind us?' I ask.

'What?' Jack frowns and lifts his eyes to the rear-view mirror. 'Which car?'

'The grey one.' I turn in the seat, crane my neck and stare at the traffic behind us until I locate it. 'Back there, in the middle lane.'

'Er… yeah, okay. You mean the Toyota?'

'I don't know,' I reply. 'Maybe. Is it grey?'

'Yup. What about it?'

'Do you think it's following us?'

'Following us?' Jack chuckles, glances sideways at me. 'Come on, Freya.'

'I'm serious.'

He shakes his head, returns his attention to the road. 'You're mad.'

CHAPTER FORTY-EIGHT

Saturday, 16 October

I'm beginning to wonder if Jack was right, and I *am*, in fact, mad. Not mad in the sense of seeing and hearing things that aren't there or believing stuff that isn't true. But mad in the sense of being hopelessly optimistic about the possibility of finding Emily and Thea here. Mad to think I can make a difference to their lives, whatever's happened to them.

Something about being outside of Weybridge and further away from London has thrown this into sharp relief. It's as if home was some kind of delusional bubble, the walls of our house a hot box that focused almost all my thoughts on my missing neighbours. Now that I'm miles away on an island, in the open air, with a sandy beach, salt breeze and lapping waves, I begin to see what all the men in my life might have meant when they warned me I was becoming obsessed. The awareness of that gives me a glimpse of what life could be like beyond this. For now, though, I've got a lead to follow. There's still work to be done.

Jack and I arrived here yesterday in the early afternoon. We checked in to our accommodation in a little chalet complex, facing the beautiful, sheer white cliffs, and immediately set out searching.

We walked along the beach for a couple of miles, before returning through the main streets of Sandown, stopping in pubs, cafés and shops to show Emily's and Thea's photographs to the staff. One or two people thought they looked familiar, but nobody was certain they'd seen them, and no one was able to offer any clues. As afternoon turned to evening, my motivation started to falter, but it lifted slightly when Jack suggested we get some fish and chips for dinner.

We sat on the sea wall, eating together and looking out towards France, somewhere past the horizon, as gulls wheeled and squawked overhead. It was still just about warm enough to be comfortable, and the night hadn't yet drawn in. When we finished our food, Jack put his arm around me and we sat like that for a while as dusk fell, until I regained my spirit and said we should carry on looking for Emily and Thea.

To my surprise, Jack agreed. He even proposed taking one more day here, extending our stay at the chalet place and moving our return ferry trip to Sunday evening. He reminded me that it was the first weekend away we'd had in well over six months. No wonder we'd both been so stressed out; alongside everything that's happened, we haven't had a holiday for almost a year. Even though we were here to look for our missing neighbours, he said, there was no shame in relaxing and having a bit of fun, too, if we could. I had to agree, although I felt guilty at the thought of us enjoying ourselves while Emily and Thea might still be in danger, so close to us that we could almost call out to them.

After another two hours of asking around last night – even messaging the woman here who claimed to have seen them – we still had nothing to show. I wanted to keep going, but Jack pointed out that everywhere was starting to close and, short of doing a police-style house to house at ten p.m., there wasn't much more we could do for now. Reluctantly, I abandoned the search for the day, and we headed back to get some sleep.

Our chalet had two single beds, which seemed more apt for me and Jack, given how close we've been lately, but Jack asked if I wanted to push them together. We did and, lying side by side, he held me as my restlessness started to recede. Before long, exhaustion had taken over my body, and I drifted off. The last thing I remember was thinking that there might be a chance for the two of us.

That all might not be lost.

I awoke this morning to the dawn light filtering through the curtains, and vague memories of bad dreams in which I was certain that someone was chasing me, but I couldn't see them. I only knew they were there, behind me. I couldn't remember any more about it than that nauseating feeling of dread, of needing to escape but being unable to run.

Today's search has been much the same as yesterday; fruitless inquiries of anyone and everyone we could think to ask in Sandown. *Have you seen this woman? She might've been with a little girl.* One or two people studied the picture for a minute, squinting and wrinkling their noses, as if there was something they recognised, but ultimately, no one could help us.

We spent long periods walking by the seafront, in hope of catching sight of Emily and Thea, but saw nothing. We went round in circles, looking for possible locations from which johnsmith12643 could be sending his threats, but there were only residential homes. We knocked on some doors, asking after John Smith as bemused occupants shook their heads. Perhaps we've got it wrong.

Perhaps I'm *mad*.

I'm trying not to lose hope, to stay positive. But I realise that this might be the end of it. If tomorrow is the same as today, then I'll have to face the possibility of going home empty-handed. If that happens, then maybe it's time I listened to Jack and Laurence and Henderson and Michael, who've all been telling me (in their own very different ways) to draw a line under it. To accept that Emily and Thea are missing, and that there's nothing I can do to bring them back.

But until that moment comes, and the ferry casts off from the island, while there's still a chance of finding them, I'm going to do everything I can to see it through to the end. And, if nothing else comes of this trip, then at least it seems to have brought Jack and I closer together than we've been for months.

That can't be a bad thing, can it?

CHAPTER FORTY-NINE

Sunday, 17 October

It's late afternoon on our third day here, and I can feel my anxiety building again as the deadline for our boat home approaches. We've only got another hour or so before we have to check out of our chalet and drive to the port. Jack has gone to pack up and get us some food for the journey, while I said I wanted to take another – perhaps final – walk along the beach, just in case. I can't quite get over the fact that this could be it. That after three months of searching, this is where I stop and leave Emily and Thea behind me. I wonder if I'll ever be able to forget them, so profound is the impact they've had on my life.

It's strange to think that I didn't even really know them that well. Perhaps it was because I saw my own future in Emily's present, that she had the life to which I aspired – marriage, child, gorgeous home – that I invested so much in finding out what had happened to her and Thea. Almost as though, if they could just disappear, the same thing might happen to me. That one day I could simply vanish, too. I wouldn't want anyone to forget about me, so I was determined not to forget about them. But maybe the time has come to move on.

I walk past the pier, where the woman said she'd seen them, towards the cliffs, knowing that my eventual return could mark the end of my search. I turn and let my gaze roam over the beach and into the distance as the waves roll in and wash over the sand.

There aren't many people here. A family or two, some older folk helping each other along, a scattering of dog walkers. And, about a hundred yards away, a woman, strolling in my direction. She's more or less my age and has a little girl beside her. Is it possible?…

I almost stumble as I begin moving towards them, oblivious to the uneven sand under my feet.

With each step forward she comes a little more into focus. The girl has the hood of an anorak up, but she looks to be about Thea's size. Soon, I'm close enough to pick out some features.

And my heart begins to sink. The hair is shorter and darker. I see a pair of glasses, which Emily never wore. My approach slows, and I'm ready to chalk it up as a final false hope, one last failure.

Then the woman stops.

We're perhaps fifty yards apart, looking at one another. There's something in her stance that suggests recognition and, as I keep walking, despite the glasses and the hair, her features resolve into the face that's seared into my mind.

I break into a run, and cry at the top of my lungs, 'Emily!'

CHAPTER FIFTY

Sunday, 17 October

Freya shouldn't have come here. She should have stayed at home instead. Of course, I'm grateful to her, at some level, for leading me to you, Emily. I would have found you eventually, but she's certainly saved me some time and effort. There was no chance of me giving up. A passion like mine, you see, isn't extinguished easily. It kept burning long after your rejection of me, and your disappearance. I'm sure you would have realised that you couldn't get rid of me that easily. That I'd track you down, one way or another. You should've understood that leaving wouldn't be the end of it. This is the end of it, for both of you.

But you don't know that yet.

And neither does she.

CHAPTER FIFTY-ONE

'It was a lie from the beginning,' Emily says, stuffing her hands into her jacket pockets and hunching her shoulders against the stiff wind that's started to pick up.

We're walking slowly along the beach as the light begins to fade, the sun veiled by cloud behind us. I wait for her to elaborate.

'Thea isn't his.'

I stop for a moment. 'Michael isn't Thea's father?'

'No. But he thought he was, at least until about five months ago.'

There's so much I want to know, I'm not sure where to begin. Normally I'm good at coaxing a story out of people, but here – reunited with Emily after three months – it just feels too personal. In the end, I settle for a simple follow-up question. 'And you knew he wasn't?'

She turns to me, and I can see tears in her eyes. 'Yes.'

We walk on in silence for a few seconds before my curiosity grows too strong to resist. 'So, who is?'

Emily sighs. 'A man I met in a club. I was in a bad place. I'd drunk far too much, and I didn't know what was going on. He took me home in a cab and… well, I never agreed to anything.'

'He – you mean, he raped you?'

Beside me, Emily sniffs. She doesn't look up, but she's nodding. 'I was too frightened and ashamed to do anything, though. I didn't even know the guy's name. He'd gone by the morning.'

'You didn't call the police?'

She scoffs. 'As if they'd believe me! He said, she said. "How much had you had to drink, madam?"' She mimics a sceptical male voice that instantly reminds me of Henderson.

'I'm so sorry,' I say.

'I'd already met Michael at that event at work,' she goes on, 'and I knew he liked me. Once I realised I was pregnant, there was no way I could go through with an abortion. I couldn't live with myself if I'd done that. Even the thought of it would put me into floods of tears…' She presses the heels of her hands to her eyes and massages them.

'So, you got together with Michael, and…'

'Yeah.' She emits a sound that's somewhere between a laugh and a sob. Then, as if she's forgotten about Thea, her head jerks up and she scans the beach for a few seconds until she locates her daughter. She's paddling in the foam at the edge of the water, picking up shells.

'Thea! Don't go too far out, darling!' she calls.

'Did he believe the timings?' I ask.

'I was only a month pregnant when Michael and I first slept together. We didn't use protection. Believe it or not, he was actually too busy to come to the first scan with me, and by the time we had the next one, there was enough margin for error in the baby's size.' She shrugs. 'I got away with it.'

'But… why?'

'Simple, really,' she replies. 'I've got nothing. No family to run to. No money of my own. I hadn't been able to get a long-term job – not one I wanted, anyway. And I needed to look after my baby. That was the only thing in my mind. Michael's well off, and he seemed reliable.'

With hindsight, it's easy to say she made a bad decision. But I've got some sympathy for her, having experienced the first few weeks of a pregnancy. The strength of the emotions it produces.

The desire to protect and nurture this tiny life inside you. I realise that Emily doesn't know about my miscarriage, though, and now probably isn't the time to tell her. I don't want to make this about me.

'It sounds insane, I know,' she continues, 'but I think I did actually come to love Michael. He's very… predictable. He loved me too, in his own, kind of distant, way. And he gave me and Thea and nice life. We had everything we needed.'

I'm not sure how I feel about this. It's one of the greatest deceptions I've heard anybody commit against another person. I'm no fan of Michael's, but I wonder if he deserved that. I can see why he had no clue, though; Thea is like a perfect miniature of Emily, as if she's been cloned from her mother without the input of a man, at all.

'Until he found out?' I prompt.

'Mm.'

Thea is making a shape in shells on the sand. We stay out of her earshot, but I can see it's a heart. I feel a sudden pang of sadness for this little girl, brought into the world through a single act of violence, and raised as part of a gigantic lie.

'Does Thea know?' I ask.

Emily shakes her head. 'No,' she says softly.

'How did Michael find out?'

She stares out to sea in silence for a moment. I watch her, waiting for her to speak.

'The guilt was too much, in the end,' she replies eventually. 'It just got the better of me.'

For some reason, that old line comes into my mind: *three can keep a secret, if two of them are dead.* Or something like that. I don't share that with Emily. Instead, I say, 'You told him?'

But she doesn't answer me. 'That's when he changed,' she says. 'The temper, violent outbursts, breaking things. I was scared; Thea was too.'

I think of the incidents that Cathy told me she'd overheard. 'I'm so sorry, that's awful.'

'He started trying to control me,' she adds.

'Money, mobile phone, your movements,' I offer.

'How do you know?' She turns to me, genuine surprise on her face.

'Well, I've spent the past three months looking for you. I ran a whole campaign online.'

'I know.' Her voice is almost a whisper. 'I've been following the webpage.'

'So, that was just a part of it,' I explain. 'I was convinced Michael had done something to you. Christ, I believed he'd murdered you and buried you in the garden.'

She barks a laugh, but it dies quickly.

'It started when I found Thea's shoe and your ring out by the shed.'

'That's where they went!' she exclaims. 'Thea had been playing at the back, and we had to leave so quickly that there was no time to properly search for them.' She massages her left ring finger, as if it's injured. 'I suppose I didn't want it, anyway.'

'There was the plot of ground, like a grave, next to the fire pit. I was sure that—'

'You mean where Seamus is buried?'

'Yeah. I, er… I dug him up.'

She gasps.

'I thought it was you,' I add. 'I only saw his ribcage and maybe, like, one long leg bone. Then there was the spade, and the blood in the shed.'

'Michael killed him,' she says, shaking her head. 'Poor boy had been hit by a car outside our house. He was bleeding badly and in so much pain. Thea was screaming and crying… it was horrible. I didn't want Michael to do it, but it was Sunday, and the vet was closed. He insisted on putting Seamus out of his misery.'

I tell her about the phone call I overheard Michael making, the words that suggested he'd killed her: *you know what she was like... it had to be dealt with.* Emily says that he was probably just talking about work. He'd been delivering a long-term project to a demanding female client he hated; it was most likely a reference to her. Again, it's something I've misunderstood. I feel relieved, but also a bit embarrassed when I think of how certain I was in my conclusions.

'I wasn't the only one who thought Michael had done something to you,' I go on. 'Cathy was adamant that he'd murdered you.'

'Oh, Cathy,' says Emily wistfully. 'She was always kind to me, but she and Michael never did get on. Two strong personalities, I suppose.'

I tell her about how I broke into Michael's man-cave and found the evidence of his monitoring. How he'd caught me, and we'd come to blows over it. She listens, rapt, her mouth opening wider with each new part of the story.

'He'd love to find me,' she says when I've finished. 'Take me to a civil court for paternity fraud, maybe get some money from me. Not that I've got any.' She snorts, shakes her head. 'Or maybe he would actually try to kill me.'

I reckon now is a good time to tell her about the violent threats from John Smith.

Emily closes her eyes briefly, takes a breath. 'I owe you an apology.'

'What for?'

'I'm John Smith,' she says.

'Sorry?'

'It's me. I'm behind the account johnsmith12643.'

'Jesus, Emily! Those messages scared the shit out of me. Why?'

Her expression is pained. 'I worked out that you were running the online campaign. The first photo posted on it was one that you took of me and Thea. You're the only person, other than me, who

has that photo. I didn't want a massive campaign of people looking
for me. I wanted to escape. I wanted to get away from them.'

'Them?' Who's she talking about? The people looking for her,
or Michael and… someone else?

She doesn't give me an answer, though. 'But I guess trying to
frighten you off didn't work.'

'Wow. You know, I thought that because this John Smith troll
knew so much about me – my name, where I lived – that it must
be Michael. I even wondered if it could be Jack, at one point.'

'Jack?'

'Yes.' Now's the time to ask her. 'You knew him, didn't you,
Emily?'

She stops walking, looks right at me. 'What?'

'You knew Jack… back at university, was it?'

She looks confused. If she's acting, she's doing a bloody good
job of it. 'No. I'd never met him before you guys moved in. I swear.'

I study her, scrutinising the features of her face for any telltale
signs of lying. Any tics or twitches, any awkwardness. But there's
nothing. She looks absolutely genuine.

'But… I found a photo of him, with your personal stuff, up
in the loft,' I counter.

'You went through my stuff?' Her tone is half-outrage, half-
amusement.

'I thought there might be something up there, you know,
some evidence or whatever.'

She smiles. 'I appreciate the effort, Freya. But I have no idea
what photo you're talking about.'

'Really?'

'Really.'

I ponder this. I can't explain it. We keep walking in silence. The
light is dimming, and there are even fewer people on the beach
than when I spotted Emily and Thea quarter of an hour ago. I
glance up, past the sea wall, to the road. There are barely any cars

passing, which is probably why this one catches my eye. It's there, crawling along for a few seconds, before it speeds up and turns out of sight, away from the beach. It's exactly the same as the one which I thought was following us from Weybridge to the coast.

My hand drops to my pocket, seeking the reassurance of the secateurs, following their contours with my fingertips. Ready to protect myself. Could Michael have hired a car? Is it possible that he's hacked my email account, seen the ferry booking? But I could easily be wrong. It's only natural that I'd be feeling a bit paranoid, after everything that's been going on.

'Are you all right?' Emily asks.

I don't want to alarm her. 'Yeah. So, does anyone else know you're here?'

She hesitates. 'I did have some help finding us a safe place to stay. There's a shelter here for… for women. We can use different names, stay off the map. It's linked to the police.'

Immediately, I think of Henderson. Emily's 'fancy man', as Cathy used to say. Was Emily in a relationship with him? The man who used to visit her regularly at home when Michael was out. Has he set all this up for her, perhaps planning a future for them together – one that she no longer wants? Suddenly, his approach to the investigation makes sense. He didn't want anyone looking for Emily because he wanted her all to himself.

'Was it the detective, Paul Henderson, who helped you?'

Emily halts, and I see her gaze roam towards the water for a moment before she spots Thea. A mother's protective instinct. She nods, and when she looks back to me the tears are gone, but there's a new emotion in her face.

It's one I recognise very well.

Fear.

'You're scared,' I say.

She nods, quickly this time.

I reach out, take her hand. 'Tell me why.'

CHAPTER FIFTY-TWO

Sunday, 17 October

I'm still reeling from what Emily's told me. Not only the story of her convincing Michael for more than five years that Thea was his child. But also what she said before we parted company, about why she had to flee, about how Michael had discovered her secret. It's shaken me, made me feel scared for myself as much as for her. To think of the danger that I've been exposed to from someone I'm supposed to be able to trust.

I've texted Jack to say I'm on my way back to the chalet, and I'm ready to head home. I don't want him to think anything's amiss. I haven't told him about finding Emily. She's sworn me not to tell a soul, but instead to let her and Thea start again, perhaps here, perhaps somewhere else, once they've got some money to move. I hope Thea will be too young to remember all this turmoil, that it doesn't scar her for life.

As we go our separate ways – me up and off the beach, Emily and Thea continuing their route towards the cliffs – I can't help but think what a powerful documentary her experience would have made. I suggested it to her, of course; that we could tell her story together, and use it as a way to raise awareness and mobilise public support, to get justice for the abuse she suffered from different men. To show the lengths that women have to go to in order to deal with sexual violence and its consequences.

The human effects of a rape, and the explanation for one of the thousands of disappearances recorded every year in the UK.

But Emily said no. And, as much as it pains me, I have to respect her wishes. Am I simply being selfish, I wonder, seeing her tragedies as a way to revive my derailed film-making career? Was I thinking only of the drama and tragedy of the story, rather than the people at the centre of it? I recall the feeling when Emily went missing that she could be me, and I have to acknowledge that I might have overinvested in it, emotionally.

After all the effort I've put in to finding her, it's tough just to let it go. But that's what I need to do. I'm going to take the *Find Emily and Thea* page down as soon as we're home again, as Emily asked. No more prompts to friends, colleagues and random members of the public for information about her, messages to look out for the two of them posted on social media and shared widely. Understandably, she's still fearful of Michael's ability to find her, and what he might do. But, now, I know that's not the whole picture.

It isn't just Michael she's scared of.

As I reach the road beside the beach and kick the sand off my shoes, I'm already starting to think about the future. About moving on from my quest to find my missing neighbours, now that I've got some level of closure on their disappearance. I'm also wondering whether Jack and I can patch things up. It'll be difficult, though not impossible.

There's still that trust issue with him, mainly over the pills he was slipping me, which is going to be hard for me to get over. But we've grown closer in the past couple of days here, and that gives me a shred of hope, like the first shoot of a fragile plant breaking the surface in search of sunlight.

From where I am, it's only a few hundred yards across to the chalet. We'll grab our bags, jump in the car and head home. I start to allow my imagination to create some of the house renovations we'd been planning, maybe alongside a fresh documentary project, too. Getting out and doing more. Making friends in Weybridge. A new start in our not-so-new home.

I let out a sigh, not of contentment but of acceptance. I stop and look over my shoulder, to get one final glimpse of Emily and Thea, both small figures now. I see them make their way over the sand towards the base of the cliffs, where the beach ends and the waves seem to possess more power, crashing against the rocks and throwing their foamy spray into the wind.

I scan the beach in the other direction, back towards the pier and beyond. It's empty, now, the last locals and straggling holidaymakers having departed as the tide comes in and the light fades. The smell of wet seaweed carries on the breeze.

I can't say what instinct makes me turn back towards the cliffs. A desire not to let go, perhaps. Or maybe it's a sound that registers below my conscious awareness. Whatever the reason, my eyes are instantly drawn to the only moving object in the landscape, other than Emily, Thea and the sea.

A grey car.

I'm sure it's the one I saw earlier. It pulls off the road, struggles a short distance over the sand and halts abruptly. The door is thrown open, and a figure emerges. Dark and angular, its movements are unmistakably aggressive. And it's striding towards Emily and Thea.

I have a fleeting premonition, or perhaps it's déjà vu. Because once more I hear myself shouting her name.

And I'm running to her.

CHAPTER FIFTY-THREE

Sunday, 17 October

By the time I reach them, he has his hands around Emily's neck. I can see from the tension in his arms that he's squeezing hard. She's already gone silent. Thea is rooted to the spot, watching her mother being strangled.

'Stop, Laurence!' I yell. 'Let her go!'

Laurence's head snaps round, his eyes wild with rage, mouth twisted in an ugly sneer. His grip loosens a fraction, and Emily gives a short gasp, then makes a kind of choking sound. Her hands lift to his wrists, but she can't dislodge them. He's too strong.

'She's mine,' he growls at me. 'I'll deal with you once she's dead.'

As he renews the force of his attack on her, she stumbles, her legs crumpling, and he falls to the sand on top of her, his weight bearing down, smothering her.

'Mummy,' Thea whimpers.

Something snaps inside of me, and the decision is made. It won't be the first time I've done it. But the difference is that this is real. I haven't imagined anything. There are no non-existent babies or buried corpses motivating me to act. Just an obsessive, jealous man who wanted Emily all to himself but couldn't have her, and who's trying to kill her right here, right now.

Moments ago, she told me the story of how Laurence mistook the closeness of their psychologist-client relationship for something more. How he broke his confidentiality as a therapist by telling Michael that he wasn't Thea's dad, in a deliberate attempt to end their marriage. How he harassed and hounded her, not taking no for an answer, until he forced her to seek the help of Detective Paul Henderson and the police to escape her life in London. And I led him right here, keeping him informed of every detail in my search for her, believing he was the only one on my side.

Laurence is lying on top of Emily, now, grunting with physical exertion. She hasn't got much time. I know exactly what I have to do.

I pull the secateurs from my pocket, grip them in both hands, lift them over my head, and then bring them down into the centre of his back with all the power I can summon.

The razor-sharp blades go right into him, and I feel the impact as my hands connect with his body. He gives a rapid intake of breath as his spine stiffens and he releases Emily's neck.

I kneel down, yank the secateurs out and lift them once more, before driving them down hard into him a second time. His body contorts, right arm jerking in the sand, wrist bent at a bizarre angle. The hooked metal beak doesn't stick in him this time, and I continue gripping the very tool which Laurence encouraged me to buy for my new gardening hobby, months ago. I'm thinking clearly, my breath steady, my grasp on the secateurs firm.

Beneath him, Emily blinks as she takes a lungful of air, and our eyes meet for a moment. As I grab his shoulder and pull him away from her, she pushes him off and between us we manage to roll him onto his back. He makes a thin, bleating sound, like a wounded sheep, but his left arm is still flailing towards Emily, clawing at her. He grabs a handful of her jacket.

'I'll fucking kill you,' he murmurs to her. 'I swear. No one else can have you. No one. Understand?'

I kneel on his stomach, and he sucks in some air, then focuses on me. His expression is more shock than pain, and his eyes widen as I raise the secateurs overhead again. There's a moment where time seems to stop. Then I swing them down with my full strength, puncturing his chest. The blades are covered in blood, now, and my hands are smeared red.

Laurence bellows in agony and releases his grip on Emily. His breathing is heavy and hard, but he's still fighting. He makes a deep gurgling sound.

'You're dead, too, you mad bitch,' he hisses at me through gritted teeth. 'I'll find you.'

I stab him again, and again, each time harder than the last. Then I let go, the secateurs embedded in his chest, their handles sticking up and out of his clothing.

His eyes roll back in his head, and I can see the tension draining from his muscles, the life ebbing from his body. There's a dribble of blood at the side of his mouth. The tide is coming in fast, now, and has almost reached us.

Emily scrambles to her feet. 'Oh fuck,' she whispers. 'Jesus Christ.'

Only now do I realise my hands have started to shake. I get to my feet and look down at Laurence. He isn't moving. I raise my head and check down the beach. There's no one else on it, and we're sheltered here by the rocks, below the level of the road. No one has seen this.

'Hey!'

The urgency and volume of the man's voice behind me is so startling that I whip round even before the adrenalin has a chance to surge through me.

It's Jack.

'Freya!' he cries, running over from where he's left the car. 'What the fuck is going on?' His gaze drops from me to the body, then back up to Emily, and it takes him a second to recognise her. 'Emily? What are you?... Did you two?—'

'He was trying to kill me,' says Emily, her face streaked with tears. 'Freya saved my life.'

'Christ, you've stabbed him. He's not moving. Is he dead?' Jack drops into a kneel beside Laurence, dips his head and places his cheek next to Laurence's parted lips. 'Who is he?'

'He's my stalker.' Emily gulps back a sob. 'And he was my therapist.'

'Mine, too,' I add. 'This is Laurence.'

'What?' Jack glances up from me to her, astounded. Then he returns his attention to Laurence, puts two fingers to his neck. 'His pulse is incredibly weak,' he states after a few seconds. Jack sits up. 'If we can get him into a pub or a shop or something – maybe even the chalet place – they might have a defib, in case his heart stops. In the meantime, we can get a paramedic. Laurence,' he says, loud and clear, 'can you hear me?'

There's no response from the body on the sand.

'Right, I'll call 999,' says Jack, producing his phone.

'No,' I say.

'What?'

'Leave him.'

'But, I…' Jack blinks. Presumably he's remembering his medical oath. *Do no harm*, or whatever it is.

'Don't do it.'

'I'm sorry,' says Jack. 'I've got to call. The police will understand, they'll—'

'They won't,' I say.

'She's right,' Emily adds.

Jack hesitates, just a few seconds, still clutching his phone. And that brief delay is all it takes. I don't see it coming until it's too late.

I thought he was dead. I guess we all did. But he isn't.

Laurence grabs the secateurs, pulls them clean out of his chest with a roar of agony, winds his arm back and thrusts the blade at Jack.

I hear myself scream.

CHAPTER FIFTY-FOUR

Sunday, 17 October

The bloodied blades arc through the air in a flash.

At the sound of my scream, Jack turns slightly, shielding himself just enough for the secateurs to glance off his arm. He cries out, and I can see his jacket is torn where they've sliced through the material. But he seems to be okay.

He swivels, drops his knee onto Laurence's arm, pinning it to the sand. The tide has almost reached us now, a large wave breaking and falling just inches short of Laurence's head.

Kneeling over him, now, Jack switches from caring to containment mode. I know from his stories that he's dealt with his fair share of violent, volatile patients over his fifteen-year career as a doctor. Drug addicts who believe you're standing in the way of their fix; psychiatric patients who think you're trying to harm them; wounded gang members determined to get out of hospital before the police arrive.

Chest upright to keep his head safe, Jack puts his weight down on Laurence, and I can see the fight drop from the body of the man I used to call my therapist. That one swing of the secateurs was his last shot.

But it isn't the last swing of the secateurs.

Before I realise what's happening, Emily has stepped around and plucked the tool from Laurence's hand. Then, with a single, almighty movement, she hurls herself down at him, the blade burying itself deep in his chest. Instinctively, I recoil, stumble back a step. Jack stays exactly where he is, continuing to pin Laurence to the ground.

'Bastard!' cries Emily.

For a few seconds, there's just the echo of her voice coming off the cliffs. Then I tune into other sounds: waves breaking and being sucked back out, gulls screeching and calling to each other, wind whipping our hair and clothing.

Thea runs to her mother, who wraps her in a hug, shielding her from the sight of the body, although she's seen everything that just happened.

'Shh, sweetie, it's okay,' Emily whispers urgently to her. 'Don't be frightened. He won't hurt us now.'

Jack touches two fingers to Laurence's throat, waits. 'He's dead,' he announces.

'We killed him,' says Emily quietly.

'What now?' I ask.

Jack wipes his hands over his face, pulls at his hair. 'Christ.'

'We… we push his body into the sea,' Emily suggests. 'It'll wash out on the tide.'

'The tide's coming in,' I counter.

'When it goes back out, it'll take him with it,' says Emily.

'Or it'll leave him on the beach for someone to find tomorrow morning,' Jack says. 'With a bunch of stab wounds in him. Fuck!'

I tear myself away from looking at Laurence's corpse and scan the beach. In the distance, I can see a couple of dog walkers. They're half a mile off, maybe more, but ambling in our direction. It won't be long before they spot us. We've got to think of something.

And then, just like that, I see it in my mind. Miniature clips from the film of my imagination, starting from this moment and playing right to the ending.

'I've got an idea,' I say. 'Jack, go and get the car. Back it up as close as you can to here.'

He stares at me for a second.

'Do it now,' I tell him.

'Okay.' He clambers to his feet, casts a final glance at Laurence, and breaks into a run. I briefly watch him head towards the vehicle before I turn back to Emily.

'You and Thea should get out of here,' I say. 'We'll sort this out.'

'But I—'

'I'm serious. Take Thea, go.'

She steps towards me, wraps her wet fingers around mine. We've both literally got Laurence's blood on our hands. I feel it, slick, as she presses her palms to my skin.

'Thank you,' she says. There are neither smiles, nor tears. Just a defiant set of her jaw, and a determination in her eyes.

'Come on, darling,' she says, guiding Thea away from the body of the man who just tried to murder her. 'Let's go.'

I watch them walk quickly off the beach, towards the rocky path at the base of the cliffs. They're already melting into the dusk as the sound of our car rises behind me. The brake lights flare and then Jack gets out, the engine still running.

'Open the boot,' I tell him. 'Then come and help me lift.'

CHAPTER FIFTY-FIVE

Sunday, 17 October

Checking that no one's watching, I remove the secateurs from my pocket. Even though it's night, and we're as far as possible from the nearest electric light, I can still see the blood on their blades, dark and dry, now, against the smooth metal. I shiver at the memory of what happened on the beach, and how far away it already seems from this car ferry, like a nightmare from which I've just woken up.

The cold air up here on deck is like a slap in the face, reminding me that the bad dream isn't over, yet. The smell of diesel wafts up from the massive engines rumbling beneath us as we chug smoothly towards Portsmouth. My gaze travels over the balustrade and down to the water below. It's almost black except for the choppy swell of grey-white spume against the ferry's gigantic iron hull.

I drop the secateurs and watch them fall silently until they're absorbed into the churning mass of seawater. I picture them sinking deeper and deeper, fifty yards or more, towards the bed of The Solent. I've just read on my phone that this stretch of the English Channel covers about eight square miles. Perhaps a deep-sea diver searching for shipwrecks will find them a decade or two from now. I wonder what they'll make of them, and whether they'd think, even for a moment, that they might have been a murder weapon.

Jack puts his arms around my shoulder and pulls me in tight. I can feel his hand trembling. Now that the adrenalin of the beach has worn off, he's as terrified as me.

'What the hell are we doing?' he asks, although I know it's a rhetorical question.

I lay my hand over his. 'We've made our choice. And we have to keep going.'

There's a brief silence before Jack speaks. 'How the fuck did it come to this?'

'He was trying to kill her,' I reply, instinctively lowering my voice, although there's nobody to overhear us. 'He would've done it if I hadn't fought back. He stabbed you. And he'd have attacked me, too, probably killed me. We had to defend ourselves.'

Jack exhales hard. 'There's defending ourselves, and there's murder.'

'Well, if you want to be technical about it, Emily's the one who actually killed him.'

'We *all* killed him,' says Jack, turning his head to me. I can see his eyes are moist. 'If we'd just called for help…'

'Then we'd each be in prison for fifteen years. Probably more.'

Jack shakes his head. 'It was supposed to be a weekend away. A chance for us to reconnect, for me to help you finish off your project.'

'You could say we did that.'

'He's fucking *dead*, Freya.' He takes his arm away from me, plants his hands on the balustrade and leans forward. 'Dead.'

'I saved her life. Maybe Thea's, too.'

'I know,' he acknowledges.

'That's worth paying a price for.'

'The price of another life?'

'I'd rather he was dead than she was,' I respond. 'If I had to choose.'

'That's not—' He stops himself, screws his eyes shut. 'Christ, I could really do with a Xanax right now.'

I stare at him, recalling his breach of my trust. 'I don't think that's very funny, Jack.'

'What do you mean? It's not a joke. I'm shitting myself here,' he admits. 'And I need a pill to calm me down.'

'I'm shitting myself, too. But I don't appreciate you talking about Xanax when you were... look, I know you were putting them in my food, okay?'

'What?' His brow creases, and the concern is so complete, so instant, that I begin to doubt myself.

'The spag bol, the porridge, the risotto... you put Xanax in mine, didn't you?'

'No.'

'But I felt calmer after those meals, then I found five pills missing from the prescription box in the bathroom. And more were gone when I looked again, later.'

Jack opens his mouth, hesitates. I wait; if he can admit it, perhaps we can deal with it and begin to move on. But if not, then—

'I took the pills,' he says.

'You?'

'Yeah.' He hangs his head. 'I mean, I got them for you – I just wanted you to feel better. I could see what it was doing to you... the miscarriage, then Emily and Thea. I only wanted to help.'

'Okay. But then?...'

'I was so stressed. About you, us, about work, the house, everything. It got too much, so I started taking the Xanax.'

'Wow.' I've heard of this; the cliché of doctors self-medicating, becoming addicted. Jack had started sliding down that path.

'They worked, for a bit. But I'd only taken a few and I was already wanting more. I had to stop. I didn't like what they were doing to me.'

'So, you didn't ever put them in my food?'

'Never.'

'You swear?'

'On my life.'

I search his face, and I'm as sure as I can be that he's telling the truth. 'Why did I feel calmer on those days, then?' I say eventually.

'Anxiety can come and go,' he offers. 'Maybe that's all it was.'

'Hm.'

He might be right. Laurence said more or less the same thing to me a couple of times. Jesus, Laurence. A brief clip plays in my mind. The beach, his hands around Emily's neck. The sound the secateurs made as I embedded them between his shoulder blades.

'Well, my anxiety's definitely back now.'

'Tell me about it.'

I slip my arm around his waist, and he hugs me close. Although we're both quivering with fear and cold, his body is warm against mine, solid. I begin daring to think, again, that I can depend on this man. I'll know for sure in the next few days.

'She had a photo of you,' I say, almost by accident, voicing my thoughts.

'Who did?'

'Emily. In the attic.'

'No. Really?' His eyebrows arch. 'Why?'

'You tell me.'

'I don't have a clue.'

'When I asked her this evening, she said you'd never met before we moved in.'

'We hadn't.'

I pause, wondering if he'll elaborate, but he doesn't. And I have no more to offer. It's a mystery. I hope they're not hiding something from me. 'I'll show you when we get back,' I tell him.

'Okay. Maybe I'll know where it's from, and we'll figure it out.'

He sounds genuine.

'All right, fine,' I say. 'It's not the main thing we need to worry about at the moment, anyway.'

He nods silent agreement, because we both know what is.

The body in the boot of our car.

CHAPTER FIFTY-SIX

Sunday, 17 October

Half an hour later, we're back below deck, sitting side by side in our car as the ferry approaches the port. We've been crammed into the hold, surrounded by other cars, less than a foot separating us from the next vehicle. That feeling of being trapped would be enough to set off a panic attack on its own, never mind the fact that Laurence's corpse is just a few feet behind us, sealed in its temporary coffin.

We're both acutely aware of the body – it's all I can think about – but we don't dare even turn around in our seats; instead fixing our gazes rigidly ahead, as if a glance behind would somehow give us away. But the truth is that these other travellers – a family of five in their estate car to my left, the older couple in a sports car to my right – don't have the faintest idea how close they are to a dead man who, just a couple of hours ago, tried to murder a woman in front of her child. When I think of it like that, it sounds so far-fetched that if I wound down my window and told them, they probably wouldn't believe me.

I'm jolted out of my absurd daydream by a thud as the boat stops. The engines give a final growl before falling silent. Then there's a loud whirring sound as the ramp ahead begins to lower. Around us, people start their cars, the dim cargo hold suddenly filled with headlights, taillights and clouds of exhaust and steam.

There's an awful sense of anticipation to it, as though it's a race we need to win; otherwise we'll be screwed for the rest of our lives.

My heart is already palpitating, my palms clammy. Beside me, I can see perspiration on the side of Jack's forehead, the muscles at his temples flexing. Despite the force with which he's gripping the steering wheel, there's a visible tremor in his hands.

'Just relax.' I lay a shaking hand on his leg, which I realise isn't exactly reassuring.

'What if they search us?'

'They won't,' I reply firmly.

'How do you know?'

'Why would they search *us*? Why would they search anyone?' I shrug, affecting a casual tone. 'It's not an international ferry.'

The unloading of cars proceeds line by line, painfully slow, and we're made to wait as those beside us go first. I imagine for a moment that they'll send everyone off the boat except us, then the police will walk up the gangway, onto the ramp and towards us, having somehow discovered our crime. But I push the image away. They don't know.

No one else knows, except Emily and Thea.

Finally, a steward in a fluorescent yellow high-vis jacket beckons us towards him. Jack releases the handbrake and the car lurches forward before immediately stalling.

'Fuck,' he mumbles.

'It's okay.'

Jack restarts the car and pulls away this time, the high-vis man directing us towards the disembarkation ramp, as if there's anywhere else we might accidentally go instead. He gives a friendly wave as we drive past, and I feel myself relax slightly.

'Nearly there,' I whisper.

We clunk our way down the big ramp and off onto solid ground again. Jack follows the *EXIT* sign painted on the tarmac, and we loop around the outside of the terminal. There are a few lorries and a smattering of cars waiting to board our ferry back to the island. People standing beside their cars, some on their phones, others smoking. Business as usual.

No one knows.

My eyes are fixed on the main gate, which will lead us out to Portsmouth and from there to the A3, the road back to London. It should be quiet at this time of night. We just have to keep to the speed limit, and then—

The man steps out in front of us, his palm raised in a 'halt' signal. He's also in high-vis, a thick jacket whose reflective patches catch the floodlights overhead, and is carrying a clipboard. He waves us over to the side of the exit route.

'Oh, shit,' says Jack. 'No, no, no. Please, no.'

I feel my guts clench, a chill spreading through me. 'Stay calm,' I say.

'Calm? What if he?—'

Jack doesn't get to finish his question, because the man has already approached his window and bent down to our level. He taps the glass, and Jack lowers it.

'Good evening, sir,' says the steward. He's middle-aged, maybe fifty, with a jowly, weather-beaten face and silvery stubble. There's a burr to his accent. He has a name badge that reads: *Ian Copeland*. 'Madam.'

'Hello there,' replies Jack, his voice tight.

'Hi,' I say, forcing myself to look happy.

'What's the purpose of your trip today?' he asks, lifting his clipboard and resting it on the car door. As he clutches the side of it, I notice a thick gold wedding band on his left ring finger.

'We're going home,' I respond before Jack can say anything. I become aware that my leg is jiggling furiously, and I clamp my hand down on it to keep it still. 'We've been on holiday.'

'Lovely,' he says, marking something on the clipboard. 'Whereabouts?'

I hesitate; should I tell him exactly where we were? Will that enable someone to connect us to the crime scene down the line? But then I remember my last image of the place where we killed Laurence. The tide washing over it, removing our footprints and other traces.

'Sandown,' I say with a smile, although my heart is pounding and part of me just wants Jack to pull away and drive out of here as fast as he can. 'It was gorgeous,' I add. 'Really relaxing.'

'Oh, yes.' He gives a cheery grin. 'Beautiful little bay down there.'

'It is.'

He marks something else on the paper.

'Right, then,' he says, straightening up. It's over. I allow myself a deep breath, and Jack starts to wind the window up.

The man's hand comes through it. 'Hold on, there.'

Jack swallows hard, the sound impossibly loud. 'Sorry?'

'If I can just take a quick look in the boot, you can be on your way.'

'The boot?'

Oh, fuck.

'Yes,' he answers. 'Just pop it open for me so I can check inside, please.'

'Er… why do you need to do that?' I ask, politely, even as I'm starting to imagine the inside of a prison cell.

'Cigarettes,' he says, as if revealing a great secret to us.

'Really?' I'm playing for time here. Next to me, Jack is actually sweating now, and I'm sure the man will see it, even though the light's off inside the car.

'Yes, we've had real trouble with smuggling the last few months. People bringing them over from France, believe it or not.'

'Is that right?' I'm desperately trying to think of a way out of this, but I have no idea what to do, other than keeping him talking. 'Why… why are they doing that?'

'It's big business,' he explains, getting into his stride. 'Customs done a crackdown at the other docks, you see, where the French boats come in direct, so some of 'em are going via the Isle of Wight, now.'

'Goodness.'

'Anyway,' he says, motioning to the rear, 'if you can just open up and let me see, I'll confirm you haven't got none of them, then that's my paperwork done, and you good people can be on your way.'

Jack and I exchange a glance. We've covered Laurence's body with anything we could find – carrier bags, cagoules, a random plastic sheet Jack had from furniture packaging. But anyone with their eyes open could see there's something else, something large, underneath them. You'd probably smell it – *him* – as soon as the boot opened.

'Give me one minute,' I whisper to Jack, taking out my phone.

'Right, okay.' Jack opens his door slowly.

'Can't you pop it open from in there?' asks the man. 'You got a lever or something?'

'No, it's, um, broken,' says Jack. 'We've been having some trouble with it. Hang on.'

I'm furiously googling the office phone number, praying it'll work. My screen displays a landline number, and I dial it immediately. I turn my head, see Jack alongside the car. He's complaining about stiff legs and lots of hiking, and our new friend Ian says he knows what he means. We can't draw this out much longer.

'Hello, Wightlink ferries,' says the voice in my ear.

As I reply, I can see them in the wing mirror, discussing which key on the fob opens the boot, and I hear Ian say, 'Just try that one, sir.'

Jack is mumbling something, anything not to have to open it.

'Let me have a go,' Ian responds, a trace of impatience in his voice, now. He holds out his palm to Jack, demanding the keys.

But he's interrupted by a bleep and a crackle. His outstretched hand drops to his coat pocket. He pulls out a walkie-talkie and says: 'Go ahead.'

A tinny voice comes through the device, speaking quickly, but I can't make out the words.

Ian raises the walkie-talkie to his mouth. 'At this time? What does she want?'

The voice gives an unintelligible, muffled reply and there's another bleep.

'You'll have to excuse me,' Ian tells Jack, 'my wife's called. Apparently it's urgent, but knowing her, it won't be. Probably something wrong with her mobile if she's ringing the office.' He sighs theatrically. 'Always some drama or other with women. Am I right, sir?'

'Yeah,' replies Jack with a dry laugh. 'Look, er, we need to be getting back. I've got an early shift tomorrow at the hospital where I work, can we just?…'

'Yeah, all right, on you go, then.' He waves us off as he marches back towards the office. Halfway to the main door, he stops, turns. 'Wait!'

I freeze in my seat. Jack has the door open. Neither of us speaks.

Ian holds up a cautionary finger. 'No cigarettes in the back, then?'

'None at all,' Jack assures him. 'Promise.'

Ian grins and flaps his hand to show he was only joking, then continues towards the building. He's disappearing through the doors as Jack climbs into the car.

I disconnect the call.

'Drive,' I tell him.

CHAPTER FIFTY-SEVEN

Thursday, 21 October

I once listened to a podcast where a forensic anthropologist half-joked that it wasn't killing someone that was the difficult part; it was getting rid of their body.

At the time, both of those activities seemed completely out of the realms of any possibility in my life, a bizarre and slightly macabre thought experiment. Little did I know that, a couple of years later, I would have done one and be in the process of doing the second. And she was right about the hard bit, too.

It's taken Jack and I the best part of a week, but we're almost there. I've lost count of the number of times I thought I was going to be sick, despite Jack doing most of the work. Even recalling it now makes me feel nauseous. As we travelled home on the ferry, I wondered if I could trust Jack. Now, although it's required the darkest, most extreme of circumstances to prove it, I know that I can.

Once we were home last Sunday night, Jack took charge. We got Laurence's body from the car to our house in a ski bag, under cover of darkness. From there, we carried him to the bathtub, where Jack… well, I don't want to think about it. I couldn't watch. Suffice to say that the extensive anatomical knowledge and strong stomach provided by Jack's medical training came into its own.

I found myself building bonfires every night, piling vegetation on top of clothing and small pieces of Laurence as, little by little, we reduced him to ash. The parts which don't burn and grind up so well – teeth, for example – went to work with Jack in a bag and were thrown in the hospital incinerator, to be obliterated with other medical waste at a thousand degrees.

We've scattered the ash in the garden, dug over the soil. Scatter, dig, repeat. The bathroom and car boot have been cleaned with the same clinical thoroughness. Jack even brought some special products back from work to make sure we get rid of every trace.

Meanwhile, I've been keeping an eye on the news, but there's nothing from the Isle of Wight, and not even anything in the local press about Laurence having disappeared. I assume he has clients who've turned up for their sessions at his little office and found him absent. Who've probably called his mobile – which by now will be as dead as he is, resting in the glove box of his rental car on the beach – and got no reply. But nobody seems to have reported him missing.

I remember wondering who Laurence shared his life with, which person was lucky enough (so I thought) to be with him. Well, I guess the answer is: no one.

I'd love to be able to say that I saw it coming – his homicidal obsession with Emily – but the truth is that I didn't have a clue. If I'm honest, I even had a crush on him. Now, the thought that I once fantasised about kissing him (and more) sends a chill through me, makes my guts lurch with disgust. Could I have worked it out? I don't think so.

I might have guessed that Emily and I had the same therapist, since she did tell me her guy was local, but that never occurred to me. And I could perhaps have deduced that the 'fancy man' who visited regularly, when Michael went out, was Laurence – but I thought it was Henderson. When Cathy spoke about him coming back, just after the detective visited, she was talking about Laurence, who'd been here earlier that week, checking in on me after I missed my session. I probably shouldn't be surprised that a stalker would be so diligent.

But, even if I'd known that Laurence was Emily's therapist, I could never have guessed what feelings he had developed for her. He was a closed book, hiding every aspect of himself so carefully from others. And yet I told him everything, believing he was my only ally. I suppose Emily must have done the same.

On the beach, she described how he'd propositioned her, after he'd initiated the breakdown of her marriage and two months of psychological abuse from Michael. How Laurence had threatened her after she'd rejected him for the last time, promising to destroy her, whatever it cost him. How she thought Henderson's police contacts on the Isle of Wight would keep her safe, even as I was pursuing her with a relentlessness whose obsession can't have been far short of Laurence's. But all I succeeded in doing was leading him right to her and giving him the chance to murder her.

I tell myself that I did a good thing, defending her like that. But I have to keep repeating it, like a mantra, reminding myself. Because it's the only way to make the guilt and the anxiety bearable.

With just a couple more bonfires, the physical traces of Laurence and that night on the beach will be gone. But I don't know whether the images of it, looping in my mind's eye, will ever leave me.

CHAPTER FIFTY-EIGHT

Thursday, 21 October

There's still one mystery I haven't solved. I've come up to the loft to get that photograph of Jack, to see if he can work out where it's from and why Emily had it in her possession. Since finding her and Thea, and knowing that Michael didn't kill them, creeping around on their side of the attic doesn't scare me any more. Or maybe the fear of trespassing here just seems like nothing, now, compared to what I've experienced over the past five days.

I go straight to where I found the photo before, by the box of Emily's things, among the workbench, DIY stuff and other containers. I shine my torch beam around. But it isn't there.

I shift a few more things, trying to recall where I put it when Jack caught me up here that time. Part of me even starts to wonder whether I might have hallucinated it. I know that's crazy, though. I saw it; I held it. Unlike some of the things I've believed in recent months, it was real.

'Henry?'

The voice snaps me out of my reverie. It doesn't have its usual steadiness, but I recognise it: Cathy.

'Henry?' she calls again. She sounds frightened.

'Cathy,' I reply gently. 'It's me, Freya.'

Slowly, I emerge from the gap between the boards where I entered the Crawfords' section of the loft (*Michael's* section, I should perhaps say now, since Emily won't be coming back).

My torch catches a spectral figure. She looks like an apparition, almost supernatural, her shock of white hair even brighter in the surrounding darkness. She grimaces and raises an arm to shield her eyes from the light.

'Sorry,' I say, dipping the beam. It picks out something in her hand. A photograph.

'I'm looking for Henry,' she says. Her voice sounds detached, as if she's speaking in her sleep. 'Have you seen him?'

She turns the photograph to me and, now it's illuminated by the torch, I can see it's the picture I thought was Jack. A memory surfaces: a photograph I saw of Henry and a young Cathy together in her home. I recall the fleeting thought that he and Jack looked similar. Then I remember how Cathy called him Henry when she first saw him. But, wherever her husband is, he's not here.

'No, I'm sorry, Cathy. I haven't seen him.'

'I've-I've got to find him,' she says, her distress palpable.

'I don't think he's up here.' I take a step towards her, my palms raised to show her I'm not a threat.

'But-but he was, I'm sure he…' she falters.

As I reach her, I can see she's trembling. 'Cathy, are you all right?'

'I've got to find him,' she repeats, just a whisper now.

I take a final step, open my arms and draw her slowly into an embrace. 'Let me help you get back downstairs,' I say.

Cathy dabs at her eyes with a handkerchief, an old-fashioned, white cotton square with her initials embroidered on it. I've made the tea for us, using her method of loose leaves in the pot, properly brewed and poured through a strainer into a cup (milk first). There's something comforting about these rituals, the traditions that Cathy preserves from a time before everything became super-fast and instantly thrown away.

'Thank you, love,' she says as I slide a cup and saucer across to her.

'Probably not as good as how you make it, but—'

'Not the tea.' She smiles briefly. 'I mean, for what you did up there. I wasn't in my right mind.' She points towards the ceiling.

'That's okay.' I pour another cup for myself. 'How are you feeling now?'

'Oh, fine. It comes and goes. Sometimes I just find myself in the loft, wandering around, and I have no memory of how I came to be there.'

'That must be scary,' I offer. I'm already thinking about the footsteps I've heard overhead at various points in the last few months, including when Michael denied he'd been in the attic. And I realise how Cathy knew that something wasn't right in the Crawfords' home, even as they were still trying to give the impression to the outside world – me and Jack included – that everything was perfect. She'd been in the attic and overheard them.

'I know he's not up there,' she continues. 'But there's obviously part of me that thinks he is.'

'What happened to him?' I ask cautiously.

Cathy takes a deep breath, wipes her eyes once more. 'He died. Just had a heart attack one day, out of the blue, when he was up there. I knew something was wrong when he hadn't come down for his lunch, so I went up to see what he was doing. I found his body. I was too late, of course.'

'I'm so sorry.' I lay a hand on top of hers.

She blinks, her eyes wet. 'I can't help wondering, if only I'd gone up there earlier, checked on him, perhaps he'd still…'

'You can't think that,' I tell her. 'It's not your fault.'

She studies the photo of Henry. Now I look at it clearly, in the cold daylight, I can tell it isn't Jack. There's a strong likeness, for sure, but it's not my fiancé. I can see how I might've thought that, though, during those confusing times a couple of months ago, after my miscarriage.

Cathy briefly manages a smile. 'You know, a while back, I found a dead bird up there, lying on the ground, exactly where my Henry was.'

I'd forgotten about the bird. 'I saw it too.'

'Well, I'm not sure what possessed me to do it, but one day I just took it with me. I didn't want it there, rotting away where Henry had been. Does that sound mad?'

'Not at all.' I pause, then ask: 'What did you do with it?'

She gives a furtive glance. 'I shouldn't have done it, but I buried it in the Crawfords' garden. If I'd put it in mine, Archie would have dug it up and brought it into the house.' She shakes her head at the thought. 'It would've been a terrible mess. But he doesn't go in theirs, you see, so I knew the bird could rest in peace over there.'

I could almost laugh. I'd constructed theories in my mind to explain why Michael had placed a dead bird in the ground above what I thought was Emily's body; symbolism and all sorts. It's incredible how our brains try to make sense of what our senses tell us, and how often we can reach the wrong conclusions.

'Don't worry,' I say. 'I won't tell Michael.'

We share a conspiratorial smile and drink our tea.

'What happened to your webpage?' she asks. 'The Emily and Thea one. It's not there now.'

'No. I, er, I took it down.'

'Why?'

I choose my words carefully. I don't want to betray Emily's trust. 'Because they don't need it any more,' I reply.

Cathy's eyes narrow as she studies me over the rim of her teacup. I can see her working it out, reading between the lines. Then she raises her eyebrows slightly, purses her lips and nods sagely. 'Well done, dear. I'm glad they're safe.'

I wonder if she's going to probe, if I'll need to dodge questions and fudge answers about Michael or the 'fancy man'. But, instead, she gets to her feet, composed and self-assured once more in her home.

'Would you like some cake?' she says.

And I know I can trust her, too.

CHAPTER FIFTY-NINE

Saturday, 23 October

I'm at the kitchen table, drinking coffee and googling doppelgangers. According to the article I'm reading, around 75,000 people in the world will share your approximate set of facial features, so it isn't as surprising as I first thought that there was a strong resemblance between Jack and a young Henry. I can understand why both Cathy and I – in our respective states of distress – mistook each of them for the other.

Jack is upstairs, giving the little second bathroom another clean. I'm about to go and check on the bonfire at the back of the garden when my phone pings. It's an alert from the doorbell camera app. I check the footage just as the buzzer sounds.

It's Detective Henderson.

I freeze. Should I answer? We could pretend not to be home, but then he might just come back tomorrow, or the day after, or call us. I have to speak to him. It's okay, I tell myself. He can't know. There's no way…

I get to my feet, the first lurches and stabs of my fight-or-flight system kicking in as I walk down the hallway. I try to keep my breathing steady, but I can feel that my palms are already clammy as I reach out and open the door. He looks the same as every other time I've seen him: stubbly jaw, tired eyes, tie knot loosened at his neck.

'Afternoon, *Ms* Northcott,' he says. 'Mind if I come in?'

'Er, sure. Of course.' I pull the door wide to let him through, pasting on a pleasant smile as he passes, even as my brain is going into overdrive. What if he walks out into the garden? What if he pokes around in the fire before it's finished?

'Everything okay?' he asks. I realise he's stopped, midway down the hall, and has turned to face me.

'Oh, yes, fine, thanks.' I probably sound completely unnatural. But then, when has Henderson ever seen me in a normal state?

'Hope I'm not disturbing,' he says, continuing down towards the kitchen.

'No, it's all right.'

'Great. Your fiancé in?'

'He's upstairs. Jack!' I call.

I hear a door shut and Jack running down the stairs. I follow Henderson into the kitchen. He glances at the laptop screen; it's a photo that appears to show identical twins, but who are in fact two total strangers who ended up sitting next to each other on a flight a few years ago. He frowns but doesn't say anything.

Jack arrives in the doorway, slightly breathless. 'Hello, Paul,' he says.

'Hello, Mr Brown.' Not *Jack*, this time, but *Mr Brown*. I'm trying to guess what Henderson knows.

'How can we help?' I ask, sitting back against the worktop to steady myself and draw his attention away from the garden.

The detective turns his head to me and our eyes lock. 'It's about Laurence Travis,' he says.

'Oh, right...'

'He's your therapist, I believe?'

'He was, yes.'

'Was?'

Shit. I've fucked up already. I read about an FBI profiling technique called statement analysis, where investigators pay attention to whether you talk about someone in the past or present tense. It's been used in murder cases. And Henderson's clocked it in my reply.

'I mean, we were having sessions together,' I say, 'but I haven't seen him for a week or more.'

He continues to regard me with suspicion, waiting. But I know that old trick – letting someone fill an awkward silence – because I use it myself when interviewing people for documentaries, so I say nothing more.

'No?'

'No.'

'When was the last time you saw him?'

'Er, Tuesday, not this week just gone, the one before.'

'Hm.' His gaze travels out of the back door, into the garden. Wisps of smoke are visible from my bonfire at the back. My stomach feels as though it's being squeezed on all sides. I hope I'm not actually sick; what the hell would Henderson make of that?

'That's confidential, isn't it?' says Jack, coming over and standing beside me.

'Normally, yes.' Henderson shoves his hands in his pockets. 'But this is a missing person's inquiry.'

'Really?' I try to affect surprise. 'Laurence is missing?'

'Yes.' He examines our faces in turn.

My heart is beating so loudly I feel as though it must be audible.

'He failed to return a rental car,' Henderson explains. 'It was discovered on a beach on the Isle of Wight. And he was subsequently uncontactable. He's not at home or work.'

Jack reaches his arm around me. We're both silent.

'Did he say anything to you about travelling there?' asks Henderson. 'Cancelling appointments, going on holiday, anything like that?'

'No.' I shrug, shaking my head quickly. Was my denial too fast, too forceful?

Henderson studies me, and I begin to think he *does* know something. They've traced Laurence's hire car to the Isle of Wight. Surely they'll be checking local hotels, ferry passenger lists… *Oh, God.*

'Will you be speaking to his other clients?' Jack asks.

'We have chatted to a couple of them, yes.' Henderson clears his throat.

'What do you think's happened?' I say. My voice is tight, strained.

'Well, we don't know yet. But…' He tilts his head, pushes out his lips, as if weighing a probability. 'An abandoned car beside some steep cliffs, and a rough sea…'

'You reckon he, um, might've killed himself?' Jack tries.

Henderson nods. 'That's certainly one possibility. I'm sorry to have to ask this, Ms Northcott, but did Laurence Travis ever behave inappropriately towards you?'

'Um, no, never.'

'Did he, er, you know, with other?…' Jack's ill-formed question tails off before it's finished.

'There have been certain allegations made.'

'Wow. Okay,' I say.

'Jesus,' adds Jack.

'When there's a possibility of that kind of thing coming out, and someone stands to lose their reputation, their career, their livelihood, even face criminal charges, then it can push them to… well, anyway, it's just one theory.'

'Perhaps he's chosen to make himself disappear,' I suggest. 'You know, to get away from it all, if he was having problems.'

'Perhaps,' Henderson notes, though I can tell he doesn't agree. He hasn't mentioned Emily, yet, although he certainly knew that Laurence was her therapist, and that he'd threatened her. She told me that. And I haven't mentioned her, either, or our trip to the Isle of Wight. But he knows that both of us were seeing Laurence, and that I was leading a campaign to find Emily, endlessly harassing him about the investigation, when he was the one who helped her escape. No wonder he constantly wanted to get rid of me and stop me digging.

'Well, we hope he's all right, whatever's happened to him,' says Jack briskly. 'Don't we, Freya?'

'Absolutely.'

Henderson looks out of the back door again. 'I see you've taken down your *Find Emily and Thea* page on social media, Ms Northcott,' he says without turning around.

'Yes, I did.'

'Why did you choose to do that this week in particular?' he asks.

I glance at Jack. 'I, er, I decided it was time to move on with my life. That's what everyone was telling me; at least, people I care about. So, I thought maybe it was time I listened to them.'

The detective nods. 'Well, good luck with it. Moving on.'

'Thanks.'

'Garden's nice,' he remarks, sending a shudder of adrenalin through me. 'Looks like you've done a lot of work in it since I was last here.'

'We've been busy.'

Henderson flashes a smile that doesn't reach his eyes. We follow him back towards the door. He stops at the bottom of the stairs and looks up towards the first floor, sniffing the air a couple of times. Has he smelled Jack's medical-grade cleaning products? We're both thinking the same thing; willing Henderson not to ask if he can go up there and use the bathroom.

But he turns smartly and reaches for the front door latch. 'Oh, one final thing,' he says. 'I'm supposed to do a quick welfare check, you know, after the, er, risk issues identified during my last visit. Did you ever see a psychiatrist in the end, Ms Northcott?'

'No, I didn't,' I reply, recalling his threatening advice after the incident where I stabbed Michael with the secateurs outside his shed, the prospect of being arrested and sectioned again. 'But thanks for asking. And I don't think I need one any more.'

Jack takes my hand in his and gives me a little squeeze.

'Good for you.' Henderson dips his head in acknowledgement, then he's gone.

EPILOGUE

The following spring

'Let me help you with that, Freya.'

Duncan, one half of the new couple next door, springs to his feet and takes the large, heavy salad bowl from me. His partner, Patrick, is at my other elbow, lifting the huge quiche I've made and setting it down in the centre of the garden table.

'Thanks, both of you, but I'm fine, honestly.'

'You should be putting your feet up,' says Patrick, nodding towards my belly. I run my hand over the bump. It's showing through my regular clothes, but not by much. We had our first scan last week. I was pretty nervous, after last time, but everything was fine. It's a little girl.

'I'm only three months along, guys,' I protest. 'I like keeping active, anyway.'

'You'll let us fuss over you though, won't you?' Duncan grins. 'Please?'

'Well…' I can think of worse things than two lovely men fussing over me.

'Freya, do we need anything else? What can I bring out?' Jack calls from the back door. Make that three lovely men.

'Salt and pepper?' I reply.

'The quiche smells incredible,' Cathy says, her eyes lighting up as she surveys the meal. 'Did you make it yourself, love?'

'I did. Using your pastry recipe.'

She beams at me. 'Marvellous.'

'Wait till you try Cathy's baking,' I tell our new neighbours.

Duncan and Patrick are making enthusiastic noises about all the food they're being offered as Jack emerges from the kitchen. He gives me a quick kiss and we all take our places, passing plates and serving our guests.

'Welcome to Sunningdale Road,' I announce, lifting my sparkling water as everyone else raises their wine glasses.

'Seems like a really lovely street,' says Patrick.

'And your garden is just beautiful,' Duncan adds.

Jack and I exchange a glance.

'Freya worked really hard on it,' Jack says.

'Well, it shows.' Duncan looks appreciatively from one fence to the other. 'We're planning to do a bit on ours, aren't we, Pat?'

'Yeah.' He chuckles. 'I mean, we're not gardeners, but…'

'Neither was I,' I say. 'You just need a bit of hard work and a lot of determination.'

'And some imagination,' adds Jack, giving me his lopsided grin.

Duncan takes a sip of wine. 'The last guy in our place – what was his name?'

'Michael,' I reply.

'Michael, that's it. He didn't do much with the area at the back. Nice that it's communal, though. Maybe we can all pitch in?'

Everyone agrees that would be nice.

It's been a month since Michael sold the house to Duncan and Patrick, departing to take up a new software design job abroad, in Finland, I think. He didn't leave a forwarding address.

'So, you guys did the place up yourselves?' Patrick is clearly impressed.

I look through the open back door and into the house. Six months of solid renovations have turned it from a run-down doer-upper into something like the home I'd envisaged us living in. The sort of place you'd want to invite friends to. Somewhere you could raise a family.

The interior might have changed, but I still remember the dark days last year, long hours of isolation, filled with anxiety and paranoia. Wondering what had happened to Emily and Thea, determined to prove Michael had murdered them. Not knowing who I could trust, even my own fiancé. It feels a little bit like a different life, now that so much has changed. But I can still see each of those moments of terror if I close my eyes and bring them to mind.

I can still feel them.

I think about Laurence quite often. His missing person's case has been shelved, I read the other week in the local paper. Henderson was quoted as saying their leading theory was that he took his own life at Sandown cliffs, but without a body, nothing could be confirmed. The article mentioned several allegations of malpractice against Laurence, asking how someone in a position of responsibility could act like that, and calling for tighter screening of independent therapists. There was nothing linking him to Emily's disappearance last summer.

'Tell us more about your new documentary, love,' Cathy says, spearing a clump of salad leaves. 'It sounds fascinating.'

'Well, er, yes, okay. So…' I'm embarrassed now that I've been put on the spot, and I'm not sure how to begin.

'She's been commissioned by the BBC,' says Jack proudly. 'It's going to be a series about women who've overcome serious adversity and rebuilt their lives and – oh, go on, Freya, you tell them.'

'I'm still just getting used to the fact that I've got a job for the next couple of years,' I say.

The chuckles are interrupted by the snap and clatter of the letterbox. I'm not expecting anything, but for some reason, I feel the urge to see what it is.

'Excuse me a second,' I say, getting to my feet and going inside. I hear Jack enthusiastically talking about the documentary project as I pad down the hallway. *She worked so hard on the pitch, it's really impressive.*

There's a postcard on the doormat. I stoop and pick it up. The photograph is a gorgeous landscape of trees beside a lake, their leaves a riot of reds, yellows and greens. In the corner it says '*CANADA*' beside a red maple leaf. I turn the card over.

On the back, my address has been written neatly in an adult's hand. Next to it is a simple drawing, which looks as though it's been done by a kid. A stick woman with long, curly hair, holding the hand of a little girl, with identical hair. There's no signature or name, just two words in a child's large, uneven script: *Thank you.*

I don't need a sign-off to know who it's from. Instantly, I see Emily and Thea walking through that forest, sitting by that lake, perhaps living in a cabin nearby or driving out from the city for a weekend hike. I can see them making a new life together, happy and safe. The pictures come easily to my mind's eye.

I've always been good at imagining things.

A LETTER FROM CHRIS

Dear reader,

I hope you enjoyed *The New Home*, my first standalone psychological thriller. If you liked it, please give it a rating online, and I'd be very grateful if you have time to leave a short review, too.

If you'd like to know more about my novels, please join my mailing list at the link below. Your email address will never be shared, and you're free to unsubscribe from the updates at any time.

www.bookouture.com/chris-merritt

There are several important real-world topics underpinning the plot of *The New Home*. The UK figures which Freya quotes on intimate partner (and ex-partner) violence are accurate, and a recent study by the United Nations Office on Drugs and Crime suggests this pattern is, unfortunately, replicated at a global scale. According to UN data, a woman is killed by her partner, ex, or a close family member somewhere in the world every ten minutes. Perhaps just as damaging are the insidious practices of coercive control in relationships – including gaslighting – which can leave their survivors with serious psychological scars. Charities such as Refuge and Women's Aid in the UK are working to assist those in need, educating people on the realities of abuse and intimate partner violence, and campaigning for change. They need our support to continue that effort, particularly since intimate partner abuse appears to have risen since the onset of lockdowns associated with the Covid-19 pandemic.

The trauma of a miscarriage is something that many women and their partners will experience, yet it is still not commonly discussed. While I was writing this book, several celebrity accounts of miscarriage appeared in the press, which may help to begin normalising conversations around it, and encouraging more women to speak to others and seek support, if they would find that helpful. Also more common than many people realise are the experiences of paranoia and delusional beliefs, which can result from a combination of life traumas, anxiety and isolation. Working in an Early Intervention Service in the UK National Health Service, I personally saw how important it was to identify the spiralling anxiety and belief changes which can lead to a psychotic episode early on, so that the person can get support as soon as possible. Many people who receive good care at that stage will recover and learn to recognise their personal signs of relapse to help prevent future episodes.

With all of these issues touched on in *The New Home*, greater public awareness is a crucial step to helping create positive change, supporting people who are suffering and alleviating their distress.

Thank you for your support to my writing. If you're new to my books and would be interested in my other crime thrillers, I have two previous series. The Zac Boateng and Kat Jones novels tackle themes of organised crime, police corruption and family loyalty, and are set in south-east London. My second trilogy, starring DI Dan Lockhart and Dr Lexi Green, is a more psychological set of serial killer stories, based in the leafy boroughs of south-west London.

Finally, if you'd like to get in touch, please drop me a line on Twitter, Facebook, or through my website. I'd love to hear from you, and I always read every message.

Best wishes,
Chris

@chrismerrittauthor

@DrCJMerritt

www.cjmerritt.co.uk

ACKNOWLEDGEMENTS

As always, I owe tremendous thanks to the Bookouture team for their energy and dedication in guiding my novels from the first spark of an idea to the final, published work. In particular, I'd like to thank my editor Helen Jenner, as well as Kathryn Taussig, for their initial suggestion that I step out of my police procedural comfort zone and attempt to write a standalone psychological thriller. I'm also grateful to Peta Nightingale, Jenny Geras, Noelle Holton, Kim Nash, Sarah Hardy, Alex Crow, Alex Holmes, and Martina Arzu for their efforts – mostly behind the scenes – in contracting, marketing and publicising my books.

Usually, I rely quite heavily on the generosity of subject matter experts who give their time and advice to make my detective stories more accurate and believable. In writing *The New Home*, however, much of the research was conducted in the same manner as its protagonist – solo and armed only with a laptop and Wi-Fi. Nonetheless, there are a small number of people I'd like to mention. Thanks to Prof Dame Sue Black, who kindly gave some thought to which part of a dog's skeleton would most readily be mistaken for human bones. Documentary film maker Pete Rudge and cardiologist Ben Dowsing inspired and informed two key professions that appear in this book – although not the characters to whom they belong, I should note. Above all, though, I want to thank the two women who kindly and bravely shared with me their experiences of having a miscarriage, and the young people at Richmond Early Intervention Service who told me their stories of recovery from delusional psychosis.

I would also like to thank readers, bloggers, bookstagrammers, fellow authors and festival organisers for reviewing, sharing and promoting *The New Home*, as well as my previous work. Your support is incredibly important to me, and your positive reactions and encouragement are a big part of my motivation for writing.

I want to reserve a particularly special thank you for my family and friends, who are not only there for me throughout the sometimes turbulent journey of a book, but also put up with hearing half-formed plot ideas and random trivia from my research along the way.

To Fiona and her family, especially, my thoughts and deepest sympathies are with you for what you've been through over the past year. I will be there for you.

Made in the USA
Las Vegas, NV
01 May 2022

48270312R10194